PLANET OF THE CARDS

Brother Paul studied the card, and the picture formed before him.

He stepped forward and suddenly he was inside the picture, advancing toward the bridge. The cloaked figure heard him and began to turn. The face came into full view.

There was no face. There was only a smooth expanse of flesh, like the face of an incomplete store-window manne-quin...

GOD OF TAROT

*The first adventure
on the miracle planet*

PIERS ANTHONY

Berkley Books by Piers Anthony

CHTHON
PHTHOR

THE TAROT TRILOGY
GOD OF TAROT (Book One)
VISION OF TAROT (Book Two)
FAITH OF TAROT (Book Three)

PIERS ANTHONY

BOOK ONE OF THE TAROT SEQUENCE

GOD OF TAROT

BERKLEY BOOKS, NEW YORK

GOD OF TAROT

A Berkley Book / published by arrangement with
the author

PRINTING HISTORY
Jove / HBJ edition / April 1979
Berkley edition / June 1981
Sixth printing / September 1983
Seventh printing / April 1984

ISBN: 0-425-07038-7

A BERKLEY BOOK ® TM 757,375
The name "BERKLEY" and the stylized "B" with design
are trademarks belonging to Berkley Publishing Corporation.
PRINTED IN THE UNITED STATES OF AMERICA

**Dedicated to
the Holy Order of Vision**

Author's Note:

This quarter-million-word novel of Tarot is published in three segments. This is the opening portion of the larger work, establishing the situation and covering the first major vision. It has its own unity, so may be read alone, though it is hoped the reader will be interested enough to peruse Books II and III also.

This novel relates to the author's Cluster series of adventures, with a number of interconnections, but is of quite a different nature; the two projects should not be confused.

An appendix defines the Animation Tarot that is the basis of this novel. The complete table of contents reflects the thirty Triumphs of that deck, from Key 0 (zero) through Key 28 (twenty-eight), which are included in the appendix.

The complex nature of this novel may lead to confusion in certain places, and some scenes may be offensive to certain readers. Yet there is a rationale: It is difficult to appreciate the meaning of the heights without first experiencing the depths.

GOD OF TAROT
TABLE OF CONTENTS

0

Folly

In 1170 A.D., *Peter Waldo, a wealthy merchant of Lyons, France, suffered a religious conversion, renounced his possessions, and wandered about the countryside in voluntary poverty. This obvious folly attracted both persecutions and followers, the latter called the "poor men of Lyons." In 1183 Pope Lucius III excommunicated the growing sect of "Waldenses," who appealed to the Scriptures instead of to papal authority, repudiated the taking of oaths, and condemned capital punishment. They never made the sign of the cross, as they refused to venerate the torture device on which Christ hung, or the painful and mocking crown of thorns. Nevertheless, the Waldenses prospered in Christian lands; many thousands of them settled in the Cottian Alps on the French-Italian border. Their dauntless missionaries covered southern France, southern Germany and northern Italy. But the Inquisition followed them, and they were savagely repressed over the course of several centuries. Their ministers had to go about in disguise, and it was hazardous for them to carry any of the literature of their faith, lest it betray them into torture and death. But it was hard to make the material clear without teaching aids, for many converts were illiterate and ignorant. Out of this impasse was to arise one of the most significant educational tools of the millennium.*

The setting is Earth of the near future. The pressures of increasing population and dwindling natural resources have brought the human scheme to the brink of ruin. There is not enough food and energy to support all the people.

But a phenomenal technological breakthrough has occurred: matter transmission. People can now be shipped instantly to habitable wilderness planets orbiting distant stars. This seems to offer relief from the dilemma of mankind; *now there is somewhere for all those people to go.*

This leads to the most massive exodus in the history of the species; so many people are leaving that within a decade no one will be left on Earth. Unfortunately, matter transmission requires a tremendous amount of energy. The planet's sources of power are being ravished. This has the peculiar side effect of reversing the technological level of human culture; people are forced to revert to more primitive mechanisms. Kerosene lamps replace electric lights; wood replaces oil; horses replace cars; stone tools replace metal ones. The industrial base of the world is shrinking as the most highly trained and intelligent personnel emigrate to their dream worlds. Yet the colonization program proceeds pell-mell, as such programs and movements have always done, heedless of any warnings of collapse.

This is sheer folly. Mankind is like the beautiful dreamer of Tarot's Key 0—the Fool—walking northwest with his gaze lifted in search of great experience while his feet are about to carry him off a precipice. He will have a great experience, oh yes! What high expectations these new worlds represent! What a marvelous goal to reduce Earth's population painlessly to an appropriate level! But what disaster is in the making, because no reasonable controls have been placed on this adventure.

Yet there are redeeming aspects. At least the Fool *has* dreams and noble aspirations, and perhaps the capacity to recognize and choose between good and evil. It may be better to step off the cliff, his way, than to stay at home without ambition. The folly of future Earth is a complex matter, with many very noble and frustrating elements that may after all salvage its greatest potential.

This is the story of just one of those elements, a single thread of a monstrous tapestry: Brother Paul's quest for the God of Tarot.

1

Skill

252 A.D.: *Emperor Decius was in power only a year, but in this time he cruelly persecuted the bothersome Christians. He seized one devout youth and coated his whole body with honey, then exposed him to the blazing sun and the stings of flies and hornets. Another Christian youth was given the opposite extreme: he was bound hand and foot by ropes entwined with flowers, naked upon a downy bed, in a place filled with the murmuring of water, the touch of soft breezes, the sight of sweet birds, and the aroma of flowers. Then a maiden of exceptionally fair form and feature approached him and bared her lovely flesh, kissing and caressing his body to arouse his manhood and enable her to envelop him in the ultimate worldly embrace. The youth had dedicated his love to God; to suffer this rapture with a mortal woman would have polluted him. He had no weapon with which to defend himself, yet his skill and courage proved equal to the*

occasion. He bit off his own tongue and spat it in the harlot's face. By the pain of this wound he conquered the temptation of lewdness, and won for himself the crown of spiritual victory. Paul, himself sincerely Christian, witnessed these torments. Terrified, he fled into the desert, where he remained alone in the depths of a cave for the rest of his life. He thus became the first Christian hermit, and was known as Saint Paul the Hermit.

The great blades of the windmill were turning, but the water was not pumping. Only a trickle emerged from the pipe, and the cistern was almost empty. It was a crisis, for this was the main source of pure water for the region.

Brother Paul contemplated the situation. "It's either a lowering of the water table or a defect in the pump," he said.

"The water table!" Brother James exclaimed, horrified. "We haven't pumped *that* much!" His concern was genuine and deeply felt; the Brothers of the Holy Order of Vision believed in conservation, and practiced it rigorously. All had taken vows of poverty, and abhorred the wasting of anything as valuable as water.

"But there has been a drought," Brother Paul said. Indeed, the sun was blazing down at this moment, although it caused no distress to his brown skin. "We might inadvertently have overpumped, considering this special circumstance."

Brother James was a thin, nervous man who took things seriously. His long face worked in the throes of inchoate emotion. "If it be God's will . . ."

Brother Paul noted his companion's obvious anxiety, and relented. "Nevertheless, we shall check the pump first."

The pump was a turning cam that transformed the rotary motion of the mill's shaft into piston motion in a rod. The rod plunged down into the well to operate the buried cylinder that forced up the water. Brother Paul brought out plumber's tools and carefully dismantled the mechanism, disconnecting the shaft from the vanes and drawing the cylinder from the depths. His little silver cross, hanging on a chain around his neck, got in his way as he leaned forward. He tucked it into his shirt pocket with a certain absentminded reverence.

He sniffed. "I trust that is not hellfire I smell," he remarked.

"*What?*" Brother James was not much for humor.

Brother Paul pried open the mechanism. Smoke puffed out. "There it is! Our wooden bearing has scorched and warped, decreasing the pump's efficiency."

"Scorched?" Brother James asked, surprised. He seemed much relieved to verify that the problem was mechanical, the result of neither the subsidence of the water level nor the proximity of hellfire. "That's a *water* pump!"

Brother Paul smiled tolerantly. The deepening creases of his face showed that this was an expression in which he indulged often—perhaps more often than was strictly politic for a man of his calling. Yet there was a complementary network of frown-lines that betrayed the serious side of his nature; some of these even hinted at considerable pain. "Not all of it is wet, Brother. This cylinder is sealed. In a high wind, when the shaft is turning rapidly—wind power varies as to the cube of wind velocity, as you know—the bearings can get so hot from friction that they actually begin to char."

16

"We did have very good winds yesterday," Brother James agreed. "Brother Peter arranged to grind flour for a whole week's baking. But we never thought the mill would—"

"No fault of yours, Brother," Brother Paul said quickly. "It is quite natural and sensible to use the mill to best effect, and a strong wind makes all its chores easy. This is just one of the problems of our declining technology. I will replace the bearing—but we would be well advised to choke down on the mill during the next gale winds. Sometimes it may be better to waste a little good wind than to lose a bad bearing." He smiled to himself as he worked, considering whether he had discovered an original maxim for life, and whether such a maxim might be worth integrating into his life's philosophy.

He fetched a suitable replacement bearing and proceeded to install it. His dark hands were strong and sure.

"You are a magician," Brother James remarked. "I envy you your proficiency with mechanical things."

"I only wish the spiritual were as easy to attain," Brother Paul replied. Now he was sweating with the pleasant effort. He was a thickset man of moderate height, with short black hair. He was inclined to chubbiness, but his muscles showed formidable delineation as he lifted the heavy unit into place.

"Wouldn't it be better to have the pump on the surface, so that it could be serviced more readily?" Brother James asked as Brother Paul struggled with the weight of the descending cylinder. Brother Paul had drawn it up without trouble, but was now occupied with easing it into its precise place.

"It would—but we would have no water," Brother Paul explained. "Surface pumps employ suction, which is actually the outside pressure of the atmosphere pushing up the fluid. That's about fifteen pounds per square inch, and that cannot draw water up more than about twenty-eight feet, what with friction and certain other inefficiencies of the system. Our water table is thirty feet down. So we employ a pressure pump set down near the water; that type of device has no such limit. It *is* more cumbersome—but necessary."

"Yes, I see that now. It is more than harnessing the windmill to the pump; it has to be done the right way."

"I suspect it is the same with the power of God," Brother Paul said musingly. "It is there, like the wind: an immense potential, often ignored or unperceived by man. Yet it is real; we need only take the trouble to understand it. It is our job to harness that potential, to apply it more directly to the lives of men. But though we seem to have all the elements right, it will not work if they are not correctly placed, and adapted to our particular situation—or if part of the mechanism is broken, even though nothing may show on the surface."

"I don't regard that as an analogy," Brother James said. "It is the literal truth. The wind *is* God, and so is the water; we can not exist apart from Him. Not for a moment, not in the smallest way."

Brother Paul paused in his labors to hold up his hands in a gesture of surrender. "You are correct, of course. Yet there must be a process of communication between the power above—" he lifted his right hand to the sky— "and the substance below." His left hand pointed toward the buried cylinder.

"I would call that process 'prayer,'" Brother James said.

18

The reassembled pump worked. A full, pure flow of water emerged from the pipe, cascading into the storage tank and cistern. Brother James was ecstatic.

Without further comment, Brother Paul walked back to his room, washed his hands, arms and face, and changed to his habit: the black robe with the reversed collar, the cross worn outside. He had a class to conduct, and he was overdue. When dealing with matters pertaining to the works of God on Earth, it was best to be punctual.

Suddenly he brightened. "Air, Earth, Water, Fire!" he exclaimed. "Beautiful. Thank you, God, for sending me this revelation." To him there was no objection to conversing with God directly; in this case, familiarity bred respect, not contempt. The Holy Order of Vision encouraged contact with God in any fashion that seemed mutually satisfactory.

The students were there before him: five young people from a nearby village. These orientation sessions were held periodically, when sufficient interest developed. As the massive energy and population depletion of Earth continued, the need for technological and social systems closer to nature intensified, so these sessions had become fairly regular. The Brothers and Sisters took turns conducting them, and this was Brother Paul's week.

"Sorry I'm late," Brother Paul said, shaking hands all around. "I was delayed, if you will, by a superimposition of elements."

One of the girls perked up. She was a slight, bright-eyed nymph with a rather pretty elfin face framed by loose, dark blonde tresses. She seemed to be about fifteen, although inadequate nutrition stunted the growth of youngsters these days, delaying maturity. A month of good feeding might do wonders for her, physically—and perhaps spiritually also. It was hard to be a devout individual on an empty stomach. At least it was hard for those not trained in this kind of discipline. "You mean something by that, don't you, sir?" she asked.

"Call me Brother," Brother Paul said. "I am Brother Paul of the Holy Order of Vision. Yes, I had an anecdote in mind, and thank you for inquiring." It was always best to begin on a personal basis; early theology could alienate young minds. He was not trying to convert, but merely to explain; even then, it had to be done appropriately. People were more complex than windmills, but there were parallels.

"Big deal," one of the boys muttered. He was a strapping lad, massive across the shoulders, but surly. He had not been stunted by hunger! Evidently he had been sent here, perhaps by parents who could not control him much longer. The Order Station was no reform school, but perhaps he would find enlightenment here. One never could anticipate the mechanisms of God, who was as much more complex in His devices as man was in relation to a windmill.

"We have a windmill that we use to pump water from the ground, among other chores," Brother Paul said. "But friction caused a bearing to burn out. Does that suggest anything to any of you?"

They all looked blank—three boys, two girls.

"In our studies at the Order we place emphasis on the elements," Brother Paul continued. "Not the atomic elements of latter-day science—though we study those, too—but the classical ones. Air, Earth, Water, Fire: we find these manifesting again and again in new ways. They show up in personality types, in astrology, in the Tarot deck—their symbolism is universal. Just now I—"

"The windmill!" the blonde girl said. "Wind is air! And it pumps water!"

"From the earth," one of the boys added.

"And it got burned," the surly one finished. "So what?"

"The four elements—all together," the first girl said, pleased. She clapped her hands together in unselfconscious joy. There was, Brother Paul noted, something very attractive about a young girl exclaiming in pleasure; perhaps it was nature's way of getting her married before she became a burden to her parents. "I think it's neat. Like a puzzle."

"What *good* is it?" the hulking boy demanded.

"It is an exercise in thinking," Brother Paul said. "As we seek parallels, coincidences, new aspects of things, we find meaning, and we grow. It is good to exercise the mind as well as the body. The ancient Greeks believed in that; hence we have the Pythagorean Theorem and the Olympic Games. We believe in it too. This, in a very real sense, is what the Holy Order of Vision is all about. 'Holy' as in 'Whole,' 'Vision' as in the vision of Saint Paul on the road to Damascus, that converted him to Christianity. He is not to be confused with Saint Paul the Hermit. We are not a church, but rather a brotherhood. We wish to bring together all people, and teach them the Universal Law of Creation, to prepare the Earth for the new age that is dawning. We try to provide for those in need, whatever that need may be, counseling them or offering material aid. We place great emphasis on practical applications—even windmills, in this day of retreating civilization."

"Hey, that's great!" the girl said. "Can anybody join?"

Bless her; she was doing his job for him! "Anybody

21

who wants to, after a student apprenticeship. We do have levels through which the novice progresses according to his ability and faith, and much of the life is not easy. You really have to understand the Order before you can know whether you want to be a part of it."

"Why do you wear the robes and study the Bible and all that?" one of the other boys asked. He was brown-skinned, like Brother Paul: that amalgam of races this culture still chose to term "black." "Can't you just go out and do good without all the trappings?"

"An excellent question," Brother Paul said. "You are really exploring the interrelationship of idea and form. A good idea is wasted without the proper form to embody it. For example, an excellent notion for a book would be ruined by clumsy or obscure writing. Or a fine idea for drawing power for the wind comes to nothing if the design of the gearing is inadequate. Perhaps man himself is an idea that exists in the mind of the Creator—yet that idea must achieve its appropriate form. So it is with us of the Holy Order of Vision; we feel that the forms *are* important, in fact indistinguishable from the basic idea."

"That's McLuhanism," the third boy said. He was a white-skinned, black-haired, clean-cut lad a little older than the others, and probably better educated. He had used a word few were now familiar with, testing the knowledge of the teacher.

"Not exactly," Brother Paul replied, glad to rise to the challenge. He liked challenges, perhaps more than he should. "The medium may be indistinguishable from the message, but it is *not* the message. Perhaps other forms of expression would serve our purpose as well, but we have a system that we feel works, and we shall adhere to it until it seems best to change." He closed his eyes momentarily, giving a silent prayer of thanks that the session was proceeding so well. Sometimes he seemed to make no contact at all, but these were alert, responsive minds. "We feel that God has found no better tool than the Bible to guide us, but perhaps one day—"

"Crap," the surly boy remarked. "God doesn't exist, and the Bible is irrelevant. It's all superstition."

Now the gauntlet had been thrown down. They all watched Brother Paul to see how he would react.

They were disappointed. "Perhaps you are right," he said, without rancor. "Skepticism is healthy. Speaking for myself alone, however, I must say that though at times I feel as you do, at other times I am absolutely certain that God is real and relevant. It is a matter for each person to decide for himself—and he is free to do so within the Order. We dictate no religion and we eschew none; we only present the material."

There was a chuckle. Brother Paul noted it with dismay, for he had not been trying to score debater's points, but only to clarify the position of the Order. Somehow he had erred, for now his audience was more intrigued by his seeming cleverness than by his philosophy.

Disgruntled, the hulking boy pushed forward. "I think you're a fake. You don't want to decide anything for yourself, you just want to follow the Order's line. You're an automaton."

"Perhaps so," Brother Paul agreed, searching for a way to alleviate the lad's ire without compromising the purpose of this session. How suddenly success had flipped over into failure! Pride before fall? "You are referring to the concept of predestination, and in that sense we are all automatons with only the illusion of self-decision. If every event in the world is precisely determined by existing forces and situations, then can we be said to have free will? Yet I prefer to assume—"

"You're a damned jellyfish!" the boy exclaimed. "Anything I say, you just agree! What'll you do if I push you, like this?" And he shoved violently forward with both hands.

Only Brother Paul wasn't there. He had stepped nimbly aside, leaving one leg outstretched behind him. The boy stumbled headlong over that leg. Brother Paul caught him and eased him down to the floor, retaining a hold on one of the boy's arms. "Never telegraph your intention," he said mildly. "Even a jellyfish or an automaton can escape such a thrust, and you could be embarrassed."

The boy started to rise, his expression murderous. He thought his fall had been an accident. But Brother Paul put just a bit of pressure on the hand he held, merely touching it with one finger, and the boy collapsed in sudden pain. He was helpless, though to the others it looked as though he were only fooling. A one-finger pain hold? Ridiculous!

"A little training in the forms can be advantageous," Brother Paul explained to the others. "This happens to be a form from aikido, a Japanese martial art. As you can see, my belief in it is stronger than this young man's disbelief. But were he to practice this form, he could readily reverse the situation, for he is very strong." Never underestimate the power of a gratuitous compliment! "The idea, as I remarked before, is valueless without the form."

Now, to see whether he could salvage the situation, he released the boy, who climbed quickly to his feet, his face red, but did not attack again. "Scientific application of anything can be productive," Brother Paul continued, "whether it is aikido or prayer." He faced the boy. "Now you try it on me."

"What?" The youth had been caught completely by surprise—again.

"Like this," Brother Paul said. "I shall come at you like this—" and he took an aggressive step forward, his right fist raised. "But you turn away from me and place your left foot back like this in the judo *tai otoshi* body drop—" He guided the boy around and got his feet placed. "Then catch my shirt and project your right foot before me like this, right across my shins. See how your body drops into position? That's why this throw is called the body drop." He more or less lifted the boy into position with a strength that was not evident to the others, but that the boy felt with amazement. "And because I am plunging forward, my feet trip over your leg while you haul my shirt—" It was not a shirt, but the loose front part of his habit, but the effect was the same. "And I am completely offbalanced and take a bad fall." Brother Paul flipped expertly over the leg and landed crashingly on his back and side, his left hand smacking into the straw mat the Station used in lieu of a rug.

The boy stood amazed, and the other four jumped in alarm. They did not know Brother Paul was adept at taking such falls, or that the noise was mostly from his hand slapping the mat to absorb much of the shock of landing. The muscular, bony arms and hands are much better able to take blows than the torso. "And if that doesn't do the job, you use hand pressure or an arm twist to keep me quiet." Brother Paul got up, and the boy moved to help him, fearing that he had been hurt. There was no longer any animosity.

"Did you study *that* here?" the brown boy asked, awed.

"Among other things," Brother Paul said. "Sometimes it is necessary for members of the Order to subdue someone who is temporarily, ah, indisposed. We do not approve the use of weapons, as they can hurt people severely, but the barehanded methods of self-defense or control—" He shrugged, smiling toward the formerly surly youth. "As you can see, he brought me down without hurting me."

They all returned his smile, and he knew it was all right again. God had guided him correctly. "Of course you do not have to join the Holy Order of Vision to receive such instruction. All of our courses in defense, reading, hygiene, farming, mechanics, figuring, and weaving are available to anyone who has the necessary interest and aptitude." He smiled again. "We can even be persuaded to teach a class or two in the appreciation of religion."

The blonde girl let out a titter of appreciation. "Do *you* teach that class, Brother?"

Brother Paul looked down. "I regret I lack the finesse or scholarship for that particular class. I am working on it, though, and in a few years I hope to be equipped." He looked up. "I thank you all for your attention to this introductory lecture. Now I will show you around the Station." He sniffed the air. "I believe Brother Peter is completing his baking. Perhaps we can pass the kitchen and sample his wares. To my mind there is nothing quite so good as bread hot from the stone oven with a little home-churned—"

But another Brother appeared. "The Reverend wishes to see you immediately," he murmured. "I will conduct the tour in your stead."

Oh-oh. Was he in trouble again? "Thank you, Brother Samuel." Brother Paul started out.

"What would you like to see first?" Brother Samuel asked the group.

As Brother Paul passed out through the doorway, he heard one of them answer, "The body drop." He smiled to himself, for poor Brother Samuel had a chronically stiff back and no training at all in the martial arts. But the delicious odor wafting from the bakery would rescue him, for young people were always hungry.

As he made his way to the Reverend's office, his thoughts became more sober. Had he done the right thing by this group, or had he merely been clever, impressing more by his physical power and rhetorical humor than by worthwhile information? It was so hard to know!

2

Memory

705 A.D.: *The daughter of an English missionary in Germany had such a genius for learning and seeming piety that she was elevated to the papal throne as John VII. Though in the guise of a male, she was—alas— female, and therefore, a vessel of iniquity. Yielding to her base female urges, she admitted a member of her household to her bed, and suffered that demonic fulfillment of her kind. In 707, during the course of a solemn Whitsun procession through the streets of Rome in the company of her clergy, at a point between the Colosseum and St. Clement's church, she who would become known as Pope Joan was delivered of a bastard son. The Popess was thus exposed as a harlot disguised as a priest. The story has, of course, been suppressed by the Church and labeled a myth, but there are those who remember it yet. This is the message of Key Two of the Tarot, entitled "The Lady Pope." Is it not, after all, a true reflection of the nature of the sex?*

Brother Paul walked past the luxurious vegetable gardens of the Station toward the office of the Reverend. It was a fine summer day. He hoped he had performed well, but he hummed nervously as he moved.

The sight of the Reverend's countenance solidified the doubts hovering about him. Some very serious matter was afoot, and he feared he had erred again. While discipline within the Order was subtle, Brother Paul had made many mistakes and done much internal penance.

The Reverend rose as he entered, and came forward to greet him. "It is good to see you, Paul. You have done well."

Glad words! So it was not one of his foul-ups, this time. "I try to do as the Lord decrees, Mother Mary," he said modestly, concealing his relief.

"Umph," the Reverend Mother agreed. She did not sit down, but paced nervously around the office. "Paul, a crisis of decision is upon us, and I must do a thing I do not like. Forgive me."

Something serious was certainly afoot! He studied her before he answered, trying to judge the appropriate response.

The Reverend Mother Mary was actually a young woman no older than himself, whose meticulous Order habit could not conceal her feminine attributes or render her sexless. She wore her dark brown hair parted down the middle, cupped to conceal her ears on either side, and pinned firmly in back—yet it framed her face like a mystical aura. Her reversed white collar clasped a very slender white neck, and her cross hung squarely on her bosom. Her robe was so long it touched the floor, concealing her feet. Occasionally it rippled and dragged behind her as she turned. Her personality, he knew, was sweet and open;

29

she was severe only in dire necessity. It would have been all too easy to love her as a pretty girl, had it not been essential to love her as a responsible woman and a fellow human being. And, of course, as the Reverend.

So it was best to allow her to unburden herself without concern for his feelings, which in any case were not easily hurt. Obviously she believed that what she had to say would cause him distress, and perhaps it would—but he was sure he could bear it. "Please speak freely, Mother."

The Reverend stepped to her desk and seemed almost to pounce on something there. "Take these, if you will," she said, proffering a small box.

Brother Paul accepted it. He had almost to snatch it, because her hand was shaking. Though her competence and position made her "Mother," at times she was more like a little girl, uncertain to the point of embarrassment. It had occurred to him before that an older person might have been better suited to the office of Reverend. But there were many Stations, and age was not the primary consideration.

He looked into the box. It contained a deck of Tarot cards, in its fashion the symbolic wisdom of all the ages.

She seated herself now, as though relieved of a burden. "Please shuffle them."

Brother Paul removed the deck from the box and spread several cards at the top of the deck. They were in order, beginning with the Fool, or Key Zero, and proceeding through the Magician, the High Priestess (also called the Lady Pope), the Empress, the Emperor, and so on through the twenty-two Trumps or Major Arcana and the fifty-six suit cards, or Minor Arcana. The suits were Wands, Cups, Swords, and

Disks, corresponding to the conventional Clubs, Hearts, Spades and Diamonds, or to the elements Fire, Water, Air and Earth. Each was a face card, beautifully drawn and colored. He had, like all Brothers and Sisters of the Order, studied the Tarot symbolism, had high respect for it, an was well-acquainted with the cards. One of the Order's exercises was to take black-and-white originals and color them according to instructions. This was no child's game; it was surprising how much revelation was inherent in this act. Color, like numbers and images, served a substantial symbolic purpose.

While he pondered, his fingers riffled the cards with an expertise that belied his ascetic calling. He had not always been a Brother, but like the Apostle Paul to whom he owed his Order name, he had set his savage prior life behind him. Only as a necessary exercise of contrition did he reflect upon the mistakes of his past. One day—when he was worthy—he hoped to seal that Pandora's box completely.

He completed the shuffle and returned the deck to the Reverend.

"Was the question in your mind the nature of my concern with you?" the Reverend inquired, holding the cards in her delicate fingers.

Brother Paul inclined his head affirmatively. It was a small white lie, since his thoughts had ranged in their unruly fashion all around the deck. Of course he had wondered why he was here; he had not been summoned from the midst of his class merely for chitchat! Still, a white lie *was* a lie.

"Let us try a reading," she said.

How quickly he paid for his lie! Her intent had been obvious when she gave him the deck; how could he have missed it? "I'm afraid I—"

31

"No, I am serious. The Tarot is a legitimate way to approach a problem—especially in this case. Let this define you."

She dealt the first card, careful to turn it over sidewise rather than end-over-end, so as not to reverse it, while Brother Paul concealed his agitation. He had made a foolish mistake that was about to cause them both embarrassment. He tried to think of some reasonable pretext to break up this reading, but all that came into his mind was a sacrilegious anecdote about Pope Joan, personification of the Whore of Babylon, epithet for the Roman Catholic Church. Such a thought was scandalous in the presence of the Reverend Mother Mary, who was completely chaste. Unless she had summoned him here to— No, impossible! A completely unworthy concept for which he would have to impose self-penance!

The card was the Ace of Wands, the image of a hand emerging from a cloud, bearing a sprouting wooden club.

"Amazing," the Reverend remarked. "This signifies the beginning of a great new adventure."

A great new adventure—with her? He tried hard to stifle the notion, fiendishly tempting as it was! In that moment he wished she were eighty years old, with a huge, hairy wart on her nose. Then his thoughts would behave. "Well, I must explain—"

"Shall we try the second?" She dealt another card from the top of the deck. She was feeling more at ease now; the cards were helping her to express herself. "Let this cross you," she said, placing the card sideways across the first.

May God have mercy! he thought fervently.

She looked at the second card, startled. "The Ace of Cups!"

32

"You see, I—I—" Brother Paul stammered.

The Reverend frowned. She was one of those women who looked even sweeter in dismay than in pleasure, if such a thing were possible. Silently she laid down the third card. It was the Ace of Swords. Then the fourth: the Ace of Coins. In each case, a hand was pictured emerging from a cloud, bearing the appropriate device.

Her gray-green eyes lifted to bear on him reproachfully.

"I did not realize what you intended," Brother Paul explained lamely. "I—old habits—I did not intend to embarrass you." No doubt Dante's Inferno had a special circle for the likes of him!

Mother Mary took a deep breath, then smiled—a burst of sunlight. "I had forgotten that you were once a cardsharp." She glanced down at the four aces and made a moue. "Still are, it seems."

"Retired," Brother Paul said quickly. "Reformed."

"I should hope so." She gathered up the cards.

"I'll shuffle them again, the right way," he offered.

She made a minor gesture of negation. "The wrong is the teacher of the right." But the ice had been broken. "Paul, it does not matter *how* you shuffled, so long as you formulated the correct question."

And of course he had *not* formulated it; he had been full of idle notions about the deck, Pope Joan, and such. His face was a mere shell, papering over the disaster of his mind.

"You are indeed about to embark on a remarkable new adventure—if you so choose."

Suddenly he realized that his penance would be to go on this mission, no matter how onerous it might prove. Today's declining civilization provided a number of most unpleasant situations. "I go where direct-ed," Brother Paul said.

"Not this time. I cannot send you on this particular round, and neither can the Order. You must volunteer for it. Knowing you as I do, I am sure you *will* volunteer, and therefore I am responsible." She looked up to the ceiling of rough-hewn logs. She was, he knew, making a quick, silent prayer. "I fear for you, Paul, and my soul suffers."

The eternal feminine! A mission had found its way down through the Order hierarchy, and she was upset because he might accept it. This was no mere rhetoric on her part; now one hand clutched the Tarot deck lightly, and now the other touched her cross. He had never seen her so tense before. It was as if she were the one with the guilty imagination, not he! "We all go where needed," he said.

"Yet some needs are stronger than others," the Reverend murmured, her eyes lifting to meet his again, her face dead serious. What could she mean by that? "It is Hell I am sending you to, Brother."

Brother Paul did not smile. He had never heard language like this from her! Of course she was not swearing; she would never do that. When she said Hell, the capitalization was audible, as it was for the Tarot; she meant the abode of the Devil. "Figurative, I trust?"

"Literal, Paul. And the returning will be harder than the going."

"It would be. Especially if it is necessary to die first." Was he being cute, implying that he might return to life, like Jesus? He had not meant to!

She did not smile. "No. Like Dante, you will be a living visitor. Perhaps you will see Heaven too."

"I don't think I'm ready for that." This time he was

completely serious. Heaven awed him more than Hell did. This had to be a really extraordinary thing she was describing!

The Reverend shook her head nervously, so that for an instant the lobe of one ear showed, like a bit of forbidden anatomy. "I am caught between the pillars of right and wrong, and I cannot tell them apart." She turned away from him; he had not realized that her chair could swivel. "Paul, I am required to present this to you as a prospective mission—but speaking as a Sister, as a friend, I must urge you to decline. It is not merely that it would sadden me never to see you again—though I do fear this, for no tangible reason—it is that this mission is a horror. A horror!"

"Now I am intrigued," Brother Paul said, his own apprehensions fading as hers increased. "May I learn more?"

"As much as we know," she said. "We have been asked to send our best qualified representative to Planet Tarot to ascertain the validity of its deity. A strong man, not too old, not too firmly committed to a single ideology, with a good mind and a fine sense of objectivity. You would seem to be that man."

Brother Paul ignored the compliment, knowing it was not intended as such. "Planet Tarot?"

"As you know, Earth has colonized something like a thousand habitable worlds in the current matter transport program. One of these is named Tarot, and there is a problem there."

"Hell, you said. I understood they did not send colonists to inclement habitats. If this planet is so hellish—"

"I did not say hellish, Paul. I said literal Hell. And the road to—"

35

"Oh, I see. It looked habitable, in the preliminary survey."

"Their surveyors must be overextended. How they managed to approve this particular planet—!" The Reverend Mother made a gesture of bafflement. "Its very name—"

"Yes, I am curious about that too. Most of the names are publicity-minded. 'Conquest,' 'Meadowland,' 'Zephyr'—how did they hit upon a name like 'Tarot'?"

"It seems a member of the survey party had a Tarot deck along. And while he waited at the base camp for his fellows to return, he dealt himself a divination hand. And—" She paused.

"And something happened."

"It certainly did. He—the card—the illustration on one of his cards took form. In three-dimensional animation."

Brother Paul's interest intensified. He had had experience with both sleight-of-hand and hallucinatory phenomena. "Had he been drinking an intoxicant?"

She shook her head. "They claim not. No alcohol, no drugs, no mushrooms or glue or extract of lettuce. That was why he happened to be entertaining himself with cards. And the other members of the party saw the animation."

"No hallucination, then. But possibly a practical joke?"

"No. No joke."

"Which card was it?"

"The Ten of Swords."

Brother Paul refrained from whistling, contenting himself with a grave nod. "Signifying ruin! Was it a literal image?"

36

"It was. Ten tall swords piercing a corpse. All quite solid."

"That should have shaken up the party!"

"It certainly did. They pulled out the swords and turned over the body. It was a man, but none they recognized. No one was missing from their crew. They buried him, saved the swords, and wrote up a report."

"Tangible evidence. That was smart."

"Not so smart. When they arrived on Earth, the objects they claimed were swords were merely so many slivers of stone, like stalactites from a cave. A second party, sent to verify the situation, dug up the body—and found only the carcass of a native animal."

"Mass hallucination?" Brother Paul suggested. "They killed an animal and thought it was a man? Because of fatigue and guilt—or because its configuration resembled that particular card? Stalactites *are* a bit like swords."

"That was the official conclusion." She paused, then girded herself to continue. "The second party brought Tarot cards and played many games, this time in the line of business, but there was no duplication of the effect. Apparently the first crew had been overworked and short on sleep, while the second was fresh. So they named the planet Tarot and approved it for colonization."

"Just like that?" Brother Paul inquired, raising an eyebrow.

"Just like that," the Reverend Mother said wryly, forgetting herself so far as to raise her own eyebrow in response. "They had a quota of planets to survey, and could not afford to waste time, as they put it, 'wild ghost chasing.' "

"How much is lost through haste!" Brother Paul remarked. But he felt a growing excitement and gratitude that this mystery had come to pass. Wild ghosts? He certainly would like to see one!

"Colonization proceeded in normal fashion," she continued. "One million human beings were shipped in the course of forty days, assigned to initial camp-sites with wilderness reduction equipment, and left to fend for themselves. Only the monthly coordination shuttle maintained contact. Colonization is," she commented with a disapproving frown, "somewhat of a sink-or-swim situation."

"Without doubt," Brother Paul agreed. "Yet the great majority of emigrants have been happy to risk it—and most seem to be swimming."

"Yes." She shrugged. "It is not the way I would have chosen—but the decision was hardly mine to make. At any rate, the colonists settled—and then the fun began."

"More Tarot animations?"

"No, not specifically. These animations were of Heaven—and of Hell. I mean the storybook Pearly Gates, with angels flying by, and harpists sitting on clouds. Or the other extreme—fiery caves with red, fork-tailed devils with pitchforks."

"Evidently literal renditions of religious notions," Brother Paul said. "Many believers have very material views of the immaterial."

"They do. There seems to be an unusual concentration of schismatic religions in this colony world. But these were rather substantial projections." She pulled out a drawer in her desk and brought forth several photographs. "Skeptics arranged to take pictures— and we have them here." She spread them out.

He studied the pictures with amazement. "There was no, ah, trick photography? They certainly look authentic!"

38

"No trick photography. There is more: the colonists organized a planetary orchestra—in any random sampling of a million people, you'll find many skills—and they practiced many semiclassical pieces. One day they were doing the tone poem by Saint-Saëns, 'Danse macabre,' and—"

"Oh, no! Not the dancing skeletons!"

"The same. The entire orchestra panicked, and two musicians died in the stampede. In fact, I believe the orchestra was disbanded after that, and never reorganized. But when cooler heads investigated, they found no trace of the walking skeletons."

"I begin to see," Brother Paul said, feeling an unholy anticipation of challenge. "Planet Tarot is haunted."

"That is one way of putting it," she agreed. "We view it more seriously." She waited until his face assumed the proper expression of seriousness. "Most haunts don't lend themselves well to motion-picture photography." She brought a reel from the drawer.

Brother Paul did a double-take. "Motion-picture film of the skeletons?"

"That's right. It seems a colonist was filming the concert. He thought the skeletons were part of the show—until the stampede began."

"This I would like to see!"

"You shall." The Reverend set up a little projector, lit its lensed lamp, and cranked the handle. The picture flickered on the wall across from her desk.

It was, indeed, the dance of death. At first there were only the musicians, playing their crude, locally fashioned violins; then the skeletons pranced onstage, moving in time to the music. There was no sound, of course; a lamp-and-hand-crank projector was not capable of that. But Brother Paul could see the breathing of the players, the motions of their hands on the instruments, and the gestures of the conductor; the beat was clear.

One skeleton passed close to the camera, its gaunt, white ribcage momentarily blotting out the orchestra. Brother Paul peered closely, trying to ascertain what manner of articulation those bones possessed; it was hardly credible that they could move without muscle, sinew, or wires. Yet they did.

Then the scramble began; the picture veered crazily and clicked off.

"I understood there was a one-kilogram limit on personal possessions for emigrants," Brother Paul commented. "How did a sophisticated device like a motion-picture camera get there?"

"They can make them very small these days," the Reverend said. "Actually, two emigrants shared their mass allotment in this case, and three others in the family collaborated by taking fragments of a matching projector that could be run by hand. Like this one." She patted it. "They yielded to need rather than philosophy; nevertheless, they were ingenious. Now we know how fortunate that was. No one on Earth would have believed their story otherwise. This film is evidence that cannot be ignored; *something* is happening on Planet Tarot, something extraordinary. The authorities want to know what."

"But why should they come to us?" Brother Paul asked. "I should think they would send scientists with sophisticated equipment."

She moved one hand in an unconscious "be patient" gesture. "They did. But the effect seems to be intermittent."

Intermittency—the scourge of repairmen and psychic investigators! How was it possible to understand something that operated only in the absence of the investigator? "Meaning the experts found nothing?" he asked.

"Correct. But they also interviewed the colonists and assembled a catalogue of episodes. They discovered that the manifestations were confined to certain times and certain places—usually. And they occurred only in the presence of believers."

"This has a familiar ring," Brother Paul said. "The believer experiences; the nonbeliever doesn't. It is the way with faith." He remembered his own discussion with the boys and girls of the village class; his belief had been stronger than their disbelief.

"Precisely. Except that the skeptics of the colony were able to witness a few of the phenomena. Whereupon they became believers."

As Saul of Tarsus had witnessed the grandeur of God on the road to Damascus, and become Christian. As the village youths had witnessed the power of martial arts. "Believers in what?"

"In whatever they saw. There may have been skeptics when the "*danse macabre*" recital began, but there were none at the end, because the skeletons were tangible. But there were other manifestations. In one case it was God—or at least a burning bush that spoke quite clearly, claiming to be God."

Presumptuous bush! "Sounds like a case for the priests, rabbis, or holy men."

"They were the next to investigate. They proceeded directly to the haunted regions." She stopped, and Brother Paul did not prompt her with another question. She stared at the desk for some time, as though probing every fissure in its rough grain, and finally resumed. "It was a disaster. Two resigned from their ministries, two had to be incarcerated as mentally in-

41

competent, and two died. It seems they experienced more Hell than Heaven. That is how the job filtered down to us."

"Those apparitions actually *killed*? Took human life? No stampede or other physical cause?"

"Those apparitions, or whatever it was those people experienced, actually did destroy minds and take human life." She faced Brother Paul squarely, and her concern for him made her almost radiant. He knew she would turn the same expression on a wounded rattlesnake or a torn manuscript; that was what made her so lovely. "Now you know what I fear. Are you ready to go to Hell?"

Ready? He was eager! "It sounds fascinating. But what exactly would be my mission there? To exorcise the Devil of Tarot?"

"No. I fear that would be beyond your powers, or mine, or any of our Order." She smiled very briefly. "The holy men who failed were prominent, devout men, thorough scholars, whose faith in their religions was tested and true. I find it strange that they should have suffered so greatly, while the large majority of the colonists, who represent a random sampling of Earth, have had few such problems."

Brother Paul nodded. "Perhaps not so strange. It may be that training and belief are liabilities in that situation."

"Perhaps. It is true that those who feel most strongly about religion obtain the strongest response from Planet Tarot. Those whose primary concern is to feed their faces—do just that."

As luck would have it, a strong waft of the aroma of Brother Peter's hot bread passed through the room, making Brother Paul's mouth water. "Are you suggesting that my concern is to feed my face?" he asked with a smile. Now that the nature of the mission had been clarified, his tension was gone.

"You know better than that, Paul! But you are not a divinity specialist. Your background is broader, touching many aspects of the human state. More than the experience of most people. You know the meaning of prayer—and of pipefitting. Of divination—and gambling."

"Those are apt parallels."

"Thank you. You are aware of things that are beyond my imagination." Brother Paul fervently hoped so; had she any inkling of the mishmash of notions that coursed through his brain, she would be shocked. He was reminded of a childhood game his friends had played, called Heaven or Hell. One boy and one girl were selected by lot to enter a dark closet. For one minute he had either to kiss her (Heaven) or hit her (Hell). Once Brother Paul had dreamed of taking the Reverend into such a closet, and he had awakened in a cold sweat, horrified. The very memory was appalling, now. Until that memory was gone, he would not be fit material for advancement within the Holy Order of Vision.

But she was unaware of this chasm within him—an innocence for which he sincerely thanked God. "I feel you would not concentrate exclusively on the religious implications of the problem," she continued blithely. "You would relate to the concerns of the colonists as well. Perhaps you will be able to ascertain not only what happened to the priests, but why it *doesn't* happen to the colonists, and why faith seems to be such a liability. But more important—"

"I think I anticipate you," Brother Paul murmured.

"We want to ascertain whether this phenomenon is ultimately material or spiritual. We have observed only the fringes of it so far, but there appear to be elements of both. One explanation is that this is a test for man, of his coming-of-age: that God, if you will, has elected to manifest Himself to man in this challenging fashion. We do not want to ignore that challenge, and certainly we do not wish to risk crucifying Christ again! But we also cannot afford to embarrass ourselves by treating too seriously a phenomenon that may have completely mundane roots."

"God has completely mundane roots," Brother Paul pointed out, with no negative intent.

"But He also has completely divine branches. The one without the other—"

"Yes, I appreciate the delicacy of the problem."

"If this manifestation should actually stem from God, we must recognize and answer the call," the Reverend Mother said. "If it is a purely material thing, we would like to know exactly what it is, and how it works, and why religion is vulnerable to it. That surely will not be easy to do!" She paused. "Why am I so excited, Paul, yet so afraid? I have urged you not to go, yet at the same time—"

Brother Paul smiled. "You are afraid I shall fail. Or that I will actually *find* God there. Either would be most discomfiting—for of course the God of Tarot is also the God of Earth. The God of Man."

"Yes," she said uncertainly. "But after all our centuries of faith, can we really face the reality? God may not conform to our expectations, yet how could we reject Him? We *must* know Him! It frightens me! In short—"

"In short," Brother Paul concluded, "you want me to go to Hell—to see if God is there."

∞

Unknown

Consciousness has been compared to a mirror in which the body contemplates its own activities. It would perhaps be a closer approximation to compare it to the kind of Hall of Mirrors where one mirror reflects one's reflection in another mirror, and so on. We cannot get away from the infinite. It stares us in the face whether we look at atoms or stars, or at the becauses behind the becauses, stretching back through Eternity. Flat-Earth science has no more use for it than the flat-Earth theologicians had in the Dark Ages; but a true science of life must let infinity in, and never lose sight of it. . . . Throughout the ages the great innovators in the history of science had always been aware of the transparency of phenomena towards a different order of reality, of the ubiquitous presence of the ghost in the machine—even such a simple machine as a magnetic compass or a Leyden jar. Once a scientist loses this sense of mystery, he can be an excellent technician, but he ceases to be a *savant*.

Arthur Koestler: *The Ghost in the Machine*

The Station of the Holy Order of Vision was, Brother Paul was forcibly reminded, well out in the sticks. It had not always been that way. This had once been a ghetto area. In the five years of the Matter Transmission program, officially and popularly known as MT and Empty respectively, several billion human beings had been exported to about a thousand colony planets. This was a rate that would soon depopulate the world.

But it was not the policy of the Holy Order of Vision to interfere in lay matters. Brother Paul could think his private thoughts, but he must never try to force his political or economic opinions on others. Or, for that matter, his religious views.

So now he trekked through the veritable wilderness surrounding the Station, past the standing steel bones of once-great buildings projecting into the sky like remnants of dinosaurs. During winter's snows the effect was not so stark; the bones were blanketed. But this was summer. His destination was the lingering, shrinking technological civilization of the planet. The resurging brush and shrubs grew thicker and taller as he covered the kilometers, as though their growth kept pace with his progress, then gave way on occasion to clusters of dwellings like medieval villages. Each population cluster centered around some surviving bastion of technology: electricity generated from a water wheel, a wood-fueled kiln, or industrial-scale windmills.

Village, he thought. From the same Latin root as *villa*, the manor of a feudal lord. Inhabited by feudal serfs called *villains*, whose ignorant nature lent a somewhat different meaning to that word in later centuries. Society was fragmenting into its original components, under the stress of deprivation of energy. Electronics was virtually a dead science in the hinterlands where there was no electricity; automotive technology was passé where there was no gasoline. Horsepower and handicrafts had quickly resumed their former prominence, and Brother Paul was not prepared to call this evil. Pollution was a thing of the past, except in mining areas, and children today did not know what the term "inflation" meant, since barter was the order of the day. People lived harder lives now, but often healthier ones, despite the regression of medical technology. The enhanced sense of community in any given village was a blessing; neighbor was more apt to help neighbor, and the discontented had gone away. Light-years away.

However, he approached each village carefully, for the villains could be brutish with strangers. Brother Paul was basically a man of peace, but neither a weakling nor a fool. He donned his Order habit when near population centers to make himself more readily identifiable. He would defend himself with words and smiles and humility wherever he could, and with physical measures when all else failed.

Though he was a Brother of an Order with religious connotations, he neither expected nor received free benefits on that account. He rendered service for his night's board and lodging; there was always demand for a man handy with mechanical things. He exchanged news with the lord of each manor, obtaining directions and advice about local conditions. Everyone knew the way to MT. Each night he found a different residence. In some areas of the country, actual primitive tribes had taken over, calling themselves Saxons, Huns, Cimmerians, Celts, or Picts, and in many respects they did resemble their historic models. The Saxons were Americans of northern European descent; the Huns were Americans of middle European admixed with Oriental descent; the Cimmerians seemed to be derived from the former fans of fantasy adventure novels. Elsewhere in the world, he knew, the process was similar; there were even Incas in Asia. He encountered one strong tribe named Songhoy whose roots were in tenth-century Black Africa. Their location, with ironic appropriateness, was in the badlands of black craters formed by savagely rapid and deep strip mining for coal. Once there had been enough coal in America to power the world for centuries; no more.

The Holy Order of Vision, always hospitable to peaceful travelers, had entertained and assisted Shamans and Druids and other priestly representatives, never challenging their beliefs or religious authority. A Voodoo witch-doctor could not only find hospitality at the Station, he could converse with Brothers of the Order who took him completely seriously and knew more than a little about his practice. Now this policy paid off for Brother Paul. The small silver cross he wore became a talisman of amazing potency wherever religion dominated—and this was more extensive every year. Political power reached only as far as the arm of the local strong man, but clerical power extended as far as faith could reach. The laity gave way increasingly to the clerical authorities, as in medieval times. Thus Brother Paul was harvesting the fruit of the seeds sown by his Order. In addition, he had rather persuasive insights into the culture of Black societies, whether of ancient Africa or modern America. He fared very well.

After many pleasant days of foot travel he entered the somewhat vaguely defined demesnes of twentieth-century civilization. Here there was electricity from a central source, and radio and telephones and automotive movement. He obtained a ride on a train drawn by a woodburning steam engine; no diesels or coal-fired vehicles remained operative, of course. The electricity here was generated by sunlight, not fossil fuel, for MT was as yet unable to preempt the entire light of the sun for the emigration program. "Maybe tomorrow," the wry joke went.

The reason for the lack of clear boundaries to the region was that the electric power lines did not extend all the way to the periphery, and batteries were reserved for emergency use. But radio communication reached some distance farther out, so that selected offices could be linked to the news of the world. At this fringe, wood was the fuel of choice where it was available.

This was a pleasant enough ride, allowing Brother Paul to rest his weary feet. He felt a bit guilty about using the Order credit card for this service, but in one day he traversed more territory than he had in a week of foot travel. He could not otherwise have arrived on time.

He spent this night at the Station of the Coordinator for the Order in this region: the Right Reverend Father Crowder. Brother Paul was somewhat awed by the august presence of this pepper-maned elder, but the Right Reverend quickly made him even less at ease. "How I envy you your youth and courage,

Brother! I daresay you run the cross-country kilometer in under three minutes."

"Uh, sometimes—"

"Never cracked three-ten myself. Or the five-minute mile. But once I managed fifteen honest pullups in thirty seconds on a rafter in the chapel." He smiled ruefully. "The chapelmaster caught me. He never said a word—but, oh, the look he gave me! I never had the nerve to try it again. But I'm sure you would never allow such a minor excuse to interfere with your exercise."

Obviously the man knew something about Brother Paul's background—especially the calisthenics he had been sneaking in when he thought no one was watching. He hoped he wasn't blushing.

"The mission you now face requires a good deal more nerve than that sort of thing," Right Reverend Crowder continued. "You have nerve, presence of mind, great strength, and a certain refreshing objectivity. These were qualities we were looking for. Yet it will not be easy. Not only must you face God—you must pass judgment on His validity. I do not envy you this charge." He turned and put his strong, weathered hands on Brother Paul's shoulders. "God bless you and give you strength," he said sincerely.

God bless you . . . Brother Paul swayed, closing his eyes in momentary pain.

"Easy, Brother," the Right Reverend said, steadying him. "I know you are tired after your arduous journey. Go to your room and lie down; get a good night's rest. We shall see you safely on the bus to the mattermission station in the morning."

The Right Reverend was, of course, as good as his word. Well rested and well fed, Brother Paul was deposited on the bus for a four-hour journey into the

50

very depths of civilization. Thus, quite suddenly, he came to the MT station: Twenty-First Century America.

He was met as he stepped down from the coach by an MT official dressed in a rather garish blue uniform. "Very good," the young man said crisply, sourly eyeing Brother Paul's travel-soiled Order robe. "You are the representative of the Visual Order—"

"The Holy Order of Vision," Brother Paul corrected him tolerantly. A Druid never would have made such an error, but this was, after all, a lay official. "Holy as in 'whole,' for we try to embrace the entire spirit of—"

"Yes, yes. Please come this way, sir."

"Not 'sir.' I am a Brother. Brother Paul. All men are brothers—" But the imperious functionary was already moving ahead, forcing Brother Paul to hurry after him.

He did so. "Before I go to the colony world, I'll need a source of direct current electricity to recharge my calculator," he said. "I'm not an apt mathematician, and there may be complexities that require—"

"There isn't time for that!" the man snapped. "The shipment has been delayed for hours pending your arrival, interfering with our programming. Now it has been slotted for thirty minutes hence. We barely—"

He should have remembered: Time, in the form of schedules, was one of the chief Gods of MT, second only to Power. Brother Paul had become too used to a day governed by the position of the sun. He had been lent a good watch along with the calculator for this mission, but had not yet gotten into the habit of looking at it. "I certainly would not want to profane your schedule, but if I am to do my job properly—"

51

With a grimace of exasperation the man drew him into a building. Inside was a telephone. "Place an order for new batteries," he rapped out, handing the transceiver to Brother Paul.

Such efficiency! Brother Paul had lost familiarity with telephones in the past few years. Into which portion of the device was he supposed to speak? He compromised by speaking loudly enough to catch both ends of it, describing the batteries. "Authorization granted," the upper part of the phone replied after a click. "Pick them up at Supply."

"Supply?" But the phone had clicked off. That seemed to be the manner, here in civilization.

"Come on," the functionary said. "We'll catch it in passing." And they did; a quick stop at another building produced the required cells. These people were not very sociable, but they got the job done!

"And this," the man at the supply desk said, holding out a heavy metal bracelet.

"Oh, Brothers don't wear jewelry, only the Cross," Brother Paul protested. "We have taken vows of poverty—"

"Jewelry, hell," the man snorted. "This is a molecular recorder. There'll be a complete playback when you return: everything you have seen or heard and some things you haven't. This unit is sensitive to quite a few forms of radiation and chemical combinations. Just keep it on your left wrist and forget it. But don't cover it up."

Brother Paul was taken aback. "I had understood that this was to be a personal investigation and report. After all, a machine can't be expected to fathom God."

"Ha ha," the supply man said without humor. "Just put it on."

Reluctantly Brother Paul held up his left arm. The man clasped the bracelet on it, snapping it in place. He should have realized that the secular powers who controlled mattermission would not cooperate unless they had their secular assurances. They did not care whether God had manifested on Planet Tarot; their God was the Machine. The Machine embraced both Time and Power, ruling all. Yet perhaps it was only fair; who could say in advance that the God of Tarot was not a machine deity? Therefore it was proper that the Machine send its representative, too.

"And this," the supply man said, holding out a set of small rods, "is a short-range transceiver. Hold it up, speak, this other unit receives. And vice versa. Required equipment for all our operatives."

"I am not your operative," Brother Paul said as gently as he could. He was, he reminded himself, supposed to be a peaceful man.

"Who's paying your fare, round trip?" the man asked.

Brother Paul sighed. He who paid the piper, called the tune. Render unto Caesar, et cetera. He took the transceivers and tucked them into a pocket. He could carry them; he didn't have to use them.

"Mind," the supply man said, his brows furrowing, "we expect this equipment back in good order."

"You can have it back now," Brother Paul said.

No one answered him. He was whisked into another building and subjected to assorted indignities of examination and preparation. In their savage velocity and callousness, these procedures reminded him vaguely of the strip mining he had seen. Then he was hurried into the thermos bottle-like capsule and sealed in. All he had to do now was wait.

He examined the chamber. It was fairly large, but

packed with unboxed equipment. Crates would have been wasteful, of course; every gram counted. Most of it was readily identifiable: hand-powered adding machines, spinning wheels, looms, treadle-powered sewing machines, mechanical typewriters, axes, handsaws, wood stoves, and the like. A sensible shipment for a colony that might be as backward as the hinterlands of Earth itself.

Those adding machines bothered him. How could he justify his fuss about the electronic calculator? He was out of tune with the technology of his mission. Perhaps he had been shortsighted. Was it rationalization to suggest that the adding machines could not readily multiply or divide numbers, do specialized conversions, or figure the cube root of *pi*? A slide rule could do those things, and it had no battery to run down. Why hadn't he brought along a slide rule? That would have been far more in keeping with the philosophy of the Holy Order of Vision. The lay powers of Earth were using calculators whose usefulness would cease when their power sources expired. He, as a Brother, should be showing his fellow man how to use slide rules that would function as long as mind and hands remained.

"I am a hypocrite," he murmured aloud. "May God correct and forgive me."

He looked at his watch—he was finally getting into that habit!—and set the elapsed-time counter. Of course mattermission was supposed to be instantaneous, the Theory of Relativity to the contrary, but there was this waiting time, and he might as well measure that. He liked to count things anyway. It was better than admitting that he was nervous.

His eye caught the silver-colored band on his wrist. It had an elaborate decoration, like a modernistic

54

painting done in relief. No doubt that was to conceal the lenses and mechanisms within it. When it was necessary to hide something, fit it into a complex container. As the crown-maker had done to conceal the amount of base metal diluting the value of the supposedly pure gold crown of Hieron, ruler of the ancient city of Syracuse. Except that Archimedes had cried "Eureka!" and found it, utilizing the principle of water displacement.

Probably the band was recording things now. How fortunate it could not record his thoughts! But what would happen when he wished to perform a natural function? Maybe he could hold that wrist up over his head so the device couldn't see anything. Yet suppose he did so, and suddenly heard it cry "Eureka!"?

He smiled at himself. Ridiculous mortal vanity! What did it matter what portion of his anatomy this device might perceive? When the lay experts played back the molecules, they would quickly be bored by the minutiae of human water displacements. Let the machine capture and contain all the information it could hold, until its cup brimmethed over.

Abruptly it struck him: a cup! This bracelet was like the Cup of the Tarot, containing not fluid but information. And the little transceivers—they were Wands. His watch was the emblem of a third suit, Disks, for it was essentially a disk with markings, and hands pointing to the time of day that in Nature was shown by the original golden disk of the sun. Three suits. What might be the fourth, that of Swords?

That stymied him for a moment. Swords were representative of trouble, violence; he had no such weapon on him. Swords were also the suit of air, and while he had air about him, this didn't seem to apply. The sword was also a scalpel, signifying surgery or medicine, and of course there was the cutting edge of thought— That was it! The sharpest, most tangible thought was the symbolism of numbers, of mathematics. The calculator! Thus he had a full roster of Tarot symbolism. Too bad he hadn't brought along a Tarot deck; that could have distracted him very nicely.

Brother Paul sat on a stove, waiting for the shipment to ship. After all that rush, they might at least have gotten on with it promptly once he was inside the capsule! But perhaps there were technical things to do, like switching coaches onto other sidings or whatever, lining everything up for the big jump. It was difficult to imagine how, in this nineteenth-century setting, he could be jolted to a world perhaps fifty light-years distant. He should have thought to inquire exactly where Planet Tarot was; that seemed much more important now that he was on the verge of jumping there. Was a jump of seventy light-years more hazardous than a jump of twenty light-years? The concept of instantaneous travel bothered him in a vague way, like the discomfort of an incipient stomach disorder that might or might not lead to retching. He would never understand how mattermission worked. Didn't old Albert Einstein know his math? Yet obviously it did exist—or did it?

His watch claimed that only another minute had passed since his last look, or a total of two and a half minutes since he had set the counter. That didn't help; subjectively he had aged far more than that!

There were chronic whispers about that objection of Relativity, rumors always denied by MT, yet persistent. Twentieth-century science had accomplished many things supposed to have been impossible in the nineteenth century; why shouldn't twenty-first century science supersede the beliefs of the twentieth? Yet he found that he now had the same difficulty disbelieving in Relativity as he had initially had believing in it. Suddenly, in the close confines of this capsule, those whispers were easy to believe. There was no doubt that Earth was being depopulated, and that such tremendous amounts of energy were being consumed that the whole society was regressing, the victim of energy starvation. But there was also no question that the emigration mechanism, MT, had been deemed impossible by the best human minds of the past. The obvious reconciliation: people *were* departing Earth—but they *weren't* arriving at other planets. The whole vast MT program could be a ruse to—

Suddenly his queasiness gave way to acute claustrophobia. He looked about nervously for nozzles that might admit poisonous gas. The Jews in Nazi Germany, half a century or so ago: they had been promised relief—

No, that didn't make sense! Why go to the trouble of summoning a single novice of a semireligious Order to this elaborate setup? Anyone who wanted him out of the way could find much less cumbersome means to eliminate him! And the Order would not suffer itself to be deceived like this. The Right Reverend Father Crowder would never countenance such a thing; of this Brother Paul was absolutely sure. And the Reverend Mother Mary, angelic in her concern for the good of all men . . .

The Reverend Mother Mary. Why fool himself? He had agreed to undertake this mission because she had asked him to. Oh, she had pleaded the opposite, most charmingly. But he would have been diminished in her eyes if he had heeded that plea.

This was no more profitable a line of thought than

the other had been. He was here neither for death nor for love. He was supposed to ascertain the validity of the God of Tarot, and the project fascinated him. Why distract himself with superficially unreasonable or impossible things, when his actual assignment surpassed the unreason or impossibility of either? How could a mere man pass judgment on God?

Brother Paul drew out his calculator, his symbol for thought, his figurative Sword of Tarot. It was an early model, perhaps twenty-five years old. An antique, but it still operated. The Holy Order of Vision took good care of those devices it preserved, perhaps fearing that one year there would be no reservoir of technology but this. The calculator had a number of square white buttons, and a number of square black ones. By depressing these buttons in the proper order he could set up any simple mathematical problem and obtain an immediate solution. Instantaneous—like the travel between worlds! This was travel between the worlds of concepts, not of space.

Idly he turned it on, watching the green zero appear in the readout window. "Two," he murmured, touching the appropriate button, and the zero was transformed miraculously into 2. "Plus three—equals five." And the green 5 was there ahead of him.

Brother Paul smiled. He liked this little machine; it might not rival the Colony computer, but it did its limited job well. "Let's remember that," he said, punching the MEMORY button, then the PLUS button. That should file the number in the memory as a positive integer. Now he touched the CLEAR ENTRY button, and the cheerful zero reappeared, as green as ever. He punched MEMORY and RECALL and the 5 returned. Good; the memory was functioning properly.

"Let's convert it from kilograms to pounds," he continued, for this was an old conversions calculator complete with the archaic measurements, as befitted the date of its origin. He touched the CONVERSIONS button, then the MINUS button, which was now understood to represent kilograms. Then the DIVIDE button, which was now pounds. These double designations were initially confusing, but necessary to make twenty buttons do the work of fifty. The answer: 11.023113.

"File that useless information in Memory Two," he said, punching MEMORY again, followed by 2, followed by PLUS, followed by CLEAR ENTRY. The readout returned to zero. Oh, he had forgotten what fun this was! "Now the number 99999999 multiplied by the number in Memory One." He punched a row of eight nines, then TIMES, then MEMORY, 1, RECALL, then EQUALS. He frowned.

A red dot had appeared in the left-hand corner of the readout. "Overload," he said. "No room for a nine-digit number! Clear it out." He struck the CLEAR button several times, then turned off the calculator so as not to waste battery power while he thought.

"Very well, he said after a moment. "Let's keep it within bounds. Multiply Memory One by Memory Two." He turned it on again and punched the necessary sequence rapidly. All he got were zeroes. "Oh, I forgot! Turning it off erases the memory! I'll have to start over." He punched in a new 5, put it in Memory One, converted it from kilos to pounds, put that into Memory Two, cleared the readout, forgot what he was doing, and punched for Memory Two Recall. The result was zero.

"Something's wrong," he said. He went through the

sequence again, watching his fingers move fleetingly over the keys—and saw his error. He had missed the 2 button for Memory Two and hit the TIMES button instead. "Can't put it in TIMES MEMORY!" he said. "That would mean I'd have to punch MEMORY TIMES RECALL to get it out, and the poor machine would think I'd gone crazy and have to flash overload lights at me to jog me out of it." As he spoke, he punched the foolish sequence he had named. The readout showed 11.023113.

Brother Paul stared at that. Then he erased the sequence and went through it all again, carefully punching the erroneous TIMES MEMORY, which was not supposed to exist. The same thing happened: he got the number back. "But that means this thing has a third memory—and it's only built for two," he said.

So he tested it methodically, for there was nothing so intriguing to him as a good mystery or paradox. He punched the number 111 into Memory One, 222 into Memory Two, and 333 into MEMORY TIMES. Then he punched out each in turn. Up they came, like the chosen cards of a sleight-of-hand magician: 111— 222—0.

"Zero!" he exclaimed. "So it *isn't* true!" But just to be certain, he repeated the process, this time checking TIMES MEMORY first—and the 333 appeared. He checked for the 222 and found it, and then the 111—and it was there too. No doubt about it; he now had three memories. But the third one was intermittent, following some law of its own, as though it were half wild.

"Half wild . . ." he repeated aloud, thinking of something else. But if he got off on that, he would not solve the present mystery. He glanced at his watch. He had really gobbled up time with his calculations! Ten minutes, forty-two seconds, give or take a second, since he had set the counter. How long would they dawdle about mattermitting this capsule?

He cleared the readout and punched MEMORY TIMES again. The 333 reappeared. "A ghost in the machine," he said. "A secret memory, unknown to—"

"So you found me," a voice responded. "Yet I was always here, to be evoked."

Brother Paul's eyes flicked from the calculator to his watch—ten minutes, forty-nine seconds—then lifted slowly. A man stood before him, on the far side of the sewing machine. He was young, but with receding hair and chin, as though he had been subjected to early stress. No, that was a false characterization; physical appearance had little to do with personality. "Sorry. I did not see you arrive," Brother Paul said. "Are you traveling to Planet Tarot too?"

The man smiled, but there was something strange about the way his mouth moved. "Perhaps—if you so choose."

"I am Brother Paul of the Holy Order of Vision." He put forth his hand.

"I am Antares," the man said, but made no motion to accept the hand.

"Well, Mr. Antares—or is it Brother Antares? Are you another investigator?"

"It is only Antares. Sexual designations have little meaning to my kind, and you would not understand my personal designation. Do you not know me?"

Brother Paul looked at him again, more carefully this time. This was just an ordinary man, wearing a dark tunic. "I regret that the only Antares I know of is a bright red star."

"Exactly."

"You associate with the star Antares?" Brother Paul asked, perplexed.

"I am the emissary from Sphere Antares, yes," the man affirmed.

"I was not aware that our colonies extended so far. Isn't Antares many hundreds of light-years distant from Sol?"

"About five hundred of your light-years, yes, in your constellation Scorpio. We are not a colony, but a separate Sphere. There are many sapient Spheres in the galaxy, and in other galaxies, each highly advanced in the center and fading in technology and competence at the fringe, owing to the phenomenon of spherical regression. Thus each empire has certain natural limits, depending on—"

"Scorpio," Brother Paul said musingly, grasping that portion of the alien's discussion to which he could relate. "The constellation."

"The scorpion that slew Orion, in your mythology," the man said agreeably. "Of course, in real history, the constellation you call Orion's Belt is the center of Sphere Mintaka, perhaps the largest and most influential Sphere in this sector of galactic space, with the possible exception of Sphere Sador. A giant, certainly, but never slain by anything in *our* rather more modest Sphere! Actually, war between the Spheres is virtually unknown, because of the problems of communication and transport."

Brother Paul was still belatedly assimilating the implications. "Perhaps I misunderstand. It almost seems that you imply you are a man from a—a regime centered in the region of the space known as—"

"Not a man, Solarian Brother Paul. I am an Antarean, a sapient creature quite alien to your type, except in intellect."

62

"An alien creature!" Was this a joke? Brother Paul looked at his watch. The counter indicated ten minutes, forty-nine seconds. Well, he would test Antares statement. "I regret that I have not encountered many alien creatures. Your form appears human—or is that a mirage?"

"This is my Solarian host. My aura was transferred to this host so that I could present to your species the technology of matter transmission. In exchange you gave us controlled hydrogen fusion."

Matter transmission! "*You* brought us that break-through technology?"

"True. It would otherwise have been some time before your Sphere developed it. The principles are foreign to the main thrust of your technology, just as the principles of hydrofusion are foreign to ours. In fact, historically, our experts believed it was theoretically impossible to accomplish such a process artificially. Our Theory of Absolutivity—"

This was a strange joke! "Antares, I would like to see you in your alien form. Would you mind materializing in that?" If this were a prank, that would expose it!

The person before him faded. In his place appeared a large amoebalike mass. On its top, it erected a pattern of spongy knobs that flexed up and down like the keys of a player piano. Then it flung out a pseudopod, a glob of gelatinous substance that landed a meter to the side connected to the main mass by a dwindling tendril. Fluid pulsed along this tendril, distending it, collecting at the end, swelling the glob until it approached the size of the main body. The process continued, making the glob even larger until at last it was the original body that was a glob, while the glob had expanded to the size of the original mass. Then the trailing tendril was sucked in. The creature now stood one meter to the side of where it had stood before. It had taken one step.

It faded, and the man reappeared. "We Antareans may be slow, but there are few places we cannot go," he said. "I have returned to the form of my human host so that I may converse with you; I doubt that you are facile in my native language."

"Uh, thank you," Brother Paul said. "That was an impressive demonstration. May I touch you?"

"I regret you cannot," the alien said. "Both my forms are insubstantial. You perceive only an animation shaped by my aura, and this is possible only while we endure in the process of transmission. You may pass your appendage through the image, but you will feel nothing."

"So you are a ghost," Brother Paul said. "An apparition without substance. Nevertheless, I am inclined to make the attempt." He reached forward slowly, over the sewing machine.

Antares did not retreat the way a joker might. He stood still, waiting for the touch.

There was no touch. Brother Paul felt a slight tingling, as of an electrical charge that gave him an odd thrill but no physical contact. This was, indeed, a ghost.

"Your aura! Amazing!" Antares exclaimed. "Never have I felt the like!"

This was strange, and far beyond the parameters of a practical joke. "My aura?"

"Solarian Brother Paul, now I know I have never touched you before, for there can be no other aura in your Sphere like yours. Or in my own Sphere. Perhaps not in the Spheres of Spica, Canopus, Polaris, or even huge Sador. I suspect there is none of greater intensity in all the galaxy, for only once in a thousand of your years is there a statistical probability of—why did you not come to me sooner?"

Brother Paul withdrew his hand, perplexed. "I do not know what you mean by 'aura.' I have never met you before—or any other ghost—and had no notion that you were to accompany me on this mission. Are you really a creature from another region of space?"

"I really am," Antares said. "More correctly, *was*. I faded out some time ago, and remain only as the captive aura of this process. As you so aptly put it, the ghost in the machine."

"I was speaking of the ghostly third memory in this little calculator," Brother Paul said. "It was designed to have only two memories, yet—"

"Allow me to examine it," Antares said.

Brother Paul held it out, and the alien passed his immaterial hand through it. "Ah, yes. That is a memory, but not precisely of the other type. It is what you call the constant: the figure retained for multiple operations. Because every element of this keyboard is dual-function, in certain cases that duality permits a direct readout of the normally hidden constant."

"The constant!" Brother Paul exclaimed. "Of course! No ghost at all, merely a misunderstood function. Like an autonomic function of the body, not ordinarily evoked consciously."

"Such comprehension comes naturally to our species," Antares said modestly.

That reminded Brother Paul. "You say your, er, Sphere traded with ours? Mattermission for hydrofusion?"

"The expense in energy of physical transport over interstellar distances makes material commerce unfeasible," Antares said. "Therefore trade is largely confined to information. Since you possess technology we lacked—"

"But if you are so advanced, why couldn't you develop controlled hydrogen fusion yourselves?"

"For much the same reason you could not develop instantaneous transmission of matter. Our mode of thinking was incapable of formulating the necessary concepts. In our framework, artificial hydrofusion is—or was—inconceivable. We are a protean, flexible species. We do not think in terms of either magnetics or lasers. We are adept at flexible circuitry, at the sciences of flowing impedences. Thus, for us, matter-mission technology is a natural, if complex, mode. You Solarians are a *thrust* culture; you poke with sticks, thrust with swords, and burn with fierce, tight lasers. For you, laser-controlled atomic fusion is natural."

That seemed to make sense, although it seemed to Brother Paul that the Antarean's ready assimilation of the calculator operation indicated a certain competence with magnetic circuitry. Probably the term "magnetic" had a different meaning for the alien, though. Man *had* been incapable of conceptualizing any physical velocity faster than that of the speed of light in a vacuum. Man's mode of thought simply could not admit the alien possibility of instantaneous travel; therefore that science had been out of the question. Thought, not physics, had been the limiting factor.

And what of God? Was man incapable of conceptualizing *His* true nature? If so, Brother Paul's present mission was doomed.

"So you traded with us," Brother Paul said, returning to a simpler level of thought. "You needed fusion for power, and we needed matter transmission for transport. Our own hydrofusion generators are now monopolized for the tremendous power needed for the MT program."

"So it would seem. This is a very foolish course you are pursuing, but it seems as though all emerging cultures must pass through it. If rationality does not abate it, the exhaustion of resources does. Only through Transfer is interSpherical empire possible. Spherical regression otherwise presents a virtually absolute limit to the extent of any culture—as you will discover."

Again, Brother Paul clung to what he could. "Transfer?"

"With your aura, you do not know of Transfer?"

"I know neither aura nor Transfer. In fact I know nothing of your society."

"Your administrators did not inform the populace?"

"Apparently not. I'd like to know about you personally, too."

"Then I shall gladly explain. It has been long since any creature expressed personal interest in me." Antares paused, and for an instant Brother Paul saw the outline of the alien protoplasm, shimmering like a hovering soul. "Every living thing we know of has an aura, a field of life-force permeating it. Solarians term it the Kirlian aura—"

"Ah, that I have heard of!" Brother Paul said. "I believe it is the same as the aura described by Dr. Kilner, and later photographed by the Russian scientist Kirlian. But I understood it was merely an effect of water vapor in the vicinity of living bodies."

"Perhaps the water vapor is associated with the photographic or visual effects," Antares said. "But the aura itself is more than this. It cannot be detected by ordinary means, although certain machines can

67

measure its imprint, and entities of intense auras can perceive other intense auras. I was a high-aura creature, and you are the highest-aura creature imaginable. Therefore our auras interact, and we perceive each other. You have no doubt perceived auras of others similarly, and supposed these to be flukes of your imagination."

"Maybe I have," Brother Paul agreed. There had been some strange phenomena in his past, now that he considered the matter in this light. Yet he was not satisfied. "Why *shouldn't* we perceive each other now, without the interaction of auras?"

"Because I am dead," Antares said.

Brother Paul had already become aware of the strangeness of this entity, so he took this statement in stride. He glanced at his watch again, noting that ten minutes and forty-nine seconds had elapsed since the setting of the counter. It had seemed longer. He fixed on a single facet, again. "You are really a ghost?"

"The ghost in the machine."

Brother Paul tried to organize his reactions, get his tongue in gear. "Actually, the human brain, with its mysterious separation of powers in its two hemispheres, has qualities that are obscure to our understanding. Nature had to have had good reason for that seeming duplication. We know that the left hemisphere relates to the right side of the body, and handles abstract analytical thought and language functions, while the right hemisphere handles space patterns, imagery, music and artistic functions. Just as two eyes provide the basis for triangulation, hence depth perception, perhaps two brains multiply the human quality as well as quantity of thought." He shook his head. "But I am babbling. My point is that the hemispheric union is as yet imperfect. Crazy-seeming things spring from it, visions and hallucinations occur at times. So while it is possible that you are what you claim to be, the ghost of an alien creature, it is rather more likely that I am suffering a similar derangement—"

"Solarian Brother!" Antares protested. "Your aura is so strong, it enables manifestations that could not otherwise occur. Your divided brain *is* imperfect, vastly complicating your thinking processes, but I am not a phantasm of your imagination. I am an aura trapped in the mechanism of the mattermission unit. We did not know the units had this property, but of course no one has ever fathomed completely the technology of the Ancients from which both mattermission and Transfer derive."

What difference did it make, really, whether this creature was real or imaginary? He was certainly entertaining! "You said you were dead."

"My Sphere, seeking trade, Transferred the auras of its most suitable members to the bodies of sapient aliens of other Spheres, animating them," Antares explained. "I was lucky enough to find this host: a Solarian who had lost his own aura and become a member of the living dead, a soulless creature. I located the Solarian authorities after some difficulty and convinced them of my authenticity, but precious time had been lost. You see, the aura of a Transferee in an alien host fades at the rate of about one intensity a day, for reasons we do not yet understand, and when it drops to the sapient norm—"

"The alien soul becomes submerged by the host," Brother Paul finished with sudden insight. All of this was incredible, yet it had its own logic, like that of non-Euclidean geometry. In this day of non-relativistic physics, why not?

"True. My natural aura was ninety times the ordinary intensity, as measured by our calibration. That is very high. Not half as high as yours, however. So I had only three of your months to act, and more than half that period was exhausted by the time I made contact. Because your scientists needed time to construct the first mattermission unit, after they had been persuaded that it was even theoretically possible—"

"You faded away to nothing before you could return to Star Antares." Brother Paul said. What singular courage this alien had had, to undertake such a mission! Traveling in spirit to an alien body, to convince people of a truth they knew was impossible—and giving his own life in the process. This creature must have had a good deal more than aura going for him; he had to have had intelligence, determination, and nerve. Brother Paul had thought his own mission special; now he saw that it was ordinary in comparison to that of Antares.

"I faded down to sapient norm," Antares agreed. "There is no fading below that, except in illness or physical death. But my native identity was gone then, as the host-body dominated. Once the first mattermission unit was ready, the Solarians shipped my Solarian host to my home Sphere, together with a nuclear fusion expert, honoring the bargain I had made. But I was dead."

"Except that you *aren't* dead!"

"My aura was enhanced by the mattermission machine, and that returned my identity to me," Antares agreed. "But my host was gone; I could not exist outside this unit. The machine is now my host, and I am now its constant, as in your calculator. I cannot manifest at all unless evoked by someone like you

70

with the interest and aura to make it possible. When you arrive at your destination—"

Brother Paul looked at his watch again. Still ten minutes, forty-nine seconds. He was certain now; no time at all had passed since Antares had appeared. He was in the process of suffering a potent hallucination. Maybe. "But if I can see you and hear you, others can too; we can open the capsule before it mattermits—"

"We are in mattermission now. Did you not comprehend?"

"Now? But I thought the process was instantaneous!"

"That it is, Solarian Brother."

Brother Paul mulled that over. An extended dialogue in zero time? Well, why not one more impossibility! "Who are these 'Ancients' you mentioned? Why don't *they* get you out of this fix?"

"They are extinct, as far as we know. They perished three million Solarian years ago, leaving only their phenomenal ruins."

"Ruins? But you said the mattermission equipment derived from—"

"Some few of their ruins have functioning components. Most of the advanced technology has been reconstituted from the far more advanced science of the Ancients by those contemporary species capable of recognizing the potential of what they discovered. There may be Ancient ruins in your own Sphere, but if your individuals did not recognize them for what they were, they may have been destroyed. Chief among these technological reconstitutions in other Spheres is Transfer—the means by which I came to Sphere Sol. That secret we will not share with you, for its value is measureless, and your species—please do

71

not take umbrage—may not be mature enough to handle this knowledge safely."

Brother Paul suddenly realized that he liked this alien ghost, even if Antares were merely a figment of his own imagination. "I take no umbrage; I regard my own species with similar misgivings, at times. I suppose you may be considered a figment of my mind, or as you put it, of my aura. Yet you have provided me comfort and interest during a nervous period."

"Do not underestimate the capacities of aura, friend Solarian," Antares replied equably. "In my brief tenure in Solarian form I came to know some of the nature of your kind, alien as it is to my prior experience. Many of your mysteries are explicable in terms of aura, as you will know when you achieve aural science. Your water-divining merely reflects the aural interaction with hidden water or metals. Your 'faith healing' constitutes a limited exchange of auras, the well one augmenting the failing one. What you call telepathy is another aural phenomenon: the momentary overlapping of aural currents such as we experience at this moment. When an entity dies, his aura may dissipate explosively, like a supernova, flooding the environment for an instant, forcing sudden awareness upon those who are naturally attuned. Close friends, or entities with very similar aural types. Thus a sleeping person may suffer a vision at the instant of his friend's demise."

Antares vanished. Brother Paul jumped up, alarmed. "Antares!" he cried. But there was nothing except the treadle sewing machine.

Then he realized that the matter transmission was over. He had arrived. The alien aura could manifest only while the Ancient reconstituted equipment was in operation. When the machine was turned off, the constant was lost—as in his calculator.

He looked at his watch. Eleven minutes, fifteen seconds. Time was moving again; the infinite expansion of instantaneity had ceased. He was back in the real world, such as it was. Whichever world it was.

Brother Paul felt a poignant loss. "If my aura is as potent as you say, brother alien, I will summon you again," he promised aloud. "Antares, you have been a good companion, and we have much more to discuss. Maybe on my return hop . . ."

But whom was he fooling? He had suffered a hallucination in transit, as he understood some people did, in this manner soothing his extreme nervousness about the mattermission. Better to shut up about it.

"Farewell, alien friend," he murmured.

3

Action

The
Statement
Below
is
TRUE

The
Statement
Above
is
FALSE

Brother Paul blinked in bright sunlight. He stood at the edge of a field of grain of an unfamiliar type. It could be a variety of wheat; Earth exported hybrid breeds of the basic cereals as fast as they could be developed, searching for the ideal match with alien conditions. There were so many variables of light and gravity and soil and climate that the only certain verification of a given type's viability was the actual harvest. This field looked healthy; the stalks were tall and green, reflecting golden at the tops, rippling attractively with the vagaries of breeze: a likely success. Of course mere appearance could be deceptive; the grains might turn out woody or bitter or even poisonous, or local fauna might infiltrate the field and consume the harvest in advance. In any event, it would be quite a job threshing by hand what wheat there was.

Not far distant rose a fair-sized mound. He was intrigued by the bright colors on one side of it. He walked out to inspect this curiosity. It turned out to be a compost pile formed from the refuse of the field: stalks and leaves shaped into a cup-shaped pile to catch and hold the rain, since water was necessary to promote decomposition.

Brother Paul smiled. He saw this mound as a living process of nature, returning to the soil the organic material that was no longer needed elsewhere, one of the great rejuvenating phenomena of existence. What better symbol could there be of true civilization in harmony with nature than a functioning compost pile? In a fundamental respect the compost did for life what the Holy Order of Vision was trying to do for mankind: restore it to its ideal state, forming fertile new soil for future generations. There could be no higher task for a man or a society than this!

The bright colors turned out to be small balloons nestling in the limited shade the mound provided. There were red, green, yellow, and blue ones, and shades between. Had some child left them here as an offering to the soil? This seemed unlikely, since the technology for making plastic balloons would hardly have been exported to this colony world in lieu of more vital processes. Had a child brought balloons from Earth, that child would hardly have left them carelessly in a field. Brother Paul put forth his hand to pick one up. It popped at his touch. It was nothing but a tenuous membrane, hardly more substantial than a soap bubble. No wonder these were in shade; mere sunlight would wipe them out! Maybe they were an alien exudation from the compost, the gas inflating a colored film. Pretty, but of limited duration. One had to expect new things on new worlds, little things as well as important ones.

Time was passing. No welcoming party? He saw no one here. Didn't they care about the shipment? Did they know about it? Apparently these transmissions were somewhat random, at the convenience of the crowded schedule of MT. With a thousand colony planets and perhaps five major settlements per world to keep track of—well, that was about five billion people, over half of Earth's pre-exodus population. Planet Tarot was lucky to get any follow-up at all! So this shipment had probably caught the colonists by surprise. The impact of arrival would have alerted them, however, and they would hustle over to unload the capsule before it shuttled back to Earth.

Should he give them a head start by carrying out some of the equipment himself? The fact that he was here on a specialized mission did not prevent him from making himself useful, and he could use the exercise.

He turned—and spied something beyond the capsule receiver building. There was a stone, a block— no, a throne, there amid the wheat! A girl was seated upon it, a lovely, fair-haired creature, a veritable princess. What was she doing here?

He started toward her. But as he did, the lady rose and fled through the field, her queenly robe flowing behind her. "Wait!" he called. "I'm from Earth!" But she continued to run, and she was surprisingly fleet. Obviously a healthy girl.

Brother Paul gave up the chase. She was frightened, and he would gain nothing by pursuing her, though he could surely catch her if he tried. This whole situation seemed even more peculiar, following his experience with the alien ghost.

He stopped short. "Key Three!" he exclaimed. The lady on the throne in the field of wheat—the card numbered the third Major Arcanum in the Tarot deck, titled the Empress.

This was Planet Tarot, where real cards had been animated. But he had not anticipated anything this soon, this literal!

Was this another ghostly manifestation? Had it all been in his mind? If so, his judgment on this mission was already suspect. What would the recorder's playback show? He wished he could peek, but of course he had no projector, and did not understand his bracelet's operation anyway. Regardless, the lady had certainly seemed genuine, and most attractive despite (because of?) her timidity.

A planet where Tarot images became literal. Brother Paul paused, thinking about that, stimulated by this sudden evidence of the fact. He had sawed pine wood, as part of his chores for the Order, and during the sometimes tedious hand labor his mind, as was its wont, had conjured a parallel between pine and the Tarot. The wood was light and white outside, easy to saw and handle, easy to burn, but not of too much substance. The heart of pine, in contrast, was rock-hard and dense, saturated with orange-colored

77

sap. It would last for decades without decaying, and the termites, whose favorite food was soft pine, would not touch the heartwood. It burned so fiercely that it soon destroyed metal grates and brick fireplaces. The queen of firewoods! The Tarot seemed like that: superficially interesting, the pictures lending themselves readily to interpretation by amateurs. But if one delved deeply enough, one encountered the heart-of-Tarot—and that was deep and dense and difficult, stretching the mind through the fourth and fifth dimensions of thought and time. Few people could handle it, but for those who persevered, the rewards were profound and lasting. Brother Paul regarded himself as on the verge between white wood and orange wood, a novice trembling at the portal of True Meaning, hardly knowing what he would discover ahead. Would he make progress, here on Planet Tarot?

Well, the throne of the Empress remained. He could check this out very quickly. He walked up to it, glancing around at the landscape as he did. This was a beautiful place, with what appeared to be a volcanic mountain rising just beyond the field, and near it a ridge of brightly colored rock. The air was warm and the gravity so close to that of Earth that he felt no discomfort at all. He would never have taken this for a haunted planet!

There was no doubt about it. This was a genuine Tarot Empress throne. Or something close to it. It was fashioned of dense, polished wood rather than stone; he was aware that there might not be suitable stone here. One side of it was carved with the design of a six-sided shield bearing a carving of a two-headed eagle. He could not safely assume such symbolism to be coincidence, but neither could he be sure it was not. So there was doubt after all. There always was.

Sturdy wooden pillars supported a pavilion roof shading the throne. A necessary precaution; even the fairest empress would suffer if she sat all day in the direct glare of the sun. Still . . .

A horrendous growl startled him. He jumped, orienting on the sound, and saw a huge, sinuous, catlike creature charging at him. The thing seemed to have five legs. Maybe its tail was prehensile.

From the lady to the tiger! Brother Paul dodged around the throne. The creature maneuvered to follow him. Catlike, but no feline; the articulation of its limbs was alien in some obscure but impressive manner. It was not that they bent backward at the joints; that did not appear to be the case. But the bending had a different aspect—

No time to cogitate on that now! This thing must mass 150 kilograms—twice Brother Paul's own weight—and there was little doubt of its intent. It regarded him either as an enemy or as prey!

It would have helped if the authorities had advised him of such details of the planetary ecology. But probably they hadn't known. He should have remained inside the capsule until a colonist-guide came for him; he had only himself to blame for this difficulty.

Brother Paul dodged around the throne again, but the tiger-thing had anticipated him. It bounded around the other way, reversing course with eerie ease, and abruptly confronted him, its forelegs outstretched.

Brother Paul suffered one of those flashes that are supposed to come to people facing sudden death. The creature's extremities were not claws or hoofs; instead,

79

they resembled leather gloves or mittens. They were forked, with the larger part hooking around in a semi-circle like a half-closed hand, but without fingers; the smaller part was like an opposable thumb. The dexterity of this "hand" could in no way approach that of the human appendage, and the calloused pads on the outside edges showed that this was primarily a running foot rather than a manipulative hand. Yet a hoof or paw would have been much better for running! What was the purpose in this wrenchlike structure?

The tiger pounced at him, its strange feet extended as though to box him, except that it was not his torso that was the target. He jumped, high and to the side, so that the creature missed him. The animal's forefeet jerked back, while the clublike hind feet struck forward. It actually landed on its hind feet, flipping over backward.

Had he remained in place, Brother Paul realized, those forefeet would have hooked his ankles, and those hind feet would have hit him with sufficient force to break his legs. Crippled, he would have been easy prey. This was not a type of attack known on Earth, but it was surely as brutally effective as teeth or tusks or claws.

The tiger wheeled about, recovering its posture with the help of its prehensile tail, and sprang again. This time it leaped higher, learning with dismaying rapidity. But Brother Paul did not jump again. He spun to face away from it, dropping simultaneously to his knees, and caught its right foreleg in the crook of his right arm. Then he rolled forward, hauling on that captive leg. This was *ippon seoi nage,* the one-arm shoulder throw—the first judo technique he had ever tried on an animal, terrestrial or alien. And with luck, the last!

The tiger's hind feet came forward in its bone-breaking reflex. They glanced jarringly off Brother Paul's back and right shoulder, and one clipped his head. Those hind feet were like sledgehammers; he saw a bright flash of light as the optic region of his brain took the shock.

He had tried the wrong technique. Since the tiger normally caught hold of its prey's limbs and broke them, he had merely set himself up for the strike by holding the creature. A man would have been thrown over Brother Paul's back, but the tiger's balance and torque were different. He was lucky it had not knocked him out; if he made another mistake, that luck was unlikely to hold.

Still, he retained a hold on its foreleg. He hauled on it and tried to roll again. This time the creature rolled with him, for its momentum was spent and it had not been able to get back to its feet. It flipped onto its back, and Brother Paul started to apply a hold-down—but realized he would then be at the mercy of those battering hind legs.

Instead, he flipped about and caught hold of the nearest hind leg. Then he leaned back, extended both of his own feet, and clamped his knees around that limb. This was a leglock that would have been illicit in judo, but what were human legality in a life-and-death struggle with an alien creature? This was not at all the type of situation he had anticipated when he had joined the Order! Brother Paul arched his back, bucked his hips forward, and drew on the captive leg, putting pressure on the joint. He had no idea whether this technique would work on such a creature, but felt it was worth a try. A man would have screamed in agony at about this time . . .

The tiger screamed in agony. Startled by this unexpected success, Brother Paul let go, just as he would for a human opponent who tapped out, admitting defeat. Too late, he remembered that this was no human sportsman, but a creature out to break his bones. Now he was in for it!

But the tiger had had enough. It rolled to its feet, steadied itself with its tail, and leaped away as rapidly as it had come. Brother Paul stood and watched it bound across the rippling sea of wheat, relieved. He hadn't wanted to hurt it, but had thought he would have no other choice. He was bruised, disheveled, and a bit lightheaded, but basically intact. It could have been worse—much worse!

Motion attracted his eye. People were approaching: half a dozen men. They were armed, carrying long spears—no, these were tridents, like elaborate pitchforks, excellent for stabbing an animal while holding it at bay. Effective against a man, too.

Somewhat nervously, Brother Paul awaited the party's approach. This, too, was not precisely the welcome he had anticipated.

As they came closer he saw that these men were being careful rather than aggressive. They looked all about, weapons ever at the ready, as though afraid something hazardous to bones might come bounding in.

"Hello," Brother Paul called. "I'm from Earth, on a special mission."

The men glanced at each other meaningfully. "What is your faith?" one asked.

"I am Brother Paul of the Holy Order of Vision. However, I'm not here to join your society. I am supposed to—" But he broke off, uncertain of their reaction.

Again, the exchange of glances. "Vision," the

spokesman said approvingly. He was a heavyset, black-haired man with fairly deep frown-lines about his mouth that showed even when he was trying to smile, as now. "A good selection. But I did not know it was a warrior cult."

Warrior cult? "The Holy Order of Vision is a pacifistic denomination, seeking always the route of least—"

"Yet you fought the Breaker."

The Breaker. A fitting description! "Self-preservation compelled me. I don't believe I damaged the creature."

A third exchange of glances. "The question is, how is it that the Breaker did not damage *you*? We must always travel in armed parties to fend off its savagery, during that part of the day when it is present."

Evidently they knew the routine of the Breaker, and this was its office hour. That would explain why they had not rushed up to greet him instantly; they had had to organize their troop and proceed with due caution. "I suspect I was pretty lucky," Brother Paul said. "I managed to frighten it away just when I thought I'd lost."

"Even so," the spokesman said dubiously—his face was very good at dour expressions—"your God surely watches over you well."

"My God is the same as your God," Brother Paul said modestly—and was amazed at the reaction this brought. Evidently he had committed a *faux pas*.

"We shall introduce ourselves," the man said, gruffly easing the awkwardness. "I am the Reverend Siltz of the Second Church Communist, spokesman for this party by consent of the participants."

Brother Paul's face never even twitched. After Antares the gelatinous alien, a living Tarot Empress, and

83

the Breaker, what was a little anomaly like a Communist Church? "Glad to make your acquaintance, Reverend Siltz," he said. The man did not offer to shake hands, so Brother Paul merely nodded affirmatively as he spoke.

The man to the Reverend's right spoke: "Janson, Adventist." And, in turn, the others: "Bonly, Mason." "Appermet, Yoga." "Smith, Swedenborgian." "Miller, Vegan Vegetarian."

"We were expecting you," Reverend Siltz said gruffly. "We were not informed of your precise time of arrival, but the matter is of some concern to us." Here one of the others stifled a snort, reminding Brother Paul again of the intricate currents that flowed beneath this troubled surface. What had he gotten into?

Reverend Siltz scowled, but continued, "Church Communist was selected by lot in accordance with the Covenant to encounter you initially and proffer hospitality for the duration of your mission. This denotes no comment on the validity of your mission, or our opinion of same. You are of course free to choose an alternate accommodation, as you please. The Order of Vision has no station here."

Currents indeed! Had the lot chosen an enemy to host him, or was this merely excessive formality? He would have to navigate his shallow craft carefully, until he knew more of this peculiar situation. "I am pleased to accept your offer, Reverend, hoping my presence will not inconvenience you or cause you embarrassment."

Now Siltz made an honest smile. "We know of your Order. Hosting you will be a privilege."

So acceptance had been the right decision. Maybe the man's gruffness had been in anticipation of demurral, so that he would not lose face when Brother Paul did the expected. But it could also have stemmed from some other factor, such as this evident individuality of gods, as though each religion had its own separate deity. Brother Paul made a silent prayer that he would not make too many wrong decisions here. How fortunate that the reputation of his Order extended even to distant planets! Of course this colony, like all the others in the human sphere, could not be more than four years old, five at the most, so the colonists would have carried their knowledge of religious sects with them from Earth. So this was really no miracle.

Reverend Siltz swung about to orient on the capsule receiver building, his motion and manner reminding Brother Paul not too subtly of the Breaker. "Now we must unload, before it mattermits out. Is it a good shipment?"

"Sewing machines, spinning wheels, stoves," Brother Paul said as they walked toward it. "Carding tools, axes—"

"Good, good!" Reverend Siltz said. "They have dowered you well." There was a murmur of agreement, surprising Brother Paul. He suffered a two-level thought: first, the confirmation that he was not completely welcome here, so had been "dowered," as though he were an unpretty bride requiring a monetary inducement to make him and his mission palatable; and second, the reaction to the shipment. Of course such artifacts were useful, but did these colonists have no yearnings for the more advanced products of civilization?

The next two hours were spent unloading. It was heavy work, but no one stinted; all the men were husky, and Reverend Siltz applied himself as vigorously as any of them. Yet throughout, Brother Paul was aware of a certain diffidence, directed not at him but occurring among the colonists themselves, as though not one of them trusted the others completely. What was the problem here?

At last the job was done. "Good, good!" Reverend Siltz said with satisfaction as he viewed the equipment piled somewhat haphazardly at the edge of the wheatfield. "Tomorrow the wagon comes." They covered each item with one of the light plastic tarpaulins provided by the shipper, and organized the return march.

As they passed the throne, Brother Paul wanted to inquire about the girl he had seen there, but hesitated; it could be that female colonists were not permitted direct contact with strange men. That would explain why she had fled, and make any question about her presence inappropriate. In a society as cult-ridden as this one seemed to be, the status of women was open to question.

Behind the ridge was a village, not much more than two kilometers from the capsule receiver. Brother Paul could have run it in six minutes or so, had he known where to go, but he doubted that the girl could have had time to arrive here, alert the village, and send this party back before he finished with the Breaker. Reverend Siltz must have been on the way the moment the capsule had arrived. Planet Tarot evidently had no electronic communications or motorized transportation, so foot power and observation were important here, just as they were on the better part of Earth, now.

A sturdy stockade of wooden posts surrounded the village, each post polished and handsome. Brother Paul had learned something about the various kinds of wood during his Order tenure, but had never seen wood like this. "The heart of heart-of-pine," he murmured.

The houses inside were of the same kind of wood, constructed of notched logs calked with mud. Their roofs were sod, in most cases, with thick grass growing on them, and even small flowers. Primitive but tight, he was sure. Here and there, in the shade, were more clusters of the colored bubbles he had noted by the compost pile. So they could not be purely a product of organic decomposition.

"What are these?" Brother Paul asked, stooping to touch one. It did not pop, so he picked it up carefully—and then it popped. Evidently some of the bubbles were stronger than others.

"Tarot Bubbles," Reverend Siltz responded. "They grow everywhere, especially at night. They are of no value, like mildew or weeds. Clever children can make castles of them on cloudy days. We keep them out of our houses so they will not contaminate our food."

How quickly a pretty novelty became a nuisance! But Brother Paul could appreciate the colonists' desire to keep proliferating growths away from their food; the residues might be harmless, but why gamble? Most germs on Earth were harmless too, but those that were not were often devastating.

In the center of the village was a pile of wood. All around it people were working. Men were sawing planks, or rather scraping them, forming mounds of curly shavings. Children gathered these shavings by armfuls, depositing them in patterns near seated women. The women seemed to be carding the shavings, stretching out the fibers of the wood so that they resembled cotton. This was some wood!

Reverend Siltz halted, and the other members of the party stopped with him, bowing their heads in silent respect. "Tree of Life, God of Tarot, we thank thee," Siltz said formally, and made a genuflection to the pile of wood.

Tree of Life? God of Tarot? Brother Paul knew the Tree of Life as the diagram of meanings associated with the Cabala, the ancient Hebrew system of number-alchemy. And the God of Tarot was what he had come to seek, but he had not expected it to be a pile of wood. What did this mean?

Reverend Siltz turned to him as the other men departed. "We are of many faiths, here at Colony Tarot. But on one thing we agree: the Tree is the source of our well-being. We do not feel that our own gods object to the respect we pay to the Tree."

"Does this resemble the Great World Tree of Norse legend, called Yggdrasil?" Brother Paul inquired. "Its roots extended into three realms—"

"There are Norse sects here that make that analogy," Siltz agreed. "But the majority of us regard it as a purely planetary expression and gift of God. Indeed, we seek to ascertain which God *is* the Tree."

"You see God as—as a physical object? A tree? Wood?"

"Not precisely. We must cooperate for survival, and only through the Tree can we accomplish this. Thus the Tree of Life is the God of Tarot." He formed a rare smile. "I perceive you are confused. Come, eat, rest at my abode, and I shall explain as well as I am permitted by the Covenant."

Brother Paul nodded, not trusting himself to speak lest he commit some additional *faux pas* in his ignorance. This nascent planetary culture was far stranger than he had anticipated.

4

Power

Before the beginning of years
There came to the making of man
Time with a gift of tears;
Grief with a glass that ran;
Pleasure, with pain for leaven;
Summer, with flowers that fell;
Remembrance fallen from heaven,
And madness risen from hell; . . .
. . . wrought with weeping and laughter,
And fashioned with loathing and love,
With life before and after
And death beneath and above,

. . .

His speech is a burning fire;
With his lips he travaileth;
In his heart is a blind desire,
In his eyes foreknowledge of death;
He weaves, and is clothed with derision;
Sows, and he shall not reap;

His life is a watch or a vision
Between a sleep and a sleep.

Algeron Charles Swinburne: *Atalanta In Calydon*

The Reverend Siltz's hut was exactly like the others, distinguished only by the hammer-and-sickle on its hewn-timber door. It was small, but cozy and well-ordered inside. The walls and ceiling were paneled with rough-sawn wood whose grain was nevertheless quite striking: the wood of the local Tree of Life, again. A wooden ladder led up the back wall to the attic. There were no windows, only air vents, slanted to exclude rain or flowing water. In the center of the room, dominating it, was the stove.

"Ah, an airtight side-drafter," Brother Paul commented appreciatively. "With cooking surfaces and attached oven. A most compact and efficient design."

"You know stoves?" Reverend Siltz inquired, suddenly more friendly.

"I get along well with mechanical things," Brother Paul said. "I would not deem myself an expert, but we do use wood at our Vision Station, and it was my task to gather the fuel from the forest. I admire a good design, if only because I deem it a shame to waste what God has grown." Yet here were these people, burning the wood of the tree they worshipped. Oh, he was getting curious about the ramifications of that!

A woman stepped forward, middle-aged and pleasant. He had not noticed her because the stove had caught his attention—which could be taken as a sign of his present confused state. Her hair was dark brown and plaited in such a way as to resemble the bark of a tree. Now Brother Paul realized that he had seen similar hairdos on several of the other women working outside. An odd effect, but not unattractive. Another salute to the Tree of Life?

"My wife," Reverend Siltz said, and she nodded. Brother Paul had not yet seen any firm indication that the woman had equal status with the men on this planet, but knew better than to make any assumptions at this early stage. "My son is at work; we may see him this evening." There was another curious inflection; either the Reverend had a number of peculiar concerns, or Brother Paul was exaggerating the meanings of inconsequential nuances of expression.

"Your house is small by Earth standards," Brother Paul said carefully. "I fear my presence will crowd you."

The Reverend unfolded a bench from the wall. "We shall make do. I regret we have no better facilities. We are as yet a frontier colony."

"I was not criticizing your facilities," Brother Paul said quickly. "I did not come here for comfort, but I would hardly call this privation. You have an admirably compact house."

The wife climbed the ladder and disappeared into the loft. "It is her sleep-shift," Siltz explained. "She must help guard the wood by night, so she must prepare herself now. This is the reason we have space for you to stay."

"Guard the wood?" Brother Paul asked, perplexed.

Reverend Siltz brought out some long, limber strips of wood and set about weaving them into something like a blanket. "Brother Paul, wood is paramount. Our houses are made from it and insulated throughout by it; it provides our furniture, our weapons, our heat. In our fashion we worship wood, because our need for it is so pressing. We must obtain it from the forest far away, and haul it by hand with guards against the

91

predators of the range. We dare not pitch our villages closer to the forest because of the Animations; they permeate that region in season, but are rare here. The other villages of this planet are similarly situated, so as to be removed from the threat. We have little commerce with the other settlements. In winter the snows come eight meters deep."

"Eight meters deep!" Brother Paul repeated, incredulous.

"Insulating us from the surface temperature of minus fifty degrees Celsius. Those who exhaust their supply of fuel wood before the winter abates must burn their furniture and supporting struts or perish, and if they burn so much that the weight of the snow collapses their houses, they perish."

"Can't they tunnel through the snow to reach the next house, so as to share with their neighbors?"

"Yes, if their neighbors happen to be of the same faith." The man frowned, and Brother Paul suspected another complication of this society. Families of differing faiths would not share their resources, even to save lives? "Those who take more than their appointed share of wood imperil the lives of others. There is no execution on this planet except for the theft or wasting of wood. The Tree of Life may not be abused!" The Reverend's face was becoming red; he caught himself and moderated his tone. "We have a difficult situation here; this is a good world, but a harsh one. We are of fragmented faiths and can hardly trust each other, let alone comprehend each other's ludicrous modes of worship. This is the reason your own mission is significant. You shall decide which God is the true God of Tarot."

Brother Paul was beginning to accept the tie-in between God and wood. Without wood, these people would perish, and they knew it. Yet this need did not seem to account for their evident fetishism. On Earth, people needed water to survive, and fresh water was scarce, but they did not worship it. "That *is* my mission, presumptuous as it may be. I gather you do not approve of it."

Siltz glanced up from his weaving, alarmed. "Did I say that?"

"No, it is merely an impression I have. You do not need to discuss the matter if you do not wish to."

"I would like very much to discuss it," Siltz said. "But the Covenant forbids it. If my attitude conveys itself to you, then I am not being a proper host, and must arrange other lodging for you."

Which surely would not be politic! "Probably I am jumping to conclusions; I apologize," Brother Paul said.

"No, you are an intelligent and sensitive man. I shall endeavor to resolve the question without violating the Covenant. I do oppose your presence here, but this does not in any way reflect on your person or integrity. I merely believe this is a question that cannot be answered in this manner. You will necessarily discover a God that conforms to your personal precepts, but whose conformance to the actual God may be coincidental. I would rather have the issue remain in doubt, than have it decided erroneously. But I am a member of the minority. You were summoned, and the lot, in its wisdom, has brought you to my house, and I shall facilitate your mission exactly as though I supported it. This *my* God requires of me."

"I do not think our concepts of God can be very far apart," Brother Paul said. "I find your attitude completely commendable. But let me qualify one aspect: it is Earth that sent me here, not Colony Tarot. We of

93

Earth are concerned as to whether the God of Tarot is genuine, or merely someone's fancy. We too are wary lest a person committed to a single view be blind to the truth, whatever that may be. I doubt that I am worthy of this mission, but it is my intent to eliminate my personal bias as much as possible and ascertain that truth, though I may not like it. I don't see that you colonists need to accept any part of my report, or let it affect your way of life. In fact I am uncertain about your references to a number of gods. Surely there is only one God."

Reverend Siltz smiled ruefully. "In reassuring me, you place me at the verge of compromising my integrity. I must acquaint you in more detail with our religious situation here, asking you to make allowance for any lack of objectivity you may perceive. We are a colony of schisms, of splinter sects. Many of us were aware of the special effects of Planet Tarot before we emigrated from Earth, and each of us saw in these effects the potential realization of God—our particular, specialized concepts of God, if you will. This appeal seems to have been strongest to the weakest sects, or at any rate, the smallest numerically. Thus we have few Roman Catholics, Mohammedans, Buddhists, or Confucians, but many Rosicrucians, Spiritualists, Moonies, Gnostics, Flaming Sworders—"

"Flaming Sworders? Is that a Tarot image—I mean the card type of Tarot?"

"Not so. I apologize for using unseemly vernacular. It is my prejudice against these faiths, which you must discount. *The Flaming Sword* is the publication of the Christian Apostolic Church in Zion, whose guiding precept is that the Earth is flat, not spherical."

"But how, then, could they emigrate to another planet? They would not believe other planets existed!"

"You must ask a member of that cult; perhaps he can provide you with a verisimilitudinous rationale. I fear my own mind is closed, but I am forbidden by the Covenant to criticize the faiths of others in your presence. Let us simply say that with faith, all things are possible. I'm sure you appreciate my position."

"I do," Brother Paul agreed. For all his gruffness, the Reverend was a sincere, comprehensible man, and a good host. "I once heard a child's definition: 'faith is believing what you know ain't so.' That now seems apropos." He paused. "Um, no offense intended, but I had not expected to encounter your own Church, either. What are its precepts?"

"I regret I can answer you only vaguely. I have vowed by the Tree of Life to make no effort to prejudice your mind by contamination with my own particular faith."

The man's attitude was coming through fairly clearly, however! "Because of the Covenant?"

"Precisely. I will not claim to agree with the Covenant, but I am bound by it. The majority feel that your continuing objectivity is crucial. I will only say that the guiding principles of Church Second Comm are essentially humanist, and that we maintain only symbolic connection to the atheistic Communists of Earth. We are *theist* Communists."

"Ah, yes," Brother Paul said, disconcerted. God-fearing Communists—and the Reverend was obviously sincere. Yet this was no more anomalous in theory than God-fearing Capitalists. "I had the impression that Planet Tarot was an English-language colony; are the religions represented here primarily Western?"

"They are. About eighty per cent derive from Occidental Christian origins; the rest are scattered. In that

95

sense, most believe in some form of the Christ, as you do; that is why I said your Order is a good one for our purpose, though I question that purpose. You will likely find a Christian God, but you have no local Church to cater to, so you are relatively objective. The reputation of your Order has preceded you; Visionists are known not to interfere with other faiths, while yet remaining true to their own faith. I believe you will be approved."

"I had not realized that my mission here was subject to local approval," Brother Paul said, a bit dryly. "What will they do if they don't like me? Ship me back to Earth?" There was, of course, no way for the colonists to do that.

"There are those whose faith is such as to destroy infidels," Siltz said. "We believe our own village is secure, but we cannot speak for other villages. We shall, of course, protect you to the limit of our means—but it is better that we stand united in this matter."

"Yes, I appreciate that." Brother Paul shook his head ruefully. Destroy infidels? That had connotations of fanatic murder! What nest of vipers had he mattermitted into? He had been warned about none of this; obviously the authorities on Earth knew little of the social phenomena of their colonies. He could not afford to rely on his limited briefings. "Yet if most sects here believe in the Christian God—who is also the Jewish and Mohammedan God, whether termed YHVH or Allah—why should there be any need to qualify Him further?"

"This is the question I have been trying to answer," Reverend Siltz said. "We are an exceedingly jealous conglomerative culture, here on Planet Tarot. Your interpretation of God surely differs somewhat from mine, and both of ours differ from that of the Church

96

of Atheism. Who is to say which sect most truly reflects God's will? There must be one group among us that God favors more than the others, although He tolerates the others for the sake of that one—and that is the one we must discover. Perhaps God has dictated the savagery of our winter climate, forcing us to seek Him more avidly, as the God of the Jews brought privation upon them to correct their erring ways. We all depend on the largesse of the Tree of Life, and so we must ultimately worship the God of the Tree, even if we don't like that God, or the sect which is that God's chosen. Whether we call Him The God, or merely One among many, is of little moment; we must address Him as He dictates. We shall do so. But first we must ascertain objectively the most proper aspect of that God."

Phew! The colonists were taking this matter much more seriously than did the scholars back on Earth. "I really cannot undertake to do that," Brother Paul said cautiously. "To me, God is All; He favors no particular sect. The Holy Order of Vision is not a sect in that sense; we seek only for the truth that is God, and feel that the form is irrelevant. While we honor Jesus Christ as the Son of God, we also honor the Buddha, Zoroaster, and the other great religious figures; indeed, we are *all* children of God. So we seek only to know whether God *does* manifest here; we do not seek to channel Him, and would not presume to pass upon the merits of any religious sect."

"Well spoken! Yet I think God Himself will be the final arbiter. He will make known His will in His fashion, and you—according to the opinion of the colony majority, which I question—shall reflect that will. God is power; none of us can stand against that, nor would we wish to."

Brother Paul was not certain he had established any solid community of concept with the Reverend, but found the discussion stimulating. Still, it was time to get more practical. "I would like to know more about your geography," he said. "Particularly where the Animations take place."

"We shall show you that tomorrow. Animations are erratic, but generally occur in the oasis three kilometers north of here. We shall have to select guards for you."

"Oh, I don't require—"

"We value your safety, Brother Paul. If you should die within an Animation, as so many do, not only would we be bereft of our answer, we should be in bad repute back on Earth."

Sobering thoughts! The Reverend Mother Mary had warned him that religious scholars had lost their minds or died exploring this phenomenon; this was the confirmation. Still, he protested, "I would not want you to be in bad repute, but—"

He was interrupted by Siltz's snort of laughter at the notion that planetary repute was more important to him than his own life. "But I understand that predatory animals avoid Animations."

"They do. But what protects you from the Animations themselves?"

"As I understand it, these are merely controlled visions—visible imagination. There would, of course, be no physical—"

Reverend Siltz shook his head emphatically. "They *are* physical! And it will be a physical God you meet, whether he be valid or invalid. You will see."

Physical imagination? There had to be some sort of confusion here! Of course there had been suggestions of this in his briefing on Earth, but he had tended to dismiss such notions as exaggerations. "I am afraid I don't—"

The Reverend raised a hand. "You will ascertain this for yourself in due course. I do not wish to violate the spirit of the Covenant, though I fear I have already compromised the letter of it. Now we must go before the storm comes."

Even as the man spoke, Brother Paul heard the imperative rumble of thunder. "Where are we going?"

"To the communal lunch. It is more efficient than home cooking, and provides for a fairer allocation of food, so we do it in summer." Naturally a Communist would feel that way! "Storm time is good eating time, since we cannot then work outside."

"Your wife—isn't she coming too?"

"She is not. She eats at another shift, as does my son. I am relieved of my community labors for the duration of your stay; my labor is to attend to you. Now I must see that you are properly fed. Come, I have delayed too long. I neglect my responsibility. We must hurry."

They hurried. Outside, Brother Paul saw the ponderously looming clouds coming in over the lake from the east, so dense that they seemed like bubbles of lava in the sky. By some freak of the local system, the wind was coming from right angles, from the north, and it looked as though rain were already falling on the wheatfield to the west. The clouds, then, must be only the most visible portion of the storm; the outer swirls of it were already upon the village. Indeed, now he spied flashes of color—Tarot Bubbles borne on the wind, popping frequently but in such great numbers that they decorated the sky. What a pretty effect!

"Too late," Reverend Siltz said. "Yet I am remiss if

I do not bring you to the others. We shall have to use the cups."

"I can stand a little rain," Brother Paul said. He rather liked bold storms; they showed the power of nature vividly.

But the man was already diving back into the house. "It is not merely water," he called from inside. "Bigfoot lurks in rain and snow."

Bigfoot? Brother Paul knew of the legends back on Earth of Yeti, Sasquatch, Abominable Snowman, Skunk Ape, and Bugbear; in fact he was somewhat of a fan of Bigfoot. With the cultural and technological regression Earth had suffered as a result of the depopulation of emigration, these legends had increased in number and force. He believed that most sightings of huge manlike monsters were merely distortions of straggling, perhaps ill human beings. An unkempt, ragged, wild-haired, dirty and desperate man could be a sight to frighten anyone, particularly when he was glimpsed only at dusk as he skulked in his search for food. Whether any nonhuman monsters existed—well, who could say? But Brother Paul hoped they did; it would certainly make Earth more interesting.

Reverend Siltz emerged with an armful of panels. Quickly he assembled two wooden hemispheres, each about a meter in diameter and girt by wicked-looking wooden spikes. Odd cups! Did this relate symbolically to the storm? Water, the Cups of the Tarot?

"You set this frame on your shoulders, and strap it under your arms," Siltz explained, helping Brother Paul into one. "When the storm breaks, angle forward into it and you will be protected. Do not let the wind catch inside the cup; it could lift you off the ground. If Bigfoot comes, use the spikes to drive him—it— off." Siltz evidently was reminding himself that the

100

monster was inhuman. "Remember, I will be beside you." And the Reverend donned his own contraption.

The umbrellalike dome came down to circle Brother Paul's shoulders, greatly reducing visibility. He wanted to get along with his host, but this was ridiculous!

Reverend Siltz led the way across the turf, around the now-deserted wood pile (except for two guards armed with tridents) toward a larger building on top of a gentle hill. Despite the cumbersome containers, they made good progress.

There were a few more minor rumbles of thunder, superfluous reminders of the intensification of the storm. The sheet of water was now within a kilometer, churning the surface of the lake with such force that no horizon was apparent there, just splash. That hardly mattered; Brother Paul could not see well anyway because of the interference of the wooden cup. So he looked at his feet and at those of his companion, and marched along, feeling somewhat like a tank with legs, while his thoughts returned to Bigfoot. Could there be a similar creature here on Planet Tarot? Or was this merely frontier superstition? With all these fragmentary religious cults, it would not be surprising to discover strong beliefs in the supernatural. Still, if there *were* a—

A sudden, quintessential crack of thunder virtually knocked him off his feet. Never before had he felt such a shock; deafened and dazed, he stood staring at the ground, feeling his hair shifting nervously, and an odd tingling all over his body. The air was electrically charged, and himself too! There would surely be more lightning strikes close by, and he didn't like it. Those had been true words, about the rigorous conditions of this planet! No wooden shields could protect them from this!

Reverend Siltz was gesturing beneath his own shield, pointing urgently forward. Yes, indeed! Brother Paul was eager to get under proper cover!

The rain struck. It was like an avalanche crushing down the cup. Rain? These were hailstones, balls of ice up to a centimeter in diameter. They rapped the shield imperatively, small but hard. No, he would not have wanted to go bareheaded among these icy bullets!

A gust of wind whipped a barrage into his legs and tugged at his shield. Quickly Brother Paul reoriented it to fend off the thrust, for indeed this storm had power.

The hail thinned to sleet, then to water. Now he was certain; he did carry a literal cup to protect him from the onslaught of water. Whether the colonists used Tarot symbolism consciously or unconsciously he could not say, but use it they did.

The field was now a river, a centimeter deep. Colored Tarot Bubbles bobbed along on it, seeming to pop as he looked at them. Probably it was the other way around: his eye was attracted to them as they popped. The surviving ones added a surrealistic luster to the scene.

Reverend Siltz brushed close. "Get out of the channel. Follow the ridges." Brother Paul saw that he was walking in a slight depression. No wonder his feet were splashing! He moved to the side, finding better footing.

"Bigfoot is near," Siltz cried. "More fast!" And he began to run.

More fast. So the language reverted some under pressure. This was no joke; the man was alarmed.

Brother Paul followed, wondering how the Reverend knew which direction to go. The rain obscured everything and showed no sign of slackening. The flash-rivers fed into the lake now, broadening out to obscure the normal fringe of the lake; all was water, below. The hailstones on the ground were turning into slush. But this business about Bigfoot—

Then he saw the footprint.

It was like that of a man, but half a meter long. The creature who had made this print, if it were similarly proportioned throughout, had to be triple the mass of a man. Two hundred twenty-five kilograms!

He felt a thrill of discovery—and of apprehension. This was a fresh print, only seconds old; already it was washing out. *There really was a Bigfoot here*— and it was within two or three meters of him!

Reverend Siltz grabbed his arm under the cup. "On!" he cried, his voice colored by something very like fear.

Brother Paul's curiosity about the monster warred against his common sense. The latter won. He plunged on. This was hardly the occasion to tangle with a two-hundred-kilo brute!

The water buffeted them, trying to twist the cups about. But the turf remained firm, and in due course they hove into the shelter of the community kitchen. Their legs were wet, but that didn't seem to matter.

"You exposed our guest to Bigfoot?" the guard at the door muttered to Reverend Siltz, holding his trident ready against the storm.

The Communist did not answer, but pushed on in. Brother Paul followed. "Actually, I'd like to meet Bigfoot," he said to the guard. "It was the lightning that scared me." But the man did not smile.

Other people were in the building, going about

103

their assorted businesses, but there were no hearty welcomes. Reverend Siltz ignored all except those wearing the hammer-and-sickle emblem of his Church. Nevertheless, he guided Brother Paul to a table where several men of differing denominations sat. Or so Brother Paul assumed from the fact that the emblems on their clothing were dissimilar.

"It is necessary that you assure these people I have not tried to compromise your objectivity," the Reverend grumbled. "I shall fetch soup."

Brother Paul seated himself and looked around. "I so assure you," he said with a smile. "I embarrassed him with a number of questions that forced him to invoke the Covenant, but he withstood the onslaught. I am wet but uncompromised."

The man across from Brother Paul nodded affably. He was middle-aged and bald, with smile-lines in lieu of Reverend Siltz's frown-lines, and bright blue eyes. "I am Deacon Brown, Church of Lemuria. We are sure you remain objective. You must forgive your host his taciturnity; he is suffering under a difficult family situation."

"I have no complaints," Brother Paul said carefully. "I am not sure I can say the same about your Covenant, but the Reverend Siltz has treated me cordially enough. I fear I kept him so busy answering my routine questions that we left his dwelling late, and so got caught in the storm. I do tend to talk too much." That should absolve the Reverend on that score. Brother Paul was tempted to inquire about this multi-sected society, but decided to wait. He already knew the colonists were not supposed to enlighten him on this matter informally, lest they be accused of proselytization. These men had clearly ignored his hints about this inconvenience.

"You see, his son is serious about a young woman of the Church of Scientology," Deacon Brown continued. "The two young people worked together this spring on a tree-harvest mission, and the Cup overflowed."

No doubt about the Tarot reference this time! Cups were not only the suit of water; they signified religion—and love. A difficult juxtaposition here, it seemed. "You do not permit marriage between churches?"

"It is permitted by some sects, and forbidden by others. You must understand, Brother Paul, that we are a jealous community." Reverend Siltz had used a similar expression; there was no doubt it was true! "We came here as individual sects to further the purity and freedom of our own selective modes of worship, and it is to our displeasure and inconvenience that we find ourselves required to interact so intimately with false believers. We find it difficult to agree on anything other than the sheer need for survival—and not always on that."

Even so! "Yes, but surely religion should not oppose common sense. I doubt that you have enough members of each sect in this village to be able to propagate freely within your own churches. There must be some reasonable compromise."

"There is some," Deacon Brown agreed. "But not enough. We understand Reverend Siltz's position; none of us would wish our children to marry Scientologists, or Baha'is, or any other heathen offspring. My daughter does not keep company with the son of Minister Malcolm, here, of the Nation of Islam." The adjacent man smiled affirmatively, the whiteness of his teeth vivid against the brownness of his skin. "Yet the Cup is powerful, and there will be serious trouble

105

unless we can soon determine the true nature of the God of the Tree."

"So I have been advised." Brother Paul was now aware of the reason for the tense relations between individuals, but it seemed to him to be a foolish and obstinate situation. With savage storms and Bigfoot and similar frontier-world problems, they did not need pointless religious dissension too. It was certainly possible for widely differing sects to get along together, as the experience of the Holy Order of Vision showed. To Brother Paul, a religion that was intolerant of other religions was by its own admission deficient. Jesus Christ had preached tolerance for all men, after all. Well, perhaps not for moneylenders in the temple, and such. Still . . .

Reverend Siltz returned with two brimming wooden bowls. He set one before Brother Paul, then seated himself on the wooden bench. There was a wooden spoon in each bowl, crude but serviceable. There must be quite a handicrafts industry here, fashioning these utensils. This was certainly in accord with the principles of the Order; wooden tableware did make sense.

Brother Paul and Reverend Siltz fell to. There was no blessing of the food; probably the several sects could not agree on the specific format, so had agreed by their Covenant to omit this formality. The soup was unfamiliar but rich; it had a pithy substantiality, like potato soup, with an unearthly flavor. "If I may inquire—" he started.

"Wood soup," Deacon Brown said immediately. "The Tree of Life nourishes us all, but it yields its sustenance more freely when boiled. We also eat of the fruit, but this is as yet early in the season and it is not ready."

Wood soup. Well, why not? This secondary worship of the Tree was becoming more understandable. Perhaps it would be best if the God of Tarot did turn out to be one with the local Tree. If it were simply a matter of interpretation—but he would have to wait and see, not prejudicing his own mind.

Brother Paul finished his bowl. It had proved to be quite filling. Reverend Siltz immediately took it away. Apparently the Reverend wanted to be quite certain the others were satisfied with the visitor's equilibrium, so left him alone at any pretext. Another indication of the strained relations here.

"If I may inquire without giving offense," Brother Paul began, aware that offense was probably unavoidable if he were to proceed with his mission.

"You are not of our colony," Deacon Brown said. "You do not know our conventions. I shall give them to you succinctly: speak no religion. In other matters, speak freely; we shall make allowances."

Hm. He would be unable to honor that strictly, since his purpose here was thoroughly religious. But all in good time. "Thank you. I notice you employ a certain seeming symbolism that resembles that of the Tarot deck. Cups, for example. The Tarot equivalent of the suit of Hearts. Is this intentional?"

Everyone at the table smiled. "Of course," the deacon agreed. "Every sect here has its own Tarot deck, or variant deck. This is part of our communal respect for the Tree of Life. We do not feel that it conflicts with our respective faiths; rather it augments them, and offers one of the few common bonds available to us."

Brother Paul nodded. "It would seem that the concept of the Tarot was always associated with this planet, with visions drawn from the cards—"

"Not visions," the deacon corrected him. "Animations. They are tangible, sometimes dangerous manifestations."

"Yet not physical ones," Brother Paul said, expecting to clarify what Reverend Siltz had claimed.

"Indeed, physical! That is why we require that you be protected when you investigate. Did the Communist not inform you?"

"He did, but I remain skeptical. I really don't see how—"

The deacon brought out a pack of cards. "Allow me to demonstrate, if there is no protest from these, my companions of other faiths." He glanced around the table, but no one protested. "We are in storm at the moment; it should be possible to—" He selected a card and concentrated.

Brother Paul watched dubiously. If the man expected to form something physical from the air . . .

A shape appeared on the table, forming as from a cloud, fuzzy but strengthening. It was a pencil, or a chopstick—

"The Ace of Wands!" Brother Paul exclaimed.

Deacon Brown did not reply; he was concentrating on his image. Reverend Siltz had quietly returned, however, and he picked up the commentary. "Now you evidently believe the Lemurian has made a form without substance, a mirror-reflection from the card he perceives. But you shall see."

Siltz reached out and grasped the small rod between his thumb and forefinger. His hand did not pass through it, as would have been the case with a mere image; the wand moved exactly as a real one might. "Now I touch you with this staff," Siltz said. He poked the end at the back of Brother Paul's hand.

It was solid. Brother Paul felt the pressure, and

then a burning sensation. He jerked his hand away. "It's hot!"

As he spoke, the wand burst into flame at the end, like a struck match. Siltz dropped it on the table, where it continued to flare. "Fire—the reality behind the symbol, the power of nature," he said. "Someone, if you please—water."

The representative of the Nation of Islam dealt a card from his own deck. He concentrated. Two ornate golden cups formed. Deacon Brown grabbed one and poured its contents over the burning stick. There was a hiss, and a puff of vapor went up.

Were they trying to fool him with magic tricks? Brother Paul knew something of sleight-of-hand; his own fingers were uncommonly dexterous. "May I?" he inquired, reaching toward the remaining cup.

To his surprise, no one objected. He touched the cup, and found it solid. He lifted it, and it was heavy. Extremely heavy; only pure gold could be as dense as this! He dipped one finger into its fluid, then touched that finger to his tongue. Water, surely! He sprinkled some on his burn, and it seemed to help. This was a solid, tangible, physical, believable cup, and physical water. Water, the reality behind the symbol, again, the female complement to the male fire. The Tarot made literal.

"Mass hypnosis?" Brother Paul inquired musingly. "Do all of you see and feel these things?"

"We all do," Reverend Siltz assured him.

"May I experiment? I confess I am impressed, but I am an incorrigible skeptic."

"Proceed," Deacon Brown said. "We approve of skepticism, in your case. We do not need yet another dedicated cultist." There was a murmur of agreement, though Brother Paul thought he detected a rueful

109

tinge to it. At least these cultists were not overly sensitive about their situation! Probably they had been chosen to deal with him because they were the least fanatical of their respective sects.

"Then if I may borrow a Tarot deck—" One was handed to him. Though he was usually observant, his fascination with the current proceedings rendered the favor anonymous; he could not afterward recall whose deck he had borrowed. He riffled expertly through the cards, limbering his fingers. There had been a time when—but those days were best forgotten.

This was one of the popular medieval-style versions, with peasants and winged figures and children, rather than the more sophisticated modern designs. In this circumstance he was glad it was this type; a surrealistic deck could only have complicated an already incredible experience.

"I shall select a card," Brother Paul said carefully. "I shall show it to all of you except one. And then that one shall have it and animate it for us, without looking at the rest of you. May I have a volunteer?"

"I will do it," Deacon Brown said. "We of Lemuria are always happy to demonstrate the reality of our—" Someone coughed, and he broke off. "Sorry. Didn't mean to proselytize."

The deacon faced away, his bald pate glistening in the dim light from a window. The storm had brought a nocturnal gloom to the landscape, but now it was easing. Brother Paul selected the Three of Swords. It was a handsome card with a straight, red-bladed sword in the center enclosed by two ornate and curving scimitars, and a background of colored leaves. Silently he showed it to the others, then passed it to the deacon.

110

In a moment the picture was reproduced with fair accuracy. Three swords and some leaves hung in the air. Brother Paul reached out and touched one of the scimitars—whereupon all three swords fell to the floor with a startling clatter.

There was silence in the hall. Everyone at the other tables was watching now, silently. "Sorry," Brother Paul said. "I fear my ignorant touch interfered. Allow me to try one more." Privately he asked himself: if he had been able to accept the presence of Antares during matter transmission, why did he have so much trouble accepting these simple objects? And the answer came to him: because there were witnesses here. He could have imagined Antares; this present phenomenon went beyond imagination.

Brother Paul glanced about. Where were the wand, the cups, the swords? He saw none of them now. Had they vanished into that limbo whence they had come, or had they never really existed? Well, if someone were tricking him, he would have the proof in a moment.

Again he selected a card: the Four of Disks, with its four flowerlike disks, each centered by a four-leafed clover, and an ornate shield bearing the device IM. After he had shown it around, he passed it to the deacon. But, unbeknownst to his audience, he exchanged cards. The actual model was the Ace of Cups.

Now, if the Four of Coins formed, he would know it was mass hypnosis, for it had to have been compelled by the belief of others. But if the cup formed—!

The cup formed, huge and colorful, with a blue rim, a red lid, and a cross inscribed on its side.

111

"I think our guest is having a little fun with us," Reverend Siltz remarked, unamused.

"Merely verifying the origin of the Animation," Brother Paul said, shaken. "Do you all see the coin?"

"Cup, not coin," Siltz said. "It is controlled by the one who makes it; our expectations are irrelevant."

Evidently so! And the cup was so large that it could not have been concealed on the deacon's person for a sleight-of-hand manifestation, even had the man been clever enough to work such a trick under Brother Paul's experienced eye. This was a larger challenge than he had anticipated. Physical, concrete apparitions, willed consciously into existence!

"Impressive," Brother Paul admitted. "Yet you seem to have good control over the situation. I had understood you were quite alarmed by untoward Animations."

Reverend Siltz smiled grimly. "We were indeed, at first. But in the past year we have come to know more about these effects. We are assured of the reality of the Animations; it is God we have yet to compass."

The deacon turned, and his cup faded out. "Any one of us might Animate God in his own image, but that would be merely opinion, not reality. It is vital that we know the truth."

"Yet would I not Animate God in *my* own image?" Brother Paul inquired, troubled. This really was the point Siltz had raised in their private discussion.

"We must trust to your objectivity—and we shall send Watchers with you to assist," Reverend Siltz said. He was not giving away any of his private attitude now! Did members of the Second Church Communist play poker? "They will also try to protect you from untoward manifestations."

And such manifestations, as had been made clear,

could be lethal! "May I try this myself? Here, now?" Brother Paul asked, feeling a slight shiver within him, as of stage fright.

"Do it quickly, for the storm is passing," Deacon Brown said. "These effects are erratic at best; this has been an unusually good run. Normally it is necessary to go into the abyss of Northole to obtain such clear Animations. And that is dangerous."

Brother Paul picked out the first of the Major Arcana: Key Zero, the Fool.

"No!" several voices cried at once.

"Do not attempt to Animate a living man," Reverend Siltz said, evidently shaken, and his sentiment seemed to be shared by the others. "This could have unforeseen consequences."

Brother Paul nodded. So they were not really so blasé about the phenomenon! If they had never attempted to Animate a man, they had not experimented very much. He knew where he had to begin. "Still, if I am to explore this phenomenon properly, I must be permitted to Animate anything that is in my power—and I would prefer to attempt it first here, under your informed guidance."

The others exchanged glances of misgiving. They might belong to many opposing religions, but they had a certain unity here! "Your logic prevails," Reverend Siltz said heavily. "If you must do this thing, it is better done here. We shall stand aside."

Brother Paul sifted through the cards. In this deck, the Fool was titled *Le Mat* and garbed as a court jester. Not at all like Waite's interpretation, in which the Fool was a noble but innocent lad about to step off a cliff, symbolic of man's tremendous potential for aspiration and error. Other versions had a vicious little dog ripping the seat from the Fool's pants, so that his bare buttock showed: the height of ridicule. He had seen one variant in which the Fool appeared to be defecating. Probably it was after all best to pass this one by, this time; to attempt it could indeed be Folly.

Key One was the Magician, or Juggler, performing his cheap tricks at a covered table. At the Order Station, Brother Paul himself was sometimes teased— very gently, of course, since no Brother would deliberately hurt anyone—about his supposed affinity with this card. They knew his background as a one-time cardsharp, and had observed his uncanny proficiency with mechanical things. Brother Paul accepted such allusions with good spirits, grateful for the camaraderie he had found within the Order after a prior life of—never mind. He preferred to think of himself as Everyman in quest of life's ultimate meanings as symbolized by the objects resting on the table in the Vision Tarot card: a wand, a cup, a sword, and a coin, meaning fire, water, air, and earth respectively in the ubiquitous symbolism of the form. In that version, too, the cosmic lemniscate, or sidewise figure-eight, the symbol of infinity, hovered like a halo above the Magician's head, and about his waist was clasped a serpent devouring its own tail: the worm Ouroborus, a symbol of eternity. All things in all space and time—that was the grandeur of the concept for which this modern Magician strived. But here in this deck, as a degraded trickster—no, pass it by also.

Key Two, here titled Juno. In Roman mythology, Juno was the wife of Jupiter and queen of the gods, counterpart to the Greek Hera. She was the special protectress of marriage and women. Her bird was the peacock, also represented in this card. Here she was a handsome female in a bright red dress, full-bosomed and bare-legged. But such an amazonian figure might not be well-received by this male-dominated assemblage. Pass her by, regretfully; even in her more common guise as the High Priestess (and the notorious Lady Pope!) she was a questionable choice.

Key Three, the Empress—a more mature and powerful woman than the preceding one. In many decks, the Priestess was the virginal figure, while the Empress was the mother figure. Here she sat on her throne; in other decks the throne was situated in a field of wheat. Had it really been her he had glimpsed when he emerged from the capsule, only hours ago? If so, he did not want to invoke her here in public. He would prefer to meet her privately, for there was something about her that attracted him. Pass her by, for now.

Key Four, the Emperor, counterpart to the Empress, symbol of worldly power, seated on his cubic throne, his legs crossed in the figure four, holding in his right hand a scepter in the form of the Egyptian Ankh or Cross of Life, and in his left hand the globe of dominion. He represented the dominance of reason over the emotions, of the conscious over the subconscious mind. Yes, this was a good symbol for this occasion! The card of power.

Though he held the medieval card, what he visualized was the Order of Vision version. The one in the present deck, that he would have to Animate, was a medieval monarch with a great concave shield a little like the wooden cup used here to guard against the threats of the storm, and a scepter that needed only three prongs added to it to become a trident. The Reverend Siltz could readily serve as a model for this one!

Brother Paul concentrated. He felt ridiculous; maybe he had taken so long to decide on a card because he knew this was an exercise in foolishness. There had to be some trick the colonists knew to make the Animations seem real; obviously he himself could not do it.

Sure enough, nothing happened. Whatever Animation was, it would not work for him. Which meant it *was* some kind of trick. "It does not seem to function," he said with a certain amount of relief.

"Allow me to try; perhaps you only need guidance," Reverend Siltz said. He took the card and concentrated.

Nothing happened.

"The storm has abated," Deacon Brown said. "The Animation effect has passed."

So the power behind Animation had fortuitously moved on. Now nothing could be proved, one way or the other. Brother Paul told himself he should have expected this.

Yet he was disappointed. It was too marvelous to be true, and he was here, perhaps, to puncture its balloon—but what incredible power Animation promised, were it only genuine! Physical objects coalesced from imagination!

Oh, well. He was here to ascertain reality. He had no business hoping for fantasy.

5

Intuition

Part-time occupation and never more in a whole
lifetime's employment, was the "eating canker" in
the lives of the queens and concubines of an
eastern harem. Unmitigated boredom, according
to one legend, and irritability arising from unmitigated boredom, according to the second,
resulted in the harem becoming the cradle of
playing cards.

In the first legend "the inner chamber" of the
Chinese imperial palace are said to have seen the
birth of cards. The "veiled ones" secluded therein
were numerous, since the Emperor had not so
much a wife as a bedroom staff, for which the
recognized establishment for some two thousand
years was: Empress 1, Consorts 3, Spouses 9,
Beauties or Concubines 27, and Attendant
Nymphs or Assistant Concubines 81. The num-

bers 3 and 9 were held in particular regard by the astrologers.

The "mistresses of the bed" kept regular night watches, the 81 Attendant Nymphs sharing the imperial couch for 9 nights in groups of 9, the 27 Beauties 3 nights in groups of 9, the 9 Spouses and 3 Consorts 1 night per group, and the Empress 1 night alone.

These arrangements lasted from, roughly, the early years of the Chou dynasty (255-112 B.C.) to the beginning of the Sung dynasty (A.D. 950-1279) when the old order broke down and had to be abandoned according to a contemporary post, because of the unbridled and ferocious competition of no less than 3000 ladies of the palace. After making every allowance for poetic licence, it is clear that by the time of the Sung dynasty the occupants of the "inner chambers" had even less to do than ever before, and time must have been wearisome to the point of inducing mental breakdown. As a result, says the legend, in the year 1120, playing cards were conceived by an inmate of the Chinese imperial harem, as a pastime for relieving perpetual boredom.

Roger Tilley: *A History of Playing Cards*

The next morning Reverend Siltz conducted Brother Paul on a geographic tour. "I trust you are strong of foot," he remarked. "We have no machines, no beasts of burden here, and the terrain is difficult."

"I believe I can manage," Brother Paul said. After yesterday's experience with the Animations, he took quite seriously anything his host told him—but it was hardly likely that the terrain alone would do him in.

He had not slept well. The loft had been comfortable enough, with a mattress of fragrant wood shavings and pretty wooden panels above (he had half expected to see the roots of the grass that grew in the turf that formed the outer roof), but those Animations kept returning to his mind's eye. *Could* he have formed a physical object himself, let alone a human figure, had he not stalled until the storm passed? If a man could form a sword from a mental or card image, could he then use it to murder a companion? Surely this was mass hypnosis! Yet Deacon Brown *had* Animated the cup instead of the four coins. . . .

He shook his head. He would ascertain the truth in due course, if he could. That was his mission. First the truth about Animation, then the truth about God. Neither intuition nor guesswork would do; he had to penetrate to the hard fact.

Meanwhile, it behooved him to familiarize himself with this locale and these people, for the secret might lie here instead of in the Animations themselves. Despite his night of doubt, he felt better this morning, more able to cope. If God were directly responsible for these manifestations, what had a mere man to fear? God was good.

As they set out from the village, a small, swarthy man intercepted them. His body was deeply tanned, or perhaps he had mixed racial roots, as did Brother Paul. His face was grossly wrinkled, though he did not seem to be older than about fifty. "I come on a matter of privilege," he said.

Reverend Siltz halted. "This is the Swami of Kundalini," he said tightly. And to the other: "Brother Paul of the Holy Order of Vision."

119

"It is to you I am forced to address myself," the Swami said to Brother Paul.

"We are on our way to the countryside," Reverend Siltz said, with strained politeness. He obviously did not appreciate this intrusion, and that alerted Brother Paul. What additional currents were flowing here? "The garden, the amaranth, the Animation region, where the Watchers will meet us. If you care to join them—"

"I shall gladly walk with you," the Swami said.

"I am happy to talk with anyone who wishes to talk with me," Brother Paul said. "I have much to learn about this planet and this society."

"We cannot spare two for the tour," Siltz insisted. "The Swami surely has business elsewhere."

"I do, but it must wait," the Swami said.

"Well, surely a few minutes—" Brother Paul said, disliking the tension between these two men.

"Perhaps the Swami will consent to guide you in my stead," Reverend Siltz said, grimacing. "I have a certain matter I could attend to, given the occasion."

"Am I the unwitting cause of dissension?" Brother Paul asked. "I certainly don't want to—"

"I should be happy to guide the visitor," the Swami said. "I am familiar with the route."

"Then I shall depart with due gratitude," the Reverend said, his expression hardly reflecting that emotion.

"But there is no need to—" Brother Paul began. But it was useless; the Reverend of the Second Church of Communism was on his way, walking stiffly but rapidly back toward the village stockade.

Looking back, Brother Paul wondered: what use was that stockade, if it did not keep out Bigfoot? Probably the monster merely swam around one end of the stockade where the wall terminated in the lake;

during a storm there would be no way to keep watch for it.

"It is all right, guest Brother," the Swami said. "We differ strongly in our separate faiths, but we do not violate the precepts of the Tree of Life. The Reverend Communist will have occasion to verify the whereabouts of his wayward son, and I will guide you while making known my exception to your mission."

Still, Brother Paul was dubious. "I fear the Reverend is offended."

"Not as offended as he pretends," the Swami said with a brief smile. "He does have a serious concern to attend to, but it would have been impolitic for him to allow that to compromise his hospitality or duty. And I *do* have a pressing matter to discuss with you. For the affront of forcing the issue I offer such token recompense as I am able. Have you any demand?"

This was a bit complicated to assimilate immediately. Was this man friend, foe, or something between? "I am really not in a position to make any demands. Let's tour the region, and I will listen to your concern, trusting that this does not violate the Covenant."

"We shall skirt the main region of permanent Animation, and the advisory party shall be there. The tour is somewhat hazardous, so we must proceed with caution. Yet this is as nothing to the hazard your mission, however sincerely intended, poses for mankind. This is my concern."

Brother Paul had suspected something of the kind. In this hotbed of schismatic religions, there was bound to be a good doomsday prophet, and someone was sure to express strong opposition to *any* community project, even one designed to help unify the community itself in the interest of survival. Brother Paul had

had experience with democratic community government. He had been shielded from the lunatic element here. Now it seemed to have broken through. Yet even a fanatic could have useful insights. "I certainly want to be advised of hazards," Brother Paul said. "Physical and social."

"You shall be apprised of both. I will show you first our mountain garden to the south; between eruptions we farm the terraces, for the ash decomposes swiftly and is incredibly rich. Our single garden feeds the whole village for the summer, enabling us to conserve wood for winter sustenance. This is vital to our survival."

The man certainly did not sound like a nut! "But what of your wheatfields that I passed through yesterday?"

"Amaranth, not wheat," the Swami told him. "Amaranth is a special grain, adaptable to alien climes. Once it was thought of as a weed, back on Earth, until the resurgence of small family farms developed the market for tough, hand-harvested grains. We have been unable to grow true wheat here on Planet Tarot, but are experimenting with varieties of this alternate grain, and have high hopes. The lava shields are also very rich here on Southmount, but decompose more slowly than the ash, and so require slower-growing, more persistent crops. The climate of the lower region is more moderate, which is a long-range benefit."

Brother Paul did not know much about either amaranth or volcanic farming, so he wasn't clear on all this and did not argue. However, he did find some of these statements questionable. The decomposition of lava was not, as he understood it, a matter of a season or two, but of centuries. The seasonal growth of plants would be largely governed by elements already available in the soil, rather than by the slow breakdown of rock.

Their discussion lapsed, for the climb was getting steep. Glassy facets of rock showed through the turf, like obsidian mirrors set in the slope. Volcanic? It must be; he wished he knew more about the subject. The volcanoes of Planet Tarot might differ fundamentally from those of Earth, however, just as did those of Earth's more immediate neighbor, Mars.

Fundamentally. He smiled, appreciating a pun of sorts. A volcano was a thing of the fundament, shaped by the deepest forces of the planetary crust. So whether different or similar—

He stumbled on a stone, and lost his train of thought. There was a path, but not an easy one. The Swami scrambled ahead with the agility of a monkey, hands grasping crystalline outcroppings with the precision of long experience. Brother Paul kept the pace with difficulty, copying the positioning of his guide's grips. In places the ascent became almost vertical, and the path was cleaved occasionally by jagged cracks in the rock. Apparently the lava had contracted as it cooled, so that the fissures opened irregularly. The slanting sunbeams shone down into these narrow clefts, reflecting back and forth dazzlingly, and making the mountain seem like the mere shell of a netherworld of illumination. A person could be blinded, he thought, by peering into this kaleidoscopic hall of mirrors.

Or hypnotized, he realized. Could this be the cause of the Animations?

Then what had he seen and touched in the mess hall, during the storm? No crevices there, no sunlight! Scratch one theory.

Cracks and gas: that suggested a gruesome analogy. The *bocor*, or witch doctor, of Haiti (and could the similarity of that name to "hate" be coincidental? Hate-Haiti—but his mind was drifting perilously far afield at an inopportune time) was said to ride his horse backward to his victim's shack, suck out the victim's soul through a crack in the door, and bottle that gaseous soul. Later, when the victim died, the *bocor* opened the grave, brought out the bottle, and gave the dead man a single sniff of his own soul. Only one sniff: not enough to infuse the entire soul, just part of it. That animated the corpse; it rose up as a zombie, forced to obey the will of the witch doctor. Could the same be done with a human aura, and did this relate to the phenomena on Planet Tarot?

Idle speculations; he would do well to curb them and concentrate on objective fact-finding. Then he could form an informed opinion. Right now he had enough to occupy him, merely surviving this hazardous climb!

They emerged at last onto a narrow terrace. The Swami led the way along this, for it was wide enough only for them to proceed single-file. The view was alarming; they were several hundred meters above the level of the village, with the top thirty an almost sheer drop. The stockade looked like a wall of toothpicks. Woe be he who lacked good balance!

The terrace opened out into a garden area. Unfamiliar shrubs and vines spread out robustly. There were no Bubbles here, however; evidently the elevation, exposure and wind were too much for them. "We have been farming this plot for twenty days this spring, since the upper snow melted," the Swami said with communal pride.

"Twenty days? These plants look like sixty days!"

"Yes. I warned you that growth was at an incredible rate, so you are free not to credit it. Soon we begin the first harvest of the season. Then no more wood soup until fall."

"We could use some of this soil back on Earth!"

"Undoubtedly. *We* could use more supplies from Earth, and not only when the mother planet wishes to bribe us to permit religious intrusion. Perhaps we can exchange some soil for such supplies."

Brother Paul was not certain how much of this was humor and how much was sarcasm, so he did not reply. The cost of mattermission made the shipment of tons of soil prohibitive. What was really needed was the formula—the chemical analysis of the soil, and some seeds from these vigorous plants. And that would be very difficult, for the importation of alien plants to Earth was forbidden. Export was without restriction, but imports had to pass rigorous quarantine; there was a certain logic to this, for those who comprehended bureaucracy. Even if he, Brother Paul, were chemist enough to work out the formula, he would probably not be able to make the authorities on Earth pay attention anyway. But he would take samples and try . . .

"This is an active volcanic region," Brother Paul observed, cutting off his own thoughts. It was a discipline he had to exert often. "What happens if there is an eruption before the harvest?"

"That depends on the vehemence of the eruption. Most are small, and the wind carries the ash away from this site. Later in the season, when the prevailing winds shift, it will become more precarious."

Brother Paul looked down the steep slope again toward the village. The scene was like that of a skillfully executed painting, with the adjacent lake brightly

125

reflecting the morning sun. Beautiful! But he would hate to be stranded here on the volcano when it blew its top! Evidently there could be both ash and lava.

That reminded him of one of his notions that had been aborted by the difficulty of the climb. "Gas," he said. "Does the volcano issue gas? That might account for—"

"There are gas and liquid and solids and enormous energy, in accordance with the laws of Tarot," the Swami said. "But none of these are of a hallucinogenic nature. Our problem is not so readily dismissed as originating in the mouth of the mountain." He stood beside Brother Paul and pointed to the north. "There, five kilometers distant, is the depression we call 'Northhole.' There is the seat of Animation for this region."

"Maybe a subterranean vent from the volcano?" Brother Paul persisted. "Strange effects can occur. The Oracle at Delphi—that's a place back on Earth—would sit over the vent of—"

"Well I know it. Yet it seems strange that there is no Animation here at the volcano Southmount itself. No, I feel that the secret is more subtle and formidable."

"Yet you object to my attempt to explore the secret?"

The Swami showed the way down the mountain. This was a less precipitous path to the west, so that they were able to tread carefully upright, occasionally skidding on the black ash lying in riverlike courses at irregular intervals. "Do you comprehend *prana*?"

Brother Paul chuckled. "No. I have tried hatha yoga and zen meditation and read the *Vedas,* but never achieved any proper awareness of either *prana* or *jiva*. I can repeat only the vulgar descriptions:

126

prana is the individual life principle, and *jiva* is the personal soul."

"That is a beginning," the Swami said. "You are better versed than I anticipated, and this is fortunate. In the Hindu, Vedic, and Tantric texts there is a symbol of a sleeping serpent coiled around the base of the human spine. This is Kundalini, the coiled latent energy of *prana,* known by many names. Christians call it the 'Holy Spirit,' the Greeks termed it 'ether,' martial artists described it as '*ki.*'"

Now Brother Paul was in more familiar territory. "Ah, yes. In my training in judo, I sought the power of *ki,* but could never evoke it. No doubt my motive was suspect; I was thinking in terms of physical force, not spiritual force."

"This is the root of failure in the great majority of aspirants." The Swami paused on the mountainside. "Do you care to break that rock?" he inquired, indicating an outcropping of crystal.

Brother Paul tapped it with his fingers, feeling its hardness. "With a sledgehammer?"

"No. Like this. With *ki.*" And the Swami lifted his right arm and brought his hand down in a hard blow upon the rock.

And the rock fractured.

Brother Paul stared. "*Ki!*" he breathed. "You have it!"

"I do not make this demonstration to impress you with my skill," the Swami said, "but rather as evidence that my concern is serious. You have looked at me obliquely, and this is your right, but you must appreciate the sincerity of my warning."

Brother Paul looked at the cracked crystal again. Some flaw in the stone? He had not observed such a flaw before, and even if there had been one, it should

127

have taken a harder blow than the human arm was capable of delivering to faze it. The power of *ki* was the most reasonable explanation. The man who possessed that power had to be taken seriously. It was not merely that he was potentially deadly; the Swami had to have undergone rigorous training and discipline, and to have achieved fundamental insights about the nature of man and the universe.

"I take you seriously," Brother Paul said.

The Swami resumed his downward trek as if nothing special had happened. "So few apply proper respect to their quest for the aura—"

"Aura!" Brother Paul exclaimed, surprised again.

The Swami glanced sidelong at him. "That word evokes a specific response?"

Brother Paul considered telling the Swami of his vision of the creature from Sphere Antares, who had informed Brother Paul of the existence of his own, supposedly potent aura. It required only a moment's reflection to squelch that notion. He knew too little of this man and this society to discuss something as personal as this, since it reflected on his own emotional competence. What sensible person would believe in the ghost in the machine, or in private, personal alien contact during the period of instantaneous matter transmission? "I have read of Kirlian photography."

"No. Photographs are not the essence. Aura permeates the gross tissues of the body, and is the source of all vital activity including movement, perception, thought, and feeling. The awakening of this force is the greatest enterprise and the most wonderful achievement man contemplates. By this means it will be possible to bridge the gulf between science and religion, between technology and truth. But there is danger, too. Grave danger."

They were now down on the plain, walking northward through the amaranth. No wonder the "wheat" had looked funny! Brother Paul was distracted by the thought of the young woman he had encountered here the day before, and his other adventure. "Speaking of danger—is it safe to come here without weapons? Yesterday I encountered a wild animal near here."

"Yes, the news is all over the village! The Breaker will not attack you again, since you mastered it. Otherwise I surely would not have brought you this way." He paused. "Though how a lone man could have defeated as horrendous a creature as that one, that none of us dares to face without a trident—"

"I was lucky," Brother Paul said. This was not false modesty; he *had* been lucky. "Had I been aware of the threat, I would not have ventured into the amaranth field."

The Swami faced him. "What exactly did you do to overcome the Breaker?"

"I used a judo throw, or tried to," Brother Paul explained. "*Ippon seoi nage* and an armlock."

"*Ippon seoi nage* should not be effective against such a creature; the dynamics are wrong." The Swami looked at him with a glint of curiosity in his eye. "I wonder—" He hesitated. "Would you show me exactly what you did?"

"Oh, I would not care to throw you on this ground," Brother Paul demurred.

"I meant the armlock—gently." There was no question that the Swami was familiar with martial arts.

Brother Paul shrugged. "As you will." They got down on the ground and he applied the armlock, without pressure. "Nothing special about it," Brother Paul said. "On the Breaker, it was really a leglock. I

129

had not expected it to work, owing to the peculiar anatomy of the—"

"Bear down," the Swami said. "Do not be concerned; my arm is strong."

He was right about that; Brother Paul could feel surprisingly formidable muscular tension in the Swami's light frame. This man was like another aspect of the ghost in the machine; he seemed fanatical because he was improperly understood, but he was merely giving his allegiance to other than the usual imperatives. Brother Paul slowly increased the force of the hold to the point where the Breaker had screamed.

"More," the Swami said.

"There is danger."

"Precisely."

Well, pain should make the man tap out before his elbow actually broke, Brother Paul thought as he put an additional surge of effort into it.

"There!" the Swami cried.

Brother Paul eased up in alarm.

The Swami smiled, obviously unhurt.

"It is what I suspected. You used *ki*!"

Brother Paul shook his head. "I have no—"

"You have a powerful aura," the Swami insisted. "I was uncertain until you focused it. You are a gentle man, so you never willingly invoke it, but were you otherwise, you would be a monster. Never have I encountered such power."

Brother Paul sat bemused. "Once another person said something of the kind to me, but I dismissed it as fancy," he said, thinking again of Antares.

"Only those who have mastered their own auras can perceive them in others," the Swami assured him. "My own mastery is imperfect, so your aura was not immediately apparent to me. But now I am certain, it was your *ki*, the focused application of your aura, that terrified the Breaker. Surely it was this aura that selected you for this mission too, though others might have rationalized it into other reasons. I had hoped this would not be the case."

Brother Paul shook his head. "If this . . . this aura protects me against threats, surely—"

"The threat of which I speak is much greater than merely a physical one. You see—"

"Hello."

Both men looked up, startled. It was the girl of the wheatfield, the Empress of Tarot. *Amaranth* field, he corrected himself. This time she was not fleeing him, and for that he was grateful. Now he could discover whom she was.

She wore a one-piece outfit, really a belted tunic embroidered with a landscape reminiscent of the local geography. Every colonist's apparel was distinctive, reflecting his religious bias, but this was something special. There were hills and valleys in color, and two volcanic mounts in front: a veritable contour map. Brother Paul tried not to stare. They were extremely lofty and well-formed volcanoes.

"We merely pass by," the Swami informed her.

"Wrestling on the ground, flattening the crop, and crying out?" she demanded. "Swami, I always knew you were a nut, but—"

"My fault," Brother Paul interposed. "I was trying to demonstrate how I discouraged the Breaker."

Her lovely eyes narrowed appraisingly. "Then I must speak with you," she said firmly. Indeed, everything about her was firm; she was a strikingly handsome young woman, with golden hair and eyes and skin, and features that were, as the narrators of the

Arabian Nights would have put it, marvels of symmetry. Brother Paul might have seen a fairer female at some time in his life, but at the moment it was difficult to call any such creature to mind.

"I have undertaken to guide this man about the premises," the Swami said gruffly, as he rose and dusted himself off. "We must arrive at Northole in due course."

"Then I shall accompany you," she said. "It is essential that I talk with our visitor from Earth."

"You cannot leave your station!"

"My station is the Breaker—who is absent today," she said with finality.

Brother Paul remained silent. It seemed that the Swami was being served as he himself had served Reverend Siltz; also, it would be wickedly pleasant having this scenic creature along. He had feared he would not see her again, but here she was, virtually forcing her company on him. Obviously she accepted no inferior status; maybe women were, after all, equal to men here. That would be nice.

The Swami shrugged, evidently suppressing his irritation. "This female is the understudy to the Breaker," he said, by way of introduction. "She alone has no fear of the monster. It is apparent in her manner."

"The Swami prefers his docile daughter," she responded, "who has few illusions of individuality."

Thrust and counterthrust! "What is your name, Breaker Lady?" Brother Paul asked. "Why did you flee from me before, if you have so little to fear?"

"I thought you were an Animation," she said. "The only way to handle an Animation is to get the hell away from it."

Hm. A candid, colloquial answer that did much to

debilitate his prior conception of her as the Empress. "But your name?"

"Call her anything you like," the Swami said. "Subtlety is wasted on the unsubtle."

The girl only smiled, not at all discommoded by the Swami's taciturnity. If she had intended to give her name, that intention was gone now. Somehow he had to defuse this minor social crisis, since he wanted to get along with both of them, though for different reasons.

"Then I shall call you Amaranth, in honor of this beautiful field where we met," Brother Paul decided that physical compliments were seldom in error, when relating to the distaff.

"Oh, I like that!" she exclaimed, melting. "Amaranth! May I keep it?"

"It is yours," Brother Paul said benignly. He liked her mode of game-playing, and he liked her. "You thought I was an Animation of the Devil, and I thought you were an Animation of the Empress. No doubt we were both correct."

She laughed, causing the volcanoes to quiver hazardously. "And I thought members of the Order of Vision were humorless!"

"Some are," Brother Paul said. "Let me hear out the Swami; then I shall be free to talk with you at leisure." Delightful prospect!

"My warning can wait upon a more propitious occasion," the Swami said sourly. "It concerns Northole."

"That's an odd name," Brother Paul observed, hoping to relieve the tension again.

"We have simplistic nomenclature," Amaranth said. "That's Southmount you came from; this is Westfield;

133

the Animation pit is Northole; and the water to the east of the village is—"

"Eastlake," Brother Paul finished. "Yes, it does make sense. What did you want to ask me?"

"Nothing," she said.

"Perhaps I misunderstood. I thought you said—"

"Never pay too much attention to what a woman says," the Swami said.

She ignored him elegantly. "I said I wished to speak with you. I am doing that."

Brother Paul smiled with bafflement. "Assuredly. Yet—"

"You overcame my Breaker with your bare hands, without hurting him or yourself. I need to study you, as I study the Breaker. This is my job: to comprehend the full nature of my subject."

"Ah. So you must comprehend the type of person who balks the animal, by whatever freak of circumstance," Brother Paul said. He had had the impression that her interest was in him personally, but this was really more realistic. What real interest would a girl of her attractions have in a sedate stranger? "Yet I remain confused," he went on.

"That's all right," she said brightly.

The Swami mellowed enough to put in an explanation. "Survival is a narrow thing here," he said. "We must labor diligently to gather wood for the arduous winter, and anything that interferes with this acquisition of fuel is a community concern. The Breaker interferes, forcing us to travel from the village in armed parties—a ruinously wasteful expenditure of manpower. Therefore we study the Breaker, hoping to neutralize it."

"Wouldn't it be simpler to kill it?" Brother Paul asked.

"Kill it?" the Swami echoed, as if baffled.

Now it was the girl's turn to make the explanation. "Many of our sects object to taking the lives of natural creatures. It is a moral matter, and a practical one. It is impossible to know what the ramifications of unnecessary killing may be. If we killed this local Breaker, another might merely move into its place. A smarter or more vicious one. If we killed them all, we could wreak ecological havoc that would in turn destroy us. Back on Earth the environment was ravaged by the unthinking war against pests, and we don't want to make that mistake here. Also, we need beasts of burden, and the Breaker, if it could be tamed and harnessed, might be an excellent one. So we protect ourselves with the tridents, not trying to kill the Breaker or any other predator. We are studying our problems before acting."

"That is what I am here to do with the problem of Animation," Brother Paul pointed out.

"Which is why you must be apprised of the danger first," the Swami said. "The Breaker is a minor menace; Animation is a major one."

"I am willing to listen," Brother Paul reminded him.

The Swami was silent, so Brother Paul addressed Amaranth. "How is it you have this dangerous job of observation? You do not carry any trident."

"Not a tangible one," the Swami muttered. "She has barbs enough."

"He sees his late wife in all young women," Amaranth said to Brother Paul. "She had a savage wit. But about me: it was the lot. No one volunteered, so we drew cards from the Tarot, and I was low. As a matter of fact, I was the Empress, Key Three; you were right about that. So they built me a protective

135

box shaped like the throne and appropriately marked—we propitiate the God of Tarot in any little way we can—and I set out to study the Breaker. And watch the amaranth, since the Breaker associates most frequently with this area. He sure keeps the grain-eaters off the field! I keep track of the temperature extremes, rainfall, and such, and measure the growth of the plants. And when an MT shipment comes, I notify the village, although the noise of arrival usually makes that superfluous. Sorry I lost my head yesterday; I had forgotten they were sending a man this time."

"But the danger—a mere girl—"

The Swami snorted. "Let the Breaker beware!"

"I had some concern myself," she admitted, again successfully ignoring the jibe. "I wanted to indulge my artistic proclivities, carving pseudo-icons and totems from Tree of Life wood and igneous stone. But that slot was filled by another, so I had to accept assignment elsewhere. When the lot put me in this dangerous and unsuitable position, I rebelled."

"She is good at that," the Swami said.

"Which is one reason I remain unmarried," she continued. "I had a prospect, but he rejected me because of my lack of community spirit. Of course, *he* didn't have to face the Breaker. Finally I had to come around, because on this planet you contribute or you don't eat; that's one of the few things our scattered cults agree on."

"An excellent policy," the Swami said.

"But do you know," she continued without even a poisonous glance at him, "I discovered that there really is a lot more to be known about amaranth than I had thought, as well as about the Breaker. Each plant is a separate individual, proceeding in its own fashion toward the harvest, requiring its own special attention.

136

Sometimes I sneak a little volcanic ash to a plant that is ailing, though I'm not supposed to. There are creatures beneath the plants, insects and even serpents sheltered by the low canopy. That makes me feel right at home."

"Most girls of Earth do not appreciate snakes, beneficial as these reptiles may be," Brother Paul observed.

"Most girls of Earth do not worship Abraxas, the serpent-footed God," she replied. "Actually, the fear of snakes is comparatively recent, historically. In the Bible, the Serpent was the source of wisdom that transformed—"

"Caution," the Swami said. "Remember the Covenant."

"Sorry," she said. "We are not permitted to go into our private beliefs, in the interest of your continuing objectivity. It's a nuisance. Anyway, I discovered unsurpassed artistry in the mountains and sunsets and storms of this unspoiled planet. Have you noticed how the Tarot Bubbles get blown by the wind? We must have the prettiest storms in this section of the Galaxy! I translated this beauty into the weaving I do in the off-hours."

"You weave also?" Brother Paul asked.

"Oh, yes, we all weave the Tree of Life fibers, especially in winter, for we must have clothing and blankets against the cold. You haven't experienced winter until you've survived it here! But even in summer I must sit still for long periods, alone, so the weaving and embroidery help distract me. This dress I designed and shaped myself," she said with pride, taking a breath that made the twin volcanoes threaten to erupt. "It is an accurate contour map of the region as seen from my station." She shrugged, causing another siege of earthquakes around the mountains. "Of

137

course, I have to be facing the right way. Strictly speaking, I should be lying down with my legs to the north—"

"Shameless!" the Swami hissed.

"Oh, come on, Swami," she said. "Doesn't Kundalini link *prana* to the sexual force, just as my God Abraxas does? There should be no shame in drawing a parallel between woman and nature. Woman *is* nature."

"I didn't realize there were two volcanoes," Brother Paul said, thinking it best to interrupt this debate. He had not believed religion could ever play too great a part in the daily lives of people, but he was developing a doubt. In every personal interaction, here on Planet Tarot, the animosities of religious intolerance were barely veiled.

"Oh, yes," she said. "Actually it is one volcano with twin cones. They normally erupt together. From the village, one cone obscures the other, and often in the mornings the haze conceals both, but from here . . ." She turned, walking briskly backward so as not to impede their progress toward Northole. "Yes, you can see them both now. Southmount Left and Southmount Right." She tapped the map appropriately, making momentary indentations in the resilient mounts.

Brother Paul yanked his eyes away from the indents and looked back. Sure enough, now two cones were apparent, and they did resemble those of the contour map: full and rounded, rather than truly conical. "Where is the mountain garden?" he inquired.

"Here in the cleft," she said, indicating a spot on the map between the cones. "The village access comes up on the east slope, here." She traced a course up the right side. "It's steep, but most direct." It certainly was! "Now we're about here—" She touched the general region of her navel. "Heading for the—"

"Enough!" the Swami cried.

"Northole," she concluded. "The passion pit."

"You are an accursed slut!" the Swami said. His face was red. Whatever control he exerted over his intellectual and spiritual powers did not seem to extend to his emotions. This was a deeply divided man, with sizable unresolved conflicts.

"Nothing wrong with me that a good man can't cure," Amaranth said blithely. Well, the Swami had started this engagement; now she was finishing it.

"You never explained about the Breaker," Brother Paul reminded her.

"Um, yes. When I studied the Breaker, I came to realize that this was the most interesting phenomenon of all. I was afraid of it at first, and I really barricaded my throne as a fortress, but after a while it got used to me. Little by little I won its respect, taming it, and now it will not attack me because it knows me. *He* knows me; I think of the Breaker as male."

"You would," the Swami muttered.

"We are friends, in our fashion," she continued. "I am closer to success than others suspect. The Breaker will come when I whistle, and I can touch him. I think he might fight for me if I were threatened. That may have been why he went after you; he thought you were chasing me."

"I was," Brother Paul said.

"I certainly would not want to see him killed. I do think that in time I will be able to harness his power for our benefit. It is a tremendous project, and I'm glad now that the lot fell to me. I'm sorry you drove the Breaker away."

"I was ignorant of—"

139

"Oh, no blame attaches to you, sir! You had to defend yourself, and you did that without actually hurting the Breaker. He will return in a day or so. Meanwhile, you can show me how you did it."

"I utilized the principles of judo," Brother Paul began, but caught the warning glance of the Swami. Yes, probably it was better not to mention the matter of *ki* or aura, yet. "*Sieroku zenyo*, maximum efficiency—"

She stopped. "Pretend I'm the Breaker, charging you. How do you react?"

Déjà vu! "It would require physical contact to demonstrate, and I have already been through this with the Swami. I'm not sure—"

"The vamp means to seduce you!" the Swami expostulated.

Brother Paul was not at all certain this was an empty warning. A forward woman who spoke appreciatively of serpents and sexual knowledge and showed off her breasts in so obvious a fashion . . . "Perhaps another time," he said. "I gather, then, that you do not feel that your assignment was a mistake." She had already said as much, but he was somewhat at a loss for suitable responses.

"It has been a revelation," she said sincerely, resuming her forward progress. She adapted to circumstances readily, whether physical or conversational. An intriguing woman to know! "The lot chose my career better than I ever could have. I believe it was the will of Abraxas."

"A heathen demon!" the Swami muttered.

"Observe the intemperate yogi," she said. "Other Indian-derived religions are supremely tolerant, but he—"

"Perhaps it was the God of Tarot who guided the

lot," Brother Paul said. "Whichever god that may be." Then, before the hostilities could resume: "I see people ahead. Swami, it may be time for you to tell me of the danger, before we are interrupted."

To his half-surprise, the Swami agreed. "The danger is this: the Animation effect is a manifestation of the fundamental power of Kundalini—the spirit force. Evoked without proper comprehension or controls, this is like conjuring Satan, like giving blocks of fissionable material to a child for play."

"Oh, pooh!" Amaranth exclaimed. "Magic like this has been known and practiced and venerated for thousands of years. The only question is, whose god is responsible? You're just afraid it won't turn out to be *your* god."

"Correct," the Swami agreed. "I worship no god; I seek only the ultimate enlightenment. This Animation is not a force of God at all, but a manifestation of uncontrolled Kundalini. In human history, Kundalini gone astray has been the cause of the evil geniuses of men like Attila the Hun and Adolph Hitler the Nazi. If you, Brother Paul of the Holy Order of Vision, evoke it now—and it is my fear that this capacity does indeed lie within you, the capacity to loose the full genie from the bottle, rather than the mere fragments of it we have hitherto seen—you may give form to a concentration of power that will destroy us all, that will exterminate the entire human colony of Planet Tarot."

"An imaginary beast!" Amaranth scoffed.

But Brother Paul was not so skeptical. The Swami had shown him some of the reasons for his concern, and they were impressive. What could the power of *ki* do, if it were to run amok? If this really were related to Animation . . . "I have seen some of the Anima-

141

tions, touched the forms myself," he said. "There is something here beyond our present comprehension. I know that other people have died exploring this mystery. Yet I am here to fathom it if I can; I believe my best course lies not in avoiding Animation, but in studying it with extreme caution and whatever safeguards are feasible. Knowledge is our most formidable weapon, especially against the unknown."

"I expected that response, and respect it," the Swami said. "My purpose is only to make certain you appreciate the possible magnitude of the threat. I can do no more. Nor would I, under the Covenant."

Brother Paul had expected a less restrained reaction. The Swami ranged from snappish intolerance to utter reasonableness without warning. "I understand there are to be assigned watchers, during my exploration. Perhaps you should be among them, to caution me where necessary."

"I am already represented," the Swami said. "Yet the watchers are as nothing against the magnitude of this force."

They had come up to the two standing figures. "Brother Paul," one said. He was an old man, white-haired but upright. "I am Pastor Runford, Jehovah's Witness. This is Mrs. Ellend, Church of Christ, Scientist."

"I am glad to meet you," Brother Paul said. Separately, to the woman, he added: "That would be Christian Scientist?"

The woman nodded. She seemed even older than the pastor, but also healthier, as befitted her calling. Christian Scientists commonly refused conventional medical attention, believing that all illness was illusory.

"We two have been assigned to watch over your experiment, remaining neutral ourselves," Pastor Runford said. "This is the edge of Northole, where Animations most frequently occur."

"If I may ask," Brother Paul said, "it seems to me that except for occasional storms, this effect remains fairly localized. Wouldn't it be simpler merely to demark the limits of Animation regions, and stay away from those areas?"

"We would do so if we could," Pastor Runford replied. "Young lady, if I may use your map . . ."

Amaranth stepped forward, smiling. The pastor used a stripped weed stem to indicate points on her map. "Our only route to the great forest to the north some leagues from here skirts Northmount. Here." He pointed to her right thigh, which was conveniently set forward. "And must veer quite near Northole, here." He gestured delicately to the obvious region, marked on her dress as a wide, shallow depression. "At times the Animation effect extends across the path, interfering with our hauling. If we do not bring down sufficient wood for the winter—"

"I understand," Brother Paul said. So there was a practical, geographic reason for neutralizing this effect, as well as the colonists' need to unify about a single God.

"We do not wish to interfere in any way with your belief or your investigation," Mrs. Ellend said. Her voice was oddly soft, yet carried well: the quiet authority of the grandmother figure. "Yet this matter is of some concern to us. Therefore it behooves us to cooperate with you, facilitating your exploration in an unobtrusive manner. While we are not, as a community, in complete agreement, common need has led us to this compromise." She glanced at the Swami. "Do you not agree, Kundalini?"

The Swami grimaced, but nodded affirmatively.

Pastor Runford's eyes traveled out over the misty hollow to the north. "Anticipating your progress, we have positioned observers within and without the Animation region. Mrs. Ellend and I are without; three colonists unknown to you are within. All are instructed by the Covenant to leave you to your own devices, except when you are in personal danger or otherwise in need of assistance. We ask you to remain near the fringe, where the effect is not strong, and to withdraw immediately if a storm should rise. Since we on the outside will be better able to detect such weather, we will signal you or send a courier at need. Are you amenable to this?"

Brother Paul considered it. "If I understand correctly, the line between reality and imagination becomes blurred within the Animation area. Thus I may perceive a storm when none is present, or overlook a genuine one. I must confess to my amazement at the manifestations evoked by Deacon Brown last night; it is apparent that my own objectivity is not proof against this sort of thing. I therefore thank you for your concern. I believe it to be well-founded, and I consider the Swami's warning quite timely also. I shall remain at the fringe today, and will respond immediately to your signal or messenger."

"We sincerely appreciate your attitude," Mrs. Ellend said with a smile that warmed him. What a gracious lady she was! "If you will also limit your initial exploration to an hour, this will serve as another safeguard."

"One hour." Brother Paul set the counter on his watch. "I'd like to take one further precaution. Because we are concerned with objective reality here, I have been provided with electronic units to enable me to communicate with persons outside of the Animation area. I propose to leave a transceiver with you, so that we will be in touch." He drew a wand from his pocket. "These are activated by pressure; just squeeze between thumb and forefinger to broadcast, and release to receive."

"I am familiar with the type," Pastor Runford said, taking the unit. "Back on Earth, we used these to coordinate our membership drives. An excellent precaution."

Membership drives. Yes, the Jehovah's Witnesses were the most persistent of recruiters, carrying their message and literature to every household. They believed the end of the world was near, and the advent of mattermission had intensified that belief. Brother Paul was not about to argue the case. "Also," he continued, "I have been cautioned against attempting to Animate the Major Arcana, but I cannot do much more with Tarot symbols like swords and cups than I have already witnessed. I would like to Animate more complex images that are still circumscribed by existing standards. It occurs to me that the picture symbolism of the Minor Arcana in the so-called Waite pack of cards—"

"You are a thoughtful man," Mrs. Ellend said. "Please accept my deck for this purpose. It is the standard Rider-Waite Tarot." She extended it.

"Thank you." Brother Paul took the deck, faced north, and started walking. The four colonists stood where they were, watching silently.

Actually he felt a bit guilty, for he had not informed them of the significance of the bracelet he wore. Yet it still seemed best merely to let this secret recorder record, and to ignore it meanwhile; it would represent the final evidence, back on Earth, of the truth of his discoveries. He could not play back its record here on Planet Tarot, so in that sense it really was irrelevant.

He wondered where the other three observers were—the ones inside the Animation region. Were they hiding? He really would not mind having them present; an objective experiment should be valid regardless of the audience, and the Animation effect did not seem to be publicity-shy. Maybe they were waiting under that tree thirty meters distant. . . .

It was a magnificent tree, possibly seventy-five meters tall, and thus larger than most that remained on Earth. The leaves formed so dense a canopy that the shade beneath it was like night. Pretty Tarot Bubbles clustered in that nocturnal shelter, exceptionally large; some were up to ten centimeters in diameter. A haze of blossoms coated the outer fringe of the upper region of the tree, and their odor drifted sweetly down to him. Could this be the source of Animation, the fragrance of the trees? No; surely anything so obvious would have been discovered long ago by the colonists. Flowers were seasonal, so the effect would be limited to springtime, and from all he had heard, Animation occurred at all seasons and in all places, though most frequently during storms and in Northole. Also, if Animation derived from the Tree of Life (assuming that this tree was a representative of that species) and remained associated with the wood, the effect would be strongest in the houses of the village. Since it was weakest there, and did not develop as the wood was being burned in winter, the Tree was an unlikely source.

The watchers were not by the tree. Brother Paul halted, physically and mentally, and pondered. "This seems like a good place to begin, nevertheless," he murmured. If this were an individual Tree of Life, allowed to stand because it was in the Animation area, it was a fitting setting for his experiment. If there were an entire forest of giants like this to the north, what a forest it would be! Perhaps he would visit that in due course. He hoped so.

He opened the pack of cards and riffled through it, his fingers nimble. He passed over the Major Arcana and stopped at the Ace of Wands. On this variant it was a picture, not a simple wand. That was why he had chosen the Waite deck. "Well, why not?" he asked himself.

He held the card before him, concentrating. Would it work, now that he was doing it alone? He wasn't sure he was far enough into the Animation area anyway, so a failure would not necessarily mean—

He looked up. And gaped. There it was: a small cumulus cloud, all gray and fleecy, hanging in the sky, its curlicues extending vertically, about a kilometer above the ground. As he watched, a white hand pushed out to the left, glowing, and in this ghostly hand was clasped a tall wooden club with little green leaves sprouting from it. The whole thing was in grandiose scale, and somewhat fuzzy and poorly proportioned, but obviously modeled upon the card he held. It was not merely a vision in the sky; there was a knoll several kilometers beyond it, on the far side of a flowing stream, and what could be a castle on this knoll. Brother Paul was sure that neither stream nor castle had been there before he had begun concentrating on the card. This meant the entire visible landscape had been coerced to conform to the card. This success was beyond his expectations; he had been ready for failure, or at best a miniature scene.

Even as he studied it, the scene wavered and faded.

147

The castle was no longer clear, and the cloud—was only a cloud. He could no longer be sure he had seen what he thought he had seen.

Brother Paul did not pause to ponder the implications. Instead he sorted out the four deuces, set aside the main deck, and shuffled the twos together until their order was random. Then he turned up the top one: the Two of Swords. The picture was of a young woman in a plain white robe, blindfolded, seated before an island-studded lake. In her hands she held two long swords. Her arms were crossed over her bosom, so that the swords pointed up and outward in a V shape. He had dealt this card reversed—upside-down— owing to the shuffling.

Before he tried to Animate it, he walked another fifty paces north, where he hoped the effect would be stronger and more persistent. He did not want another wavering, distorted picture to sap his certainty. He concentrated on the card as it was, then looked up.

Sure enough, the blindfolded lady was there, in every detail. Also the lake, the islands, and the crescent moon showing in the V. *And the whole scene was inverted*—like the card. The lake was overhead, the moon below; it was as if she were supported by the projecting swords.

Reversal could be highly significant in Tarot. In divination—the polite term for fortune-telling—it meant the message of the card was diminished in impact or changed. Muted. Brother Paul knew that according to the author of this deck, Arthur Waite, the reversed Two of Swords was an omen of imposture, falsehood, or disloyalty. A bad sign?

No, this was no divination! It was only an experiment, a testing of a specific effect. Besides, he did not believe in omens. For his purpose, this inversion was

148

invaluable, because no such thing would have happened naturally. He *had* Animated it! Having verified this, he let it fade out.

Brother Paul sorted and shuffled the four threes, and dealt one. Cups, reversed. He concentrated, and the three maidens appeared, dancing in a garden, with cups held high, pledging one another. Upside-down.

If he were a believer in divination, he would be feeling rather doubtful now. The Trey of Cups signified the conclusion of any matter happily; reversed, it would mean—

Frowning, he put away the card, and watched the vision fade. He set up the fours. He walked farther north as he mixed them. The Animation effect did seem to be getting stronger, despite the inversions; it could be the intensification of the field or whatever enabled the effect, or it could be increasing proficiency on his part as he gained experience. This time he would really test it, by producing something he could touch.

He turned up the Four of Pentacles, Waite's name for Disks or Coins. Yet again, the card was reversed. And the image formed before him, without his consciously willing it. Inverted. It was a young man, seated, with a golden disk on his head, the disk inscribed with a five-pointed star, and another disk like it held before him, and two more under his feet. *Over* his feet, in this position.

"Damn it!" Brother Paul swore, in most un-Vision-like ire. He was tired of inversion and its theoretic warnings of trouble that he didn't believe in. He strode forward, moving his arm as if to sweep the vision away. Half certain that he would encounter nothing, he fixed his gaze on the fair city in the distance, also upside-down, like a mirage.

His outflung hand struck the front disk. It flew wide, reminding him momentarily of Tennyson's Lady of Shalott, whose spindle had flown wide and cracked the mirror from side to side. Was he, like that Lady, living in fantasy? The disk bounced and rolled along the ground. The man fell over, his feet coming down to touch the ground. He looked surprised. He opened his mouth as if to cry out—and faded away.

Shaking, Brother Paul stood looking at the spot where the Four of Pentacles had been. The Animation *had* been solid! Just as the symbols yesterday in the mess hall had been solid. There was now no question: belief in an image caused it to become real, here. Faith was the key.

Brother Paul put the deck away. It was evident that he could Animate what he saw on the cards, and these constructs seemed to pose no threat to him personally. But was there really any significance beyond this? If this were simply a work of art—reproducing pictures in three dimensions, converting pictures to sculptures—then there was surely no special god involved.

"Brother Paul," a small voice murmured.

If there were no god—at least none directly controlling the Animation effect—his task was simple. He could declare the problem solved and go home. But surely the colonists would not have been cowed by the Animation effect, if it were only an art form, any more than they were cowed by the volcanoes or the Tarot Bubbles. And what was the specific cause of the effect? His will controlled a particular image, but something else had to make it possible here, while it remained impossible elsewhere.

"Brother Paul," the small voice repeated, "do you perceive me?"

He knew he had to work this out very carefully. He

150

believed in God, and this was a most powerful and pervasive belief, the realization of which had transformed his life eight years ago. Yet he had never presumed to define that God too specifically. It was essential that he keep his mind objective, and not create any deity here, as it were, in his own image. That had been Reverend Siltz's caution, and a proper one. For this mission, as in life, his God was Truth: the most specific, objective, explicable truth he was capable of mustering.

If God Himself should manifest via the medium of Animation, surely He would make Himself known in His own fashion, indisputably, as someone had already suggested. Brother Paul merely had to hold himself in readiness for that transcendent revelation, that supreme intuition.

"Lord," he murmured, "let me not make a fool of myself, in my quest for Thee." But he had to reprove himself: it was a selfish prayer. If it were necessary to make a fool of himself to discover God, then it would be well worth it. In fact, was this not the nature of the Fool of Tarot?

His hour was passing; if he were to progress beyond yesterday's point, he had to do it soon. He brought out the deck again and riffled through it, seeking inspiration. The Minor Arcana were not sufficient; should he Animate a Court Card? Perhaps a King or a Queen?

A figure showed. Female, coming toward him. But he hadn't attempted another Animation! Unless—

That was it. He was going through the Suit of Swords, and there was the Eight: a woman bound and hoodwinked among a forest of standing swords. It meant bad news, crisis, interference. He had unconsciously Animated it. He would have to watch that; he was in the depths of the Animation region now, and with practice was developing such ready facility that any card he glimpsed could become physical, even without his conscious intent.

Well, time for the big one. He would see if he could make the Tarot deck itself respond to his queries. Brother Paul brought out the deck again, sorted through the Major Arcana, and selected the Hierophant. This was Key Five of this deck, the great educator and religious figure known in other decks as the High Priest or the Pope, counterpart to the High Priestess. It all depended on the religion and purpose of the person who conceived the particular variant. The title of the card hardly mattered anyway; some decks used no titles. The pictures carried the symbolism. Surely this august figure of Key Five would know the meaning of Animation, if there were a meaning to be known.

Brother Paul concentrated, and the figure materialized. He sat upon a throne, both hands upraised, the right palm out, two fingers elevated in benediction, the left hand holding a scepter topped with a triple cross. He wore a great red robe and an ornate golden headdress. Before him knelt two tonsured monks; behind him rose two ornate columns.

Brother Paul found himself shaking. He had conjured the leading figure of the Roman Catholic Church, by whatever name a Protestant deck might bestow. Had he the right?

Yes, he decided. This was not the real Pope, but a representation drawn from a card. Probably a mindless thing, a mere statue. That mindlessness needed to be verified, so Brother Paul could be assured that there was no intellect behind the Animation effect.

"Your Excellency," he murmured, inclining his

152

head with the respect he gave to dignitaries of any faith. One did not need to share a person's philosophy to respect his dedication to that philosophy. "May I have an audience?"

The figure's head tilted. The left arm lowered. The eyes focused on Brother Paul. The lips moved. "You may," the Hierophant said.

It had spoken!

Well, his recorder-bracelet would verify later whether or not this was true. Voice analysis might reveal that Brother Paul was talking to himself. That did not matter; it was his mission to make the observations, evoking whatever effects could be evoked, so that the record was complete. He could not afford to hold back merely because he personally might not like what manifested. He was already sorry he had Animated the Hierophant; now he had to *talk* with the apparition, and that seemed to commit him intellectually, legitimizing a creation he felt to be illegitimate. Well, onward.

"I seek information," he said, meekly enough.

The holy head inclined. "Ask, and it shall be given."

Brother Paul thought of asking whether God was behind the Animation effect, and if so, what was His true nature? But he remembered an event of his college days, when a friend had teased the three-year-old child of a married student by asking her, "Little girl, what is the nature of ultimate reality?" The child had promptly replied, "Lollipops." That answer had been the talk of the campus for days; the consensus of opinion had been that it was accurate. But Brother Paul was not eager for that sort of reply from this figure. First he had to verify the Hierophant's nature. So he asked it a challenging but not really critical question, a test question. "What is the purpose of religion?"

"The purpose of religion is to pacify men's minds and make them socially and politically docile," the Hierophant replied.

This caught Brother Paul by surprise. It was certainly no reflection of his own view of religion! Did this mean the figure did possess a mind of its own? "But what of the progress of man's spirit?" he asked. "What happens to it after it passes from this world?"

"Spirit? Another world? Superstitions fostered by the political authorities," the Hierophant said. "No one in his right mind would put up with the corruption and cruelty of those in power, if he believed this were the only world he would experience. So they promise him a mythical life hereafter, where the wrongs of *this* life will be compensated. Only a fool would believe *that*, which shows how many fools there are. Barnum was wrong; a fool is not born every minute. A fool is born every second."

"Lord have mercy on me, a fool," Brother Paul murmured.

"Eh?" the Hierophant demanded querulously.

"I merely thought there was more to religion than this," Brother Paul clarified. "A person needs some solace in the face of the inevitable death of the body."

"Without death, there would be no religion!" the Hierophant asserted, waving his scepter for emphasis. It almost struck the pate of one of the monks. The Hierophant frowned in annoyance, and both monks disappeared. "Religion started with the nature spirits—the forest fire, flood, thunder, earthquake and the like. Primitive savages tried to use magic to pacify the demons of the environment, and made blood sacrifices to the elements of fire, water, air, and earth, hoping to flatter these savage powers into benign behavior. Read the Good Book of Tarot and you will find these spooks lurking yet, in the form of the four suits. Formal religion is but an amplification of these concepts."

Brother Paul's amazement was giving way to ire. "This is an idiot's view of religion," he said. "You can't claim—"

"You have been brainwashed into conformity with intellectual nonsense," the Hierophant said with paternal regret. "Your whole existence has been steeped in religious propaganda. Your memory is imprinted with the face of Caesar and the message 'In God We Trust.' Your pledge of allegiance to your totemic flag says 'One nation under God indivisible.' Why not say 'In Satan We Trust,' for Satan has far more constancy than God. Or 'One nation, embracing a crackpot occult spook, indivisible except by lust for power—'"

"Stop!" Brother Paul cried. "I cannot listen to this sacrilege!"

The Hierophant nodded knowingly. "So you admit to being the dupe of the organized worldwide conspiracy of religion. Your objectivity exists only so long as the truth does not conflict with the tenets of your cult."

Brother Paul was angry, but not so angry that he missed the kernel of truth within the religious mockery. This cardboard entity was baiting him, pushing his buttons, forcing him to react as it chose. The Animation was in control, not he himself. He had to recover his objectivity, to observe rather than proselytize, or his mission was doomed.

Brother Paul calmed himself by an effort of will that became minimal once he realized what was happening. "I apologize, Hierophant," he said, with a fair

155

semblance of calmness. "Maybe I have been misinformed. I will hear you out." After all, freedom of speech applied to everyone, even those with cardboard minds.

The figure smiled. "Excellent. Ask what you will."

This was now more difficult than before. Instead of a question, Brother Paul decided to try a statement. Maybe he could gain the initiative and make the Animation react instead; that should be more productive. Obviously there was a mind of some kind behind the facade; the question was, *what* mind?

"You say I can tolerate only that truth which does not conflict with the tenets of my personal religion," he said carefully. "I'm sure that is correct. But I regard my religion as Truth, and I do my best to ascertain the truth of every situation. I support freedom of speech for every person, including those who disagree with me, and I endorse every man's right to life, liberty, and the pursuit of happiness. This is part of what I mean when I salute my country's flag, and when I invoke God's name in routine matters."

"Few nations support these things," the Hierophant said. "Certainly not the monolithic Church. A heretic is entitled to neither life nor liberty, and no one is entitled to happiness."

"But happiness is the natural goal of man!" Brother Paul protested, privately intrigued. Now he was baiting the figure! He considered happiness only a part of the natural goal of man; he himself did not crave selfish happiness. Once, perhaps, he had; but he had matured. Or so he hoped.

"The salvation of his immortal soul is the proper goal of man," the Hierophant said firmly. "Happiness has no part of it."

"But you said man's immortal soul was superstition, a mere invention spawned by political—"

"Precisely," the figure agreed, smiling.

"But then it is all for nothing! All man's deeds, man's suffering, unrewarded."

"You are an apt student."

Brother Paul shook his head, clearing it. This thing was not going to mousetrap him! "So the destiny of man is—"

"Man must eschew joy, in favor of perpetual mortification."

"But all basic instincts of man are tied to pleasure. The satisfaction of abating hunger, the comfort of rest after hard labor, the acute rapture of sexual union—"

"These are temptations sponsored by Satan! The ascetic way of life is the only way. The way of least pleasure. A man should feed on bread and water, sleep on a hard cot, and have contact with the inferior sex only for the limited purpose of propagating the species, if at all."

"Oh, come now!" Brother Paul protested, laughing. "Sex has been recognized as a dual-function drive. Not only does it foster reproduction, it enhances the pleasure of a continuing interpersonal relationship that solidifies a family."

"Absolutely not!" the Hierophant insisted. "The pleasures of fornication are the handiwork of Satan, and the begetting of a child is God's punishment for that sin, a lifelong penance."

"Punishment!" Brother Paul exclaimed incredulously. "If I had a child, I would cherish it forever!" But he wondered whether this were mere rhetoric; he had no experience with children.

The Hierophant frowned. "You are well on the way to eternal damnation!"

"But you said there was no afterlife! How can there be eternal damnation?"

"Repent! Mortify yourself, throw yourself upon the tender mercy of the Lord in the hope that He will not torture you too long. Perhaps after suitably horrendous chastisement, your soul will be purged of its abysmal burden of guilt."

Brother Paul shook his head. "I am trying very hard to be open and objective, but I find I just can't take you seriously. And so you are wasting my time. Begone!" He turned away, knowing the figure would dissipate. Maybe he had lost this engagement by calling it off, but he didn't regret it.

These Animations were fascinating. There was a tremendous potential for physical, intellectual, and spiritual good here, if only it could be properly understood. So far he had not succeeded in doing that. The Hierophant Animation had spoken only a pseudo-philosophy, as shallow as that of a cardboard figure might be expected to be. If he had Animated a lovely woman, would she have been as bad?

A lovely woman. That intrigued him on another plane. Some men considered intellect a liability in a woman, and indeed some supposedly stupid women had made excellent careers for themselves by keeping their legs open and their mouths closed. This was not really what Brother Paul was looking for, yet the interest was there. Would an Animation woman be touchable, kissable, seducible?—a construct of air, like a demon, a succubus?

He wrenched his speculation away. It was *too* intriguing; maybe he *was* too far on the road to damnation! To utilize a phenomenon like Animation merely to gratify a passing lust! Of course there was nothing wrong with lust; it was God's way of reminding man that the species needed to be replicated, and it provided women of lesser physical strength with a means to manage otherwise unmanageable men. But lust directed at a construct of air and imagination could hardly serve those purposes. "Get thee behind me, Satan," he murmured. But even that prayer was useless, for Satan was also the master of buggery: not the type of entity a man would care to have standing near his posterior.

Brother Paul looked at his watch. His time was up; in fact he was already overdue. Why hadn't the watchers notified him? He must return to the non-Animation area.

But which way was out? Clouds were swirling close; a storm was in the neighborhood. Why hadn't he noticed it coming? This too should have caused the watchers to—

Suddenly he remembered. They *had* called him—and he had been too preoccupied to notice it consciously. The pastor must have assumed that the signal wasn't getting through. Still, he might have sent someone in. . . .

The hoodwinked girl, representing the Eight of Swords! Had Amaranth come in to warn him, after the transceiver contact had failed, and been incorporated into that mute image? There was some evidence that Animations were ordinary things, transformed perceptually, so maybe an Animation person was a real person, playing a part. But that didn't make sense either; why would a person play such a part? No one claimed that Animation affected the inner workings of the mind; it only changed perceptions of external things.

Maybe Amaranth had come in, and been deceived by the various images he had conjured, and lost her way. Now he and she—and probably the various hidden watchers—were stranded in the Animation region, in a storm, unless he got out in a hurry, and brought them out with him.

How to do it? He should call out, of course! Establish contact with those outside, obtain geographic directions. "Pastor Runford!" he said to his transceiver.

There was static, but no answer. This was not surprising; the range of the tiny wand was limited, and terrain and weather could interfere. Probably the watchers had been forced to retreat before the storm, lest they be caught in the spreading Animation region.

His predicament was his own fault. He had been careless, when he should have been alert. He was only sorry that he had involved others in it, assuming they had not gotten out safely. What next?

Well, the Tarot deck had gotten him into this, to a certain extent; maybe it could get him out. He brought out the deck again and sorted through it.

Maybe one of the fives—

The first five he encountered was the Five of Cups, pictured by three spilled and two standing cups. Symbolic of loss, disappointment, and vain regret.

Precisely.

He studied the card, uncertain as to what to do now. And the picture formed before him. A man stood in a black cloak, his head bowed in the direction of the spilled cups, ignoring the two that remained standing. In the background a river flowed by—the stream of the unconscious, symbolically—and across it stretched a bridge leading to a small castle. Could that be the same castle he had seen in the Animation of the Ace of Wands? If so, he could use it for orientation. It was probably just the background, like a painted setting, representing no more than the orientation of the painting. Still, if he held the scene in mind, maintaining its reality, the others caught in this region might be able to orient on it, and then they all could find their way out together. The colonists would know the real landscape better than he did.

Was this crazy? Probably, but it was still worth a try. If *he* could approach that distant castle, so could *they*. Maybe they knew their way out, and were trying to locate him, to guide him out too, and the castle could serve as a rendezvous. At least he could test that hypothesis.

First, he would check with the black-cloaked figure. Maybe it was just the Hierophant, in a new role. On the other hand, it could be a watcher, impressed into this role, if that were possible.

Brother Paul stepped forward. And suddenly he was inside the picture, advancing toward the bridge. The cloaked figure heard him and began to turn. The face came into full view. And there was no face, just a smooth expanse of flesh, like the face of an incomplete store-window mannequin.

6

Choice

There seems to be a human fascination with secrets. Secrets and secret societies have abounded throughout history, some relating to entire classes of people, as with initiation rites for young men; some relating to religion, as with the "mystery" cults of the Hellenic world; and some relating to specialized interests, such as deviant sexual practices, fraternities, and the occult. The arcana of the Tarot reflect this interest: the word "arcanum" means a secret. The Major Arcana are "Big Secrets," the Minor Arcana "Little Secrets." So it is not surprising that the Tarot has been the subject of exploration by some "secret societies." The most significant of these was conducted by the Hermetic Order of the Golden Dawn, founded in 1887 as an offshoot of the English Rosicrucian ("Rosey Cross") Society, itself created twenty years before as a kind of spinoff from Freemasonry, which in turn originated with the Masons, or builder's guild. The Golden

Dawn had 144 members—a significant number in arcane lore—and was formed for the acquisition of initiatory knowledge and powers, and for the practice of ceremonial magic. Many leading figures of the day were members, such as Bram Stoker (the author of the novel Dracula) *and Sax Rohmer (the creator of Fu Manchu). One of its "grand masters" was the prominent poet William Butler Yeats. He presided over meetings dressed in a kilt, wearing a black mask, and with a golden dagger in his belt. But the Golden Dawn is remembered today for the impact some of its members had on Tarot. Arthur Edward Waite, creator of the prominent Rider-Waite Tarot deck, was a member; so was Paul Foster Case, a leading Tarot scholar; and so was Aleister Crowley, said to be the wickedest man in the world, who created the Thoth Tarot deck under the name Master Therion. Crowley was a highly intelligent and literate man, the author of a number of thoughtful books, but he had strong passions, indulged in drugs like cocaine and heroin, practiced black magic (one episode left one man dead and Crowley in a mental hospital for several months; they had summoned Satan), and had homosexual tendencies that led him to degrade women. He set up a retreat in Italy called the Abbey of Thelema where his darker urges were exercised, and this became notorious. Yet for all the faults of the author, Crowley's Thoth Tarot remains perhaps the most beautiful and relevant of contemporary decks, well worth the attention of anyone seriously interested in the subject.*

The picture about him wavered and faded. Brother Paul hesitated, but immediately realized the problem: his entry into the Animation had changed it. Maybe the legendary Chinese artist—what *was* his name?—had been able to enter his own realistic painting and disappear from the mundane world, but very few others had acquired such status! Brother Paul could only look, not participate.

Yet why *not*? These Animations were governed by his own mind. If he wanted to paint a picture with himself in it, who was there to say he could not? He dealt the Six of Swords.

The picture formed. The stream of the unconscious had grown to the river of consciousness. The bridge was gone; this water was too broad for it. He could not see the castle at all. Of course this was a different picture, for a different card; the Five of Cups had stood for loss, while the Six of Swords represented a journey by water. He had lost the Five, appropriately, but gained the Six.

He spied a small craft on the water. It was a flat-bottomed boat, containing a woman and a child, and a man who was poling the boat across the river. "Wait!" Brother Paul cried, suddenly anxious, but also conscious of the possible pun: wait—Waite, the author of this deck. "I want to go, too!" But they did not heed him; probably they were out of earshot, if they existed at all as people. They were, literally, of a different world, one he could not enter.

He thought of the vacuous mouthings of the Hierophant, and felt his ire rising again. *He* was Animating these pictures; he would have his answer! He had intended to ascertain whether there was any objective validity to these Animations, or whether they all merely represented a sequence of solidified visions from his mind. If the latter, he had his answer: there was no specific God of Tarot. If the former . . .

But right now he was merely trying to find his way

164

out of this situation. He had intended merely to taste the water, not to drown in it!

Water—an excellent symbol. Why not put it to the proof?

He plunged into the river, half expecting to feel the scrape of ground against his body as he belly-flopped on reality. But his dive was clean; it was the shock of physical water that struck him. It foamed around his face and caught at his clothing; he should have stripped before entering! Yet he had not really believed . . .

If faith were the key to Animation, how was this water real, despite his unbelief?

But already his entry was changing the Animation. The water was vaporizing, the river diminishing. Brother Paul fixed his gaze on the people in the boat, striving to hang onto them, to prevent the entire image from evanescing. If only he could *talk* to them, these people of the Tarot background, and ask them—

The boat shivered. The man flew up into the air, sprouting wings, and perched upon a low-hanging cloud. The woman aged rapidly into a hag. The child grew up into an extremely comely young lady.

As Brother Paul approached them, they turned to face him. He halted a few paces away, discovering that he was back on his feet and soaking wet. His glance traveled from one woman to the other, the young and the old. He realized that this was no longer an image from the Minor Arcana, but one from the Major Arcana. This was Key Six, known as The Lovers.

Well, not necessarily. There was a certain haziness about the scene, an impression of multiple images.

Naturally. He had dealt no card of the Major Ar-

165

cana, had sought no specific "Big Secrets," so had laid down no dictum for the scene. The Animation was trying to form itself from chaos. He must not permit that; he had to retain control of it!

Brother Paul raised the deck of cards that was still in his hand—but hesitated. There were many established variants of the Tarot, and the Major Arcana were powerful cards. Which variant of Key Six would be best?

His own Holy Order of Vision variant, of course. The scholars of the Order had refined the symbolism developed by the researchers of the Golden Dawn and clarified the illustrations until this deck was as precise as the Tarot could be: a marvelous tool for self-enlightenment.

Yet the Holy Order of Vision did not restrict its Brothers and Sisters to its own Tarot deck, any more than it confined them to its own religious teaching. The heart of its philosophy, like that of Jesus Christ and the Apostle Paul, was service to man. Freedom of faith was one such service. Those who wished to pursue the Order positions were free to do so, and to become Ministers of Vision. But individual members like Brother Paul were encouraged to seek their own understandings, for dedication to the Order had to be freely given. The Order asserted that there was no freedom without enlightenment, so they were expected to study widely before orienting on any particular creed. Thus Brother Paul had investigated many aspects of religion and life, although so far these studies had been necessarily shallow: there was not time enough in a single human life to grasp thoroughly the full ramifications of any one of Earth's multiple faiths, let alone all of them. Had he focused his interest more narrowly, he could have moved beyond the "Brother" stage of his Order by this time—but that was not his way. Now he had to ask himself: should he take the familiar Vision Tarot, or should he use the generally similar Waite deck in his hand, or should he seriously consider other Tarot decks?

Phrased that way, the question admitted only one answer. If he used the Tarot at all, he should use the one best suited to the need. He always tried to research the full range of a problem, never accepting one solution blindly. The Vision Tarot was good, no doubt of it—but was it the best for this situation? Since other decks reflected other beliefs, and the whole problem of Planet Tarot was one of conflicting beliefs, he could make no quick assumptions.

He had not planned to go this deeply into Animation, on this first attempt. Discovering himself in over his head, as it were, he had the impulse to pull out immediately, and give himself the chance to consider more objectively, at leisure, what he had discovered, and to organize a more disciplined program of investigation. He still felt that haste would be foolish. He had the feeling that if he spoke to one of these two women, she would reply—and that this time the answer would be more meaningful than the response of the Hierophant had been. That did not mean he should speak now; he had to consider which woman to ask, and what to ask her. His choice of person might be highly significant. So he should withdraw, and recreate this scene only when he was properly prepared to exploit it.

One problem remained, however: how would he find his way out of this Animation? Should he ask one of these women? Then he would be committing himself to dialogue with them, as he had with the Hierophant. Better to leave them both strictly alone for now.

Then he realized why he believed he would have an answer. One of the aspects of Key Six was choice— the choice between virtue and vice. One woman was the right one, but which was which? Fuzzy as they both were, he could not tell. And he was by no means certain that external appearance would provide the necessary clue. Virtue was not necessarily lovely, and vice not always ugly; if they *were*, few people would ever make the wrong choice! This was another thing to work out carefully.

He had played with numbers and pictures, and gotten nowhere, *because* he had been playing. Now, at last, he was *in* the Animation, and the choice was far more precarious. He did not know whose God, if any, was manifesting here, and he would never learn if he allowed his preconceptions to dominate his investigation. God might well manifest through some quite unexpected medium. Perhaps he had an inadequate tool in this Tarot concept, or even a ludicrous one, but now he seemed closer to the truth he sought than he had been before, and closer than he might be in the future, and he was not sure he should waste the opportunity. God would not necessarily wait on his private convenience. Therefore he might be best advised to take what was offered and follow this up right now.

Yet his innate sense of caution cried out like a fading conscience; he could not allow himself to be unduly influenced by minor considerations. He had been intrigued by his fleeting glimpse of the Empress, the Girl of the Wheatfield, who had turned out to be Amaranth, and who might be one of these figures before him. If he left this Animation now, would she come with him? Or would she be lost? How could he be sure?

Sure of what? He shook his head. Sure he was not pursuing this vision because he suspected he might have some sort of power over her here, some way to make her amenable to . . . to what? He had no legitimate business with her, unless it was to use her relief-map torso to find his way out of here. Since she was not an assigned watcher, her very presence here threatened to distort his whole mission, especially since her body and personality were so . . .

He was going around in circles! Was it better to try to escape this Animation, so as to be able to set it up properly at another time instead of more or less by accident, or should he plunge ahead, now that he was this far along? He was hopelessly confused, now, about his own motives. He needed more objective advice. But he could not seek it without vacating this Animation (the Key Six scene seemed to be frozen obligingly in place, in all its foggy detail, while he wrestled with his uncertainties), and that would be a decision in itself, perhaps an error. That meant he was on his own, regardless. Unless, somehow, he could obtain a guide within the Animation itself.

Well, why not? "I want," he said aloud, clearly, "to select an adviser, who will then guide me through this Animation."

"Don't we all!" a voice agreed.

Brother Paul looked around. It had been a male voice, yet both figures before him, though obscure, were definitely female. "Where are you?"

"Up here on cloud nine."

Brother Paul looked up. The former boatman looked down. "Are you up there by choice?" Brother Paul inquired.

"Not that I'm aware of. I was poling my wife and kid across the river, when suddenly—" The man paused. "I don't even *have* a wife or kid! Am I going crazy?"

"No," Brother Paul reassured him. "You are part of a scene I conjured from the Tarot cards."

"*You* conjured it? I thought *I* conjured it!" The man scratched his head. "But if it fits your notions, it must be yours, because I never set out to fly!"

Was this a real man, a colonist, participating, like Brother Paul himself, in the Animation? Or was he entirely a figment of the evoked picture? Brother Paul hesitated to inquire, since he was not sure he could trust the answer. He should be able to work it out for himself in due course. "Well, maybe we can get you down from there. I'm about to deal another card."

"Wait!" the man cried in alarm. "If you deal away this cloud, I'll fall and break my leg!"

Brother Paul started to laugh, but immediately reconsidered. There was little doubt that these Animations were three-dimensionally projected visions, that even a camera's lens could see (and he hoped his recorder was watching well, because who on Earth would otherwise believe this story?)—but within them, there had to be some core of physical reality. People *did* die while experiencing Animations. If this man was real, he might actually be perched up in a tree, and if his "cloud" disappeared so that he believed he had to fall, he might very well topple from his branch and suffer serious injury. Brother Paul did not want to be responsible for that!

"Very well. I will leave this card, and merely summon spokespersons for each separate Tarot deck, if that turns out to be possible. I'm sure you will be secure." If the man believed him, he *would* be safe.

Faith was the key, if his present understanding were correct.

"Couldn't you just conjure me a ladder, so I can climb down?" the man asked plaintively.

Brother Paul considered. "I'm not sure I can do that. So far, I have formed these scenes by laying down cards and concentrating on the scenes they depict. I have no card with a ladder. If I try to put a ladder in *this* card, where it does not belong—well, when I introduced myself into a scene before, it changed. I fear it is not possible to make any change in an existing scene without breaking up the whole pattern. So the attempt to introduce a ladder might abolish the ground on which the ladder rests and lead to the very fall we seek to avoid. Maybe spot changes would be possible if I had greater experience with Animation, but right now I'm afraid to—"

"I get the message," the man said. "Do it your way. I'll wait. This cloud is pretty comfortable, for now."

Brother Paul concentrated. "Oldest Tarot, bring forth your spokesman," he intoned, suddenly quite apprehensive. This business of Animating visions was tricky in detail, like donning roller skates for the first time. One might master the basic principle, but lack the coordination for proper performance, and take a painful tumble. He was not at all sure he was following the rules of the game, now, for this was an indefinite command rather than a pictorial image.

A figure appeared. Had it actually worked? This seemed to be a king, garbed in suitably rich robes. The king spoke. But the words were incomprehensible. It was a foreign language! He should have known he could not glean information from cardboard; it was balking him again. Still . . .

Brother Paul listened carefully. In the course of his

schooling, he had taken classes in French and German, and had had a certain flair for linguistics. But that had been a decade ago. He had been better at German, but this figure did not look German. French? Yes, possibly the French of six centuries ago, the time of the earliest known authentic Tarot deck! This must be King Charles VI of circa 1400, who commissioned the famous Gringonneur decks of cards.

The figure gestured, and a scene materialized. An Animation figure making a new Animation? Maybe so! This new scene was full of people. Three couples were walking gaily, as in a parade. The young men were dressed in medieval garb, the young ladies in elegant headdresses and trailing skirts. Above them, the cloud-borne man had fissioned into two military figures with drawn bows. They were aiming their arrows down at the happy marchers. What carnage had he loosed now?

Brother Paul smiled. This was not an ambush or a symbol of split personality, but romance. The cloudmen were adult Cupids, striking people with the arrows of love. He hardly needed the running French commentary to understand this card! But his purpose was to find a guide, not to evoke detailed derivatives of a particular Tarot concept. In any event, a guide whose advice he could not properly understand, because it was in a barely familiar language, would not do.

"Sorry," he said. "You may be the original Tarot, with impeccable taste, but I shall have to pass you by. Next!"

The scene faded, including the king, to be replaced by what Brother Paul took to be an Italian, though he could not say precisely on what evidence he made this judgment. It was a man, advanced in years, partially armored with sculptured greaves and wearing a sword. He had a thigh-length cape or topcoat, intricately decorated, and a crownlike headdress. Obviously a person of note.

The man made a formal little bow. "Filippo Maria Visconti," he said.

So this was the famous (or infamous) Duke of Milan about whom Brother Paul had read, who had commissioned the beautiful Visconti-Sforza Tarot to commemorate the marriage of his daughter to the scion of Sforza. A rigorous, brutal man, the Duke, but intelligent and politically powerful. He had paid a small fortune for the paintings, and the deck was the handsomest of the medieval Tarots.

Brother Paul returned the bow. "Brother Paul of the Holy Order of Vision," he said, introducing himself. "Pleased to make your acquaintance." Yet his pleasure was tempered by a nagging memory: hadn't this Duke fed human flesh to his dogs?

Visconti commenced his presentation—in Italian. Another linguistic barrier! The Duke gestured, and another scene materialized. This one had just three figures: the young couple, and a winged Cupid on a pedestal between them—which got the poor man down from the cloud—but Cupid was blindfolded, and held an arrow in each hand, that he was about to fling at the people below. *Love is blind!* Brother Paul thought.

"Francesco Sforza . . . Bianca Maria Visconti . . ." The names leaped out of the opaque commentary. The betrothed young couple, uniting these two powerful families. A truly pretty picture. But old Filippo Maria Visconti would not do as a guide.

"Next," Brother Paul said.

This time a small figure appeared: a child. There

173

was a haunting familiarity about it; did he know this person? Brother Paul shook his head. This child was perhaps four or five years old, six at the most, and not quite like any he had seen on Earth.

The child spoke in French, and though Brother Paul was able to make out more words than before, this was still too much of a challenge for him. However, his lingering curiosity about this child caused him to listen politely. Was it a boy or a girl? Female, he decided.

She gestured, and a scene appeared. "Marseilles," she said clearly. And this most closely approached the original, fuzzy picture: a young man between two women, with a winged Cupid above, bow drawn and arrow about to be loosed. If Brother Paul didn't get that man safely down from that cloud pretty soon, he might be provoked actually to let that shaft fly!

But this picture was more like a cartoon than the previous two had been. Though the figures were three-dimensional and solid-seeming, they were obviously artificial, as though shaped crudely from plastic and painted in flat blue, red, yellow, and pink. This was the kind of scene a child would appreciate, almost devoid of subtle nuances of art. But by the same token, its meaning was quite clear: the man had to choose between the pretty young woman and the ugly old one. Or was the old hag the mother, officiating benignly at the romance of her son or daughter? Doubtless the child's narration explained this, but Brother Paul could not make out enough of it.

Regretfully he turned down this potential guide. "I'm sure I would enjoy your company, little girl," he said gently. "But since I cannot understand your words, I must seek other guidance. Next."

A lady appeared, garbed quite differently. She

174

seemed to be Egyptian, wearing the ancient type of headdress held in place by an ornament shaped like a little snake, and an ankle-length dark dress with black bands passing horizontally around it at intervals. She tended to face sidewise, to show her face in profile, in the manner of Egyptian paintings.

"I hope you speak my language," Brother Paul murmured. Egyptian was entirely out of his range!

"Oh, I do," she said, startling him. "I represent the Sacred Tarot of the Brotherhood of Light."

Brother Paul had some familiarity with the Church of Light Tarot, but it differed in rather fundamental respects from the Vision Tarot. For one thing, the Hebrew letter associated with this Key differed. Brother Paul knew it as Zain, meaning Sword; the Light deck listed it as Vau, meaning Nail. The astrological equivalence also differed; to the Holy Order of Vision it was Gemini, while to the Brotherhood of Light it was Venus.

The woman gestured, her arm moving in a stylized manner, and her card manifested. A man stood between two women. All were clothed in ancient Egyptian garb. The man's arms were crossed, his hands on his own shoulders; the ladies' arms were bent upward at the elbows, the hands leveled at shoulder height. Thus each woman had one hand touching a shoulder of the man, though she faced away from him, while he looked at neither. Above, a demonic figure within a sunlike circle drew an ornate bow, aiming a long arrow.

"This is Arcanum Six, entitled 'The Two Paths,'" the female announcer said. "Note the two roads dividing, as in the poem by Robert Frost; the choice of paths is all-important. This Arcanum relates to the Egyptian letter *Ur*, or Hebrew *Vau*, or English letters

175

V, U, and W. Its color is yellow, its tone E, its occult science Kabalism. It expresses its theme on three levels: in the spiritual world it reflects the knowledge of good and evil; in the intellectual world, the balance between liberty and necessity; in the physical world, the antagonism of natural forces, the linking of cause and effect. Note that the woman on the left is demurely clad, while the one on the right is voluptuous and bare-breasted, with a garland in her hair and her translucent skirt showing her legs virtually up to the waist. Remember, then, son of Earth, that for the common man the allurement of vice has a far greater fascination than the austere beauty of virtue."

Brother Paul was impressed. "You have really worked out the symbolism," he commented. "But most scholars regard this card as symbolizing love rather than choice."

"Venus governs the affections and the social relations," she replied, undismayed. "It gives love of ease, comfort, luxury, and pleasure. It is not essentially evil, but in seeking the line of least resistance it may be led into vice. When it thus fails to resist the importunities of the wicked, it comes under the negative influence of Arcanum Two, Veiled Isis—"

"Wait, wait!" Brother Paul protested. "I don't want to get tangled up with the High Priestess or other cards at the moment; I just want to understand this one as a representative of your Tarot deck, so I can compare it to the equivalent cards of the other decks. Are you saying this is a card of love, or of choice? A simple yes or no will do—I mean, one description or the other."

She glanced at him reproachfully. "If you seek simplistic answers to the infinitely complex questions of eternity, you have no business questioning the Brotherhood of Light."

Brother Paul had not expected such a direct and elegant rebuff from a conjured figure. "I'm sorry," he apologized. "It's just that I'm not really looking for the full symbolism, but for a guide who can bring me most rapidly and certainly to the truth. I know I shall never master the Tarot as thoroughly as you have done, but perhaps you could show me—"

She softened. "Perhaps so. I will try to provide your simplistic answers. This is a card of love *and* choice, for the most difficult decisions involve love. Note that the man stands motionless at the angle formed by the conjunction of the two roads, as it seems you stand now. Each woman shows him her road. Virtue carries the sacred serpent at her brow; Vice is crowned with the leaves and vine of the grape. Thus this represents temptation."

"Temptation," Brother Paul echoed. Her "simplistic" answer did not seem very simple to him, but he appreciated her attempt to relate to him on his own level. He saw that she herself most closely resembled, in dress and manner, the figure of Virtue, yet her demure apparel did not entirely conceal the presence of excellent breasts, legs, and other feminine attributes. She reminded him of—well, of the colonist Amaranth. And there was temptation again! But logic did not concur.

"I like your rationale," he said. "I am sorry I have not paid more attention to the Tarot of the Brotherhood of Light before. I suppose when I saw the demon Cupid in the sky, I jumped to the conclusion that—"

"That is neither demon nor Cupid," she said. "It is the genie of Justice, hovering in a flashing aureole of

177

twelve rays of the zodiac, crowned with the flame of spirit, directing the arrow of punishment toward Vice. This ensemble typifies the struggle between conscience and the passions, between the divine soul and the animal soul; and the result of this struggle commences a new epoch in life."

Brother Paul nodded thoughtfully. There was much in this presentation that appealed to him. Certainly Venus related well to the love aspect, and the interpretation of the image as representing choice related extremely well to his present situation. And if this were the girl Amaranth, describing what must be the Tarot deck she used, he would be very glad to have her as his guide. Still, he should look at the remaining offerings before making his decision. Apologetically, he explained this to the lady.

She smiled. "I am sure you will do the right thing," she said, and faded out.

So she could wait her turn without fretting. She looked better and better.

The next presentation was by a male figure that reminded him strongly of his alien acquaintance, Antares, in his human host. But the scene itself was instantly recognizable: it was The Lovers, by Arthur Waite, perhaps the best known expert on Tarot. The scene was of a naked man and woman standing with spread hands, front face, while a huge, winged angel hovered above the clouds, extending his benediction. To the right was the Tree of Life, bearing twelve fruits; to the left, behind the woman, was the Tree of the Knowledge of Good and Evil, with the serpent twining around it. The Tarot of the Holy Order of Vision was derived from that of Paul Foster Case, which was refined in turn from that of Waite. Thus this picture was extremely comfortable in its familiarity.

Yet the points of the apologist for the Light deck were well-taken. "Sir," Brother Paul said diffidently to the Waite figure, "I have just viewed an Egyptian variant of this Key—"

"Preposterous!" the figure snapped. "There is not a particle of evidence for the Egyptian origin of Tarot cards!"

"But a number of other experts have said—"

The figure assumed what in a lesser man would resemble an arrogant mien. "I wish to say, within the reserves of courtesy belonging to the fellowship of research, that I care nothing utterly for any view that may find expression. There is a secret tradition concerning the Tarot, as well as a secret doctrine contained therein; I have followed—"

"But the aspect of choice, of temptation, two roads—"

The figure was unrelenting. "This is in all simplicity the card of human love, here exhibited as part of the way, the truth, and the life. It replaces the old card of marriage, and the later follies that depicted man between vice and virtue. In a very high sense, the card is a mystery of the covenant and Sabbath."

"But—"

"The old meanings fall to pieces of necessity with the old pictures. Some of them were of the order of commonplace, and others were false in symbolism."

Brother Paul had always had a great deal of respect for Waite, but this arrogance reminded him uncomfortably of the Animated Hierophant. The Lady of Light had been complex but reasonable; Waite seemed only complex.

Still, he was a leading Tarot figure. Brother Paul

tried again. "According to the Brotherhood of Light, the Hebrew letter assigned to this card is *Vau*, rather than—"

"That would be the handiwork of Eliphaz Levi. I do not think that there was ever an instance of a writer with greater gifts, after their particular kind, who put them to such indifferent uses. He insisted on placing the Fool toward the *end* of the Major Arcana, thereby misaligning the entire sequence of Hebrew letters. Indeed, the title of Fool befits him! There was never a mouth declaring such great things—"

"Uh, yes. But astrologically, Venus does seem to match the card of Love."

"Nonsense. The applicable letter is *Zain*, the Sword. A sword cleaves apart, as Eve was brought from the rib of Adam, flesh of his flesh, bone of his bone. *Zain*, following the *Vau* of the Hierophant: the nail that joins things together. Astrologically, Gemini naturally applies. The sign of the twins, of duality, male and female. There is no question."

Brother Paul sighed inwardly. He had agreed with Waite's analysis before he had encountered that of the Light Tarot; now both conflicting views seemed reasonable. He was in no position to debate symbolism with these experts, and that was not his present purpose anyway. Why was such a seemingly simple project becoming so complex? To choose a single expert from among six, some of whom had already been eliminated because of language or age. Too bad he couldn't evoke both Light and Waite together, and let them thrash it out themselves.

Why not? It might be worth a try.

No, they would merely argue interminably, and this was really his own decision to make.

"I do have one more card to consider," Brother

Paul said, conscious of the numerical symbolism: six variants of Key Six.

Waite faded out with a grimace of resignation. He obviously felt that the mere consideration of alternative decks was frivolous. He was replaced by a portly, unhandsome man, bold and bald, whose aspect was nevertheless commanding. "I am the Master Therion, the Beast 666," he proclaimed. "I overheard your previous interview. Isn't old Arthwaite an ass? It's a wonder anyone can stomach him!"

Brother Paul was taken aback once again. These Animation figures were showing a good deal more individuality than he had expected. "Arthur Waite is a scholar. He—" He paused. "What did you call yourself?"

"The Beast 666. The living devil. The wickedest man on Earth. Is it not immediately apparent?"

"Uh, no. I—"

"Call me Master Therion, then, as you will. Do what thou wilt shall be the whole of the law. Love is the law; love under will."

Brother Paul was impressed again. "Love is the law. What an excellent thought for this Key of Love!"

Therion smiled approvingly. "Indeed. Did you notice old Arthwaite's slip about Adam and Eve? He actually *believes* the hoary tale about Adam's rib. Rib, hell! Eve was formed from the foreskin excised from Adam's pristine penis when he was circumcised. Look it up in the Babylonian Talmud, from which so much of the Old Testament was pirated. And expurgated. A neat little bloody ring of skin, the original symbol of the female. God formed it into a living, breathing tube of flesh typified by circles, from the two globes perched ludicrously on her chest to the very manner in which her elliptical mind works. She was fashioned

181

for one purpose only, and that was to embrace again that member from which she was so blithely cut, making it whole once more. Any man who permits her to distract his attention for any other purpose is a fool."

Brother Paul appraised Therion. It had been a long time since he had heard so concentrated and unprovoked a denunciation of woman. "You really *are* a beast!"

"Correct!" Therion agreed, pleased.

"I think I'd better have a look at your card."

"Do what thou wilt!" Therion gestured, and the scene formed.

It was—different. It was filled with figures, yet not crowded. A man and a woman stood centrally, each in royal robes. They stood facing a huge, headless figure whose great, dark arms stretched forward in benediction, massive sleeves accordion-pleated like those of an old-fashioned robot or space suit. Where the head should be, the winged Cupid flew instead, an arrow notched to his bow. A naked man and woman stood in the upper corners, two children stood in the foreground, and there were also a lion, a bird, and snake. Eleven living entities in all—yet they were integrated so harmoniously that it all seemed normal. The whole effect was absolutely beautiful.

Still, it was not art he sought, but good advice. "Two prior versions of this card differ in certain details," Brother Paul began cautiously.

"Arthwaite is ludicrous, but in the matter of the Hebrew equivalence he is more or less correct," Therion said. "Even a stopped clock is right on occasion! This card is The Lovers, matching with *Zain* the Sword, and Gemini astrologically."

"More or less correct?" Brother Paul repeated questioningly.

"He transposed the cards for Adjustment and Lust. That cannot be justified rationally."

Brother Paul was perplexed. "Adjustment? Lust? These are not symbols of the Tarot."

"Formerly known as Temperance and Strength," Therion explained. "Arthwaite simply switched them on his own initiative, exactly as he garbled their symbolism. He denied the Egyptian origin of the Tarot."

"You say it *is* Egyptian?"

"Absolutely. I call it the Book of Thoth. Of course others have arrived at more speculative derivations. The phrase *Ohev Tzarot* is Hebrew for a 'lover of trouble.' That seems to relate in several ways, but I regard it as coincidence. After all, if we start spelling the word with a 'Z', we could derive it from Tzar, or use 'Cz' for Czar, deriving it from the Roman emperor Caesar. Thus 'Czarot' could be taken to mean a device of supreme power, dominating an occult empire. That convolution of logic is almost worthy of Arthwaite! But the actual origin of the Tarot is quite irrelevant, even if it were certain. It must stand or fall as a system on its own merits. It is beyond doubt a deliberate attempt to represent, in pictorial form, the doctrines of the Qabalah."

"The Kabala?"

"Qabalah."

"Let's return to Key Six."

"Very well. Atu Six is, together with its twin Atu Fourteen, Art, the most obscure and difficult of the—"

"Please," Brother Paul interrupted. "I need a fairly simple analysis." He wondered whether he would receive another rebuke.

But the Master Therion smiled tolerantly. "Of course. I will start at the beginning. There is an Assyrian legend of Eve and the Serpent: Cain was the

183

child of Eve and the Serpent of Wisdom, not of Adam. It was necessary that he shed his brother's blood, so that God would hear the children of Eve."

"This cannot be!" Brother Paul cried in horror. "The son of the *Serpent*?"

Therion glanced at him, frowning. "I took you for a seeker after truth."

"I—" Brother Paul was stung, but did not care to be the target of obscenity or blasphemy.

"Surely you realize it was not general knowledge that Adam and Eve were denied, but *carnal* knowledge. The Serpent is the original phallic symbol."

"I do want to be objective," Brother Paul said. "But can you give me a more specific summary of the meaning of the card? For example, do you feel it represents Choice?"

"It represents the creation of the world. Analysis. Synthesis. The small figures behind the shrouded Hermit are Eve and Adam's first wife, Lilith."

Brother Paul realized that he was getting nowhere. However fascinating the symbolism might be, it was not helping him to make his decision. Probably the Light card was best, and therefore the pretty woman should be his guide. "I'm afraid I—"

"Do what thou wilt," Therion said.

To do what he really willed, Brother Paul realized, now required the presence of the woman. He believed he could justify choosing her on the basis of what he had seen in these sample cards, and by the attitudes of their presenters. Waite had been too arrogant and inflexible, while Therion was—well, a bit of a beast. . . .

Then he noticed something else about the central figures of the scene. The female was very like the girl of the wheatfield, and the man was black. Not demon-black, but Negro-black. This was an inter-racial union!

Brother Paul himself was only about one-eighth black, but that eighth loomed with disproportionate importance in his home world. Suddenly he identified.

He stepped into Therion's picture, his choice made.

It was a mistake.

7

Precession

Those who read the standard editions of the Bible may wonder why there is a gap of two or three hundred years in the record between the Old and New Testaments. Did the old scholars, historians, philosophers, and prophets simply stop creating for a time? As it turns out, this was not the case. Material was recorded, and was known to the scholars of Jesus's time, and perhaps to Jesus himself, but it was not incorporated into the Bible. In the succeeding millennia, much of it was buried in old libraries and largely ignored. Then, in 1947, the discovery of the Dead Sea Scrolls transformed the picture, for these documents, dating from the time of Jesus, contained much of this same material, authenticating it. Now the story of the lost years could be unraveled:

After Alexander the Great conquered the world, many Jews were scattered from Israel to all the countries of the Mediterranean. This was the Diaspora—

not the first or the last Jewish dispersion, for a number of conquerors used this method to deal with these intractable people—significant because it happened to make a cutoff date of about 300 B.C. for the assorted books of the Bible. Many displaced Jews now spoke Greek rather than Hebrew, and there were actually more Jews in Alexandria than in Jerusalem. But only narrowly defined Hebrew-language texts were accepted for the Bible as it now stands. Thus much material was excluded by both Jews and Christians, although it was generally recognized to be parallel to the included books. The complete assembly consists of the thirty-nine books of the Old Testament, fourteen books of the Apocrypha (meaning "hidden"), about eighteen books of the Pseudepigrapha ("false writings"), and twenty-seven books of the New Testament. That makes the record continuous.

The chariot raced across the plain. Brother Paul grabbed for support, but found his hands encumbered by the monstrous cup he was carrying. There were no reins.

He braced his legs against the metallic supports of the chariot's canopy, and discovered that he was in armor. His helmet visor was open and his gauntlets were flexible; it was a good outfit. For combat. The chariot was solid and well made; there was no danger of its falling apart, despite the pounding of its velocity. The horses—

Horses? No, these were four incredible monsters in harness! One had the head of a bull, another that of an eagle, a third that of a man, and the fourth that of a lion. The four symbols of the elements! Yet the bodies did not match. The man-head had eagle's talons; the lion-head had eagle's wings, woman's breasts, and bull's feet. All the components of the sphinx, yet none of these *was* the sphinx.

"What am I doing here?" Brother Paul cried out in confusion.

The man-head turned to him, and framed by its Egyptian headdress was the face of Therion. "You are the Charioteer!" the monster cried. "I am guiding you through the Tarot, as you requested."

"But I didn't mean—" Brother Paul broke off. What *had* he meant? He had asked for guidance, and the Chariot was the next card, Key Seven. The symbol of victory, or of the Wheels of Ezekiel, drawn by two sphinxes representing the senses: part lion, part woman. The occult forces that had to be controlled so that they would power man's chariot. Without such control, he could not find his way out of the morass these Animations had led him into, let alone separate God from chaos.

So why were there four steeds instead of two? Because this was not the card Brother Paul knew, but the one Therion knew. No wonder this was hard to manage! "Give me the other variant!" Brother Paul cried.

The composite creatures shifted and merged into two white horses. The chariot became medieval. "No, not that one!" More shifting, and two sphinxes appeared, one black, one white. "Yes, *that* one!" he cried, and the variant became fixed.

The white sphinx turned its head to face him. "How nice to see you again," she said.

"Light!" Brother Paul cried in recognition. "I mean, the apologist for the Tarot of the Brotherhood of Light! I thought this was the Waite deck."

She wrinkled her pert nose. "I hoped you had given up on that discredited innovation."

"Now you sound like Therion."

She snorted delicately. "Why choose between evils, when truth is available? Be yourself, the Conqueror; use the Sword of Zain to break through all obstacles, crush your enemies, and achieve sovereignty of spirit."

Brother Paul caught on. "You call Key Seven 'The Conqueror'!"

"Arcanum Seven, yes. This is historically justified in the Bible."

Oh-oh. Brother Paul did not want to get involved in another technical discussion, but his curiosity had been piqued. "The Bible?"

"Joseph, sold into Egypt, overcame all obstacles and rose to great power, as indicated by the sword." Brother Paul discovered that he was holding a curved blade in his right hand, not a cup. He set the sword down, afraid he would inadvertently cut the starry canopy. He remembered that the Hebrew alphabet for the Light Tarot differed from what he was used to. In that deck, Key Seven was Zain, the Sword. So the lady was correct, by her definitions. "He was tempted by Potiphar's wife, in Arcanum Six, but he triumphed over the temptation. He interpreted the dream of Pharaoh about the seven fat kine and the seven lean kine, and the seven good ears and the seven bad ears. And Pharaoh told him: 'See I have set thee over all the land of Egypt,' and made him to ride in a chariot, and made him ruler over—"

"Bullshit!" the black sphinx cried.

The white sphinx froze, shocked.

"Oh, Therion," Brother Paul said, trying to sound reasonable, although he too was upset by the interjection. "Now look, she didn't interfere in *your* presentation."

"*I* never uttered such nonsense! Women are such

189

brainless things; if they didn't have wombs they'd be entirely useless."

The man was certainly contemptuous of the fair sex! What was the matter with him? In other respects he seemed to be quite intelligent and open-minded. "Still," Brother Paul admonished him, "you should not interrupt."

The lady sphinx turned her head toward the black sphinx, and then her body. The chariot veered, for they were both still galloping forward at a dismaying velocity. "No, I want to hear his objections. Does he challenge the validity of the Bible?"

"The Bible is hardly an objective account, and what there is is both incomplete and expurgated. Naturally the Hebrews and their intolerant, jealous God colored the record to suit themselves. How do you think the poor, civilized Egyptians felt about this barbaric conqueror?"

"They *welcomed* the Hebrews! Pharaoh raised up Joseph, put his own ring on Joseph's hand, arrayed him in fine linen, put a gold chain about his neck—"

"Bullshit!" Therion repeated. He seemed to enjoy uttering the scatological term in the presence of the lady. "Pharaoh gave away nothing! The Hebrew tribesmen and their cohorts came in, a ravening horde from the desert, overrunning the civilized cities, burning houses, pillaging temples and destroying monuments. They were the nefarious Hyksos, the so-called 'shepherd kings,' who ravaged cultured Egypt like pigs in a pastry shop for two hundred years before their own barbaric mismanagement and debauchery weakened them to the point where the Egyptians could reorganize and drive them out. *That* is why you call this *Atu* 'The Conqueror.' Joseph was a rabble-spawned tyrant, thief, and murderer. What little civilization rubbed off on his ilk was Egyptian, such as the Qabalah—"

"Kabala?" Light inquired.

"Qabalah. This was stolen from Egyptian lore, just as the golden ornaments were stolen from Egyptian households. The ones these thieves melted down to form the Golden Calf, a better deity than they deserved, before they settled, by the fiat of Moses, on a bloodthirsty, competitive, nouveau-riche God whose name they were ashamed to utter."

"I don't have to listen to this!" Light exclaimed. The scene began to change.

"Wait!" Brother Paul cried, suffering a separate revelation. This unrelenting attack on the roots of the Judeo-Christian religion—he recognized the theme, from somewhere.

"Waite? That does it!" the white sphinx snapped. She veered away, making the chariot tilt alarmingly.

Why had he chosen Therion as a guide, instead of Light? How much better he empathized with her! Now, when he had almost gotten her back into the scene, she was going again. The chariot was rocking perilously, about to overturn, a victim of this religious debate. The sphinxes phased into two great horses again, white and black, then these animals fragmented into the composite monsters of Therion's Thoth *Atu*. Again Brother Paul found himself clutching the huge cup, which somehow he knew he dare not drop.

"Seven!" he cried. "I deal the Seven of Cups!"

The cup he was holding, which had given him this emergency inspiration, expanded. It was made of pure amethyst, its center a radiant, blood red. It was the Holy Grail.

The Cup expanded to encompass him, its radiance

spreading out like the sunrise. Brother Paul felt himself falling into it. . . .

And he was splashing, swimming in a sea of blood. Thick, gooey, greenish ichor—the blood of some alien creature, perhaps from Sphere Antares, rather than of man. Great, cloying drops of it pelted down, forming slowly expanding ripples in the ocean. The drops fell from other cups: ornate blue vessels, six of them, set about a metallic support that rose from a larger cup resting on the surface of this awful sea. The green goo overflowed from each cup, and especially from the large one. Flowers lay inverted atop each cup, tiger lilies or lotuses; it was from them that the slime seemed to issue. The smell of corruption was awful.

"Thus the Holy Grail is profaned by debauchery," the voice of Therion said. It seemed to come from the largest cup, the seventh one, as though the man himself were immersed in its septic fluid.

"I have no interest in debauchery," Brother Paul protested, gasping. He was weighed down by his armor, trying to tread water, and the stench hardly helped his breathing. "I dealt the Seven of Cups."

"Indeed you did! Note how the holiest mysteries of nature become the obscene and shameful secrets of a guilty conscience."

Brother Paul opened his mouth to protest again, then abruptly realized the significance of the framework holding the cups. It was a convoluted, overlapping double triangle, shaped into the stylized outline of the female generative organs. Womb projecting into vagina, the largest cup being the vulva, overflowing with greenish lubrication from the sex organs of the plant. Flowers were of course copulatory organs, made attractive so that other species, such as bees, would willingly aid the plants to reproduce. How many prudish women realized the full significance of what they were doing when they poked their noses into bright flowers to sniff the intoxicating perfume? Nature laughs at the pretensions of human foibles.

Still, enough was enough. Brother Paul did not care to remain bathed in these thick juices. "The *Waite* Seven of Cups!" he cried.

"Oh, very well," Therion said grouchily. "It *is* one of Arthwaite's better efforts, for all that he misses the proper meaning entirely."

The sea boiled, releasing great clouds of steam. From a distance came Therion's voice: "You'll be sorry!" And it echoed, "Sor-ry! Sorr-rry!"

The sea evaporated into clouds of greenish vapor, leaving Brother Paul standing on a gummy film of green that became a lawn. The cups retained their positions, however, turning golden yellow. The flowers above them dropped inside, mutating into assorted other objects that showed over the rims. At last he stood before this display of seven cups supported by a gray cloud bank.

"There it is," Therion said, now standing beside him. "Confusing welter of images, isn't it?"

"Are you still here? I thought Waite would—"

"You chose *me* as your guide, remember? Way back in Key Sex. I mean Six. You may view any cards you wish, but *I* shall do the interpretations."

So that choice had been permanent, at least for the duration of this vision. Brother Paul feared he had chosen carelessly. Well, he would carry through, and be better prepared next time. *This* time, confronted with the choice between Virtue and Vice, it seemed he had chosen Vice. At least he had some familiarity with this particular image, although the Holy Order of Vision did not put much stress on the Minor Arcana.

193

First, he had to orient himself. Why, exactly, was he here? He had wanted to get out of the careening chariot, of course, and out of the slime-soup of Therion's Seven of Cups, but what was his *positive* reason?

Answer: he was here to discover the ultimate ramifications of these Animations. His short-range objective of getting out of this particular sequence was passé; no matter how he struggled, he only seemed to be getting in deeper, as a man mired in quicksand only worsens his situation by thrashing about. (Though he had always understood that, since sand was denser than water, a man should readily float in quicksand, and so was in no danger if he merely relaxed. Could he float, here in Animation, if he just went along with it?) So he might as well follow through now, on the theory that it was as easy to move forward as backward.

When God manifested for him, as He had for others, whose God was it? Questioning the Hierophant had not helped; Brother Paul had first to comprehend the specific nature of the manifestations. Once again he reviewed it, hoping for some key insight. Were the visions purely products of his own mind, or was there some objective reality behind them? This remained a very difficult question to resolve, for how could he judge the validity of material drawn from his own experience? It was like trying to find a test for whether a person was awake or dreaming; he could pinch himself—and dream he was being pinched. If he knew what any given detail of an Animation was, that detail would be authentic; if he suffered from misinformation, how could he correct the image? Yet now it certainly seemed as though there were input from other minds, for Brother Paul had not before known all the details of the Tarot variants he had perceived in this Animation. Some of the concepts this Therion character had put forward were entirely foreign to Brother Paul's belief, yet again, these might be his own suppressed notions coming out, all the more shocking because he had always before denied their existence. The hardest thing for a man to do was to face the ugly aspects of himself.

So maybe he should face those aspects. Maybe the thing to do was to plunge all the way into this vision and grasp his answer before it faded. Surely it was in one of these displayed cups. At any rate, he owed it to himself and to his mission to look.

He inspected the cups more closely. One contained a tall miniature castle, another was overflowing with jewels, and others had a wreath, a dragon, a woman's head, a snake, and a veiled figure. All were symbols whose significance he had reviewed in the course of his studies at the Holy Order of Vision. But never before had they been presented as tangibly as this, and he knew now that these Animated symbols would not submit passively to conventional analysis.

The castle was similar to the one he had seen on prior cards, probably the same edifice. Symbolism in the Tarot tended to be consistent; a river was always the stream of the unconscious, originating in the trailing, flowing gown of the High Priestess, and the cup was always a vessel of emotion or religion. The castle represented for him a rallying point, an initial answer. Suppose he entered it now?

Well, why not *try*? He tended to spend too much time pondering instead of acting.

And the castle expanded, bursting out of its cup, becoming a magnificent edifice with banners flying from its lofty turrets, situated atop a precipitous mountain. Beautiful.

Brother Paul set out for it. Therion accompanied him, humming a tune as though indifferent to the proceedings.

"I've heard that song," Brother Paul said, determined not to let the man escape involvement so easily. "Can't quite place it, though."

"The 'Riddle Song,'" Therion answered promptly. "One of the truly fine, subtly sexual folk expressions."

"Yes, that's it. 'I gave my love a cherry'—but how is that sexual? It's a straightforward love song."

"Ha. The cherry was her maidenhead, that he ruptured. You have led too cloistered a life, and never learned proper vernacular."

"Oh? He also gave her a chicken without a bone, and a ring without end, and a baby without crying."

"The boneless chicken was his boneless but nevertheless rigid penis, thrusting through her ring-shaped orifice, producing in due course the baby—who naturally was not crying at the time."

That was one way of looking at it. "I should have stayed with the stream of the unconscious," he murmured.

"Oh, yes. That water Arthwaite says flows through the whole deck of the Tarot, starting with the gown of the harlot, yet. What crap!"

Here it went again! "I always thought it was a beautiful concept. How do you manage to see, ah, crap in it?"

"More ways than one, Brother! It is crap in that it is errant nonsense; water symbolizes many things besides the unconscious, and it is ridiculous to pretend that it can only stand for that one thing. But more directly, that euphemism he foists off on his fans—do you really think it is her *gown* that originates the fluid?"

"Well, that may be artistic license, but—"

"Her gown merely covers the real, unmentionable source, which is her body. A woman is a thing of flowing fluids, as I tried to make clear in *my* Seven of Cups. Milk from her tits, and blood from her—"

"Milk and blood are chemically similar," Brother Paul said quickly. "In fact, chlorophyll, the key to plant metabolism, is also surprisingly close to—"

"Flowing out from her orifices, bathing the whole Tarot in its hot, soupy—"

"Let's change the subject," Brother Paul said, not eager to argue the case further. What a case of gynophobia!

"Coming up."

A dragon appeared. Brother Paul whirled, gripping the sword he discovered at his hip. "That's the Dragon of Temptation!" he exclaimed. "It belongs in a different cup; I did not invoke it!"

"You must have invoked it, Paul," Therion said, without alarm. "For *I* did not do the dastardly deed."

Ha! "I Animated the castle; that was the only cup I emptied!"

Therion smirked. "*You* know that; *I* know that. But does *it* know that?"

Unfunny cliché! But the great Red Dragon of Temptation was charging across the plain. No time now to debate who was responsible; he had to stop it. "At least the Knights of the Round Table were mounted," Brother Paul muttered. "A lance and an armored charger—"

"You have to battle Temptation by yourself," Therion reminded him. "It has been ever thus."

So it seemed. Therion wore no armor and carried

no weapon; obviously he could not oppose the dragon, and had no intention of trying. Brother Paul retained his chariot armor, although he had lost the chariot itself. So it was up to him.

The dragon had a huge wedge-shaped head from which a small orange flame flickered. No, that was only its barbed tongue. Its two forelegs projected from immediately behind its head, almost like ears, and two small wings sprouted from its neck not far behind, like feathers or hair. It seemed an inefficient design, but so did the design for Tyrannosaurus Rex, on paper. The rest of the monster trailed away into wormlike coils. Only its foreparts possessed a menacing aspect; when this creature retreated, it would be harmless. Which was of course the nature of Temptation, or any other threat.

The dragon was not retreating. It was galumphing directly at him, its serpentine body bouncing like a spring-coil after the awful head.

Brother Paul went out to engage it, his sword shining like Excalibur. Yet he wondered: he considered himself to be a fairly peaceful man, not a warrior; why should he attack a living creature with a brute sword? This wasn't a living thing; it was an Animated symbol. Still, the matter disconcerted him.

The Dragon of Temptation drew up about two meters away. It glanced contemptuously at him. It had big yellow eyes, and its glare was quite striking. Its red snout was covered with great, hairy green-and-blue warts, and gnarled gray horns projected from its forehead. Its tusks were twisted and coated with slime. Brother Paul wondered idly if it had been mucking about in one of Therion's gooey cups before coming here.

The barbed tongue flicked about, striking toward

198

Brother Paul like an arrow but stopping short of the target. The small wings flapped slowly back and forth, the thin leathery skin crinkling between the feathered ribs. Brother Paul could not recall ever having seen anything uglier than this.

"Whatsamatter?" the dragon demanded. "Chicken?"

Brother Paul felt a tingle of anger. What right had this filthy thing to call him names? He gripped his sword firmly and stepped forward.

And paused again. This was Temptation—the urge to violence for insufficient cause. So the monster had called him "chicken"; why should he react to the archaic gibe? This was the lowest level of social interaction, and violence was the refuge of incompetence. "I merely wish to visit that castle, for I suspect that the information I need is inside. If you will kindly stand aside, there need be no strife between us."

"Temptation never stands aside!" the creature snorted. It was very good at speaking while snorting. "You must conquer me before you can complete your mission, chicken."

"But I don't want to slay you. I shall be satisfied to pass you by."

"You *can't* slay me; I am eternal. You can't pass me by. In fact, you can't even fight me; you're a natural coward. Why don't you get out of this scene and let the air clear?"

As if he hadn't been trying to do just that! "I would, if I had no mission to perform. I will, after it is done. Now please stand aside." Brother Paul strode forward.

The dragon held its ground. "Temptation cannot be bluffed," it said.

Brother Paul refused to strike it with the sword without some more definite provocation. Though he knew it to be a mere symbol, its semblance of a living, intelligent (if ugly) entity was too strong.

He sidled around it—and the dragon was before him again. It had jumped magically to block him. He changed direction again—and it blocked him again.

So that was the way of it; the thing was trying to provoke him into striking. And if he struck first, he would have succumbed to Temptation.

This time Brother Paul walked straight into the dragon. And bounced off its warty face.

Therion still stood a little apart, watching with morbid interest. "It didn't bite me," Brother Paul said, surprised.

"Temptation does not attack physically," Therion explained. "It merely offers a more intriguing alternative. Still, it must be conquered."

Brother Paul failed to see anything intriguing in the dragon. He tried again to avoid it, and failed again. He was becoming more than mildly angry, and felt the urge simply to smash the thing out of his way, but he suppressed the impulse. Instead, he sheathed his sword and tried to heave Temptation out of the way with his hands. But the dragon was too heavy and low-slung to budge. "You can't conquer me by halfhearted measures," it said with a phenomenal yard-long sneer.

Brother Paul found himself sweating. Apparently this thing *could* balk him if he refused to fight it directly. Yet he remained reluctant to do so. He turned to Therion. "You're my guide. What do you recommend?"

"You must find common ground on which to meet it. Temptation assumes many guises. Maybe one will suit you."

Brother Paul considered this. Many guises—could that be literal here? Physical? "I don't care to take the sword to you, beast," Brother Paul told it. "Yet you must be moved. Isn't there some less devastating way to determine the issue?"

"I'll meet you on any front, chicken," the dragon said. Part of its sneer remained, having failed to clear the far end of its long mouth.

"How about barehanded? Can you meet me in human form?"

The dragon vanished. In its place stood a man, huge and muscular, with yellow eyes, a red face, blue horns and a warty nose. And that lingering sneer. "What say now, coward?" the demon demanded.

"I say that if Jacob could wrestle with the Angel of the Lord, I may wrestle with Temptation," Brother Paul replied. He felt better now. This was a judo situation, and he was competent. He could subdue his opponent without hurting him.

"I don't know no Jacob!"

" 'And Jacob was left alone; and there wrestled a man with him until the breaking of the day.' It's from the Bible, the first book of Moses, called Genesis, chapter thirty-two." Brother Paul paused, expecting the demon to flinch at the Biblical reference, but was disappointed. But of course this was not a demon of the infernal regions, but the demon that was within every man; it would be conversant with the holy as well as the unholy. Except that it did not seem to know about this particular episode.

"Oh, *that* Jacob!" the demon said sneeringly. "He was a pretty puny angel, not to be able to beat a mortal man. In fact he would have lost if he hadn't struck a low blow."

Brother Paul remembered. " 'And when he saw that he prevailed not against him, he touched the hollow of his thigh; and the hollow of Jacob's thigh was out of joint, as he wrestled with him.' But that sounds more like a leglock than a low blow—leverage on the thigh to throw out the hip joint."

"The 'hollow of the thigh' is a euphemism for the crotch," the demon insisted. "The angel popped Jacob's crotch."

"Perhaps so," Brother Paul admitted. "It is a debatable point. Yet further along it is referred to as 'the sinew which shrank' and since he did sire a good family—"

"Not after he wrestled with the angel!"

Brother Paul spread his hands. He had thought his combat with the demon-dragon would be physical, but he was glad to settle for this Biblical arena instead. He had done a lot of Bible reading in the past few years, being fascinated with it as both religion and history. He was also intrigued by the continuity of the Bible, in the forms of the Apocrypha and Pseudepigrapha. "At any rate, the Angel did not defeat him, and he won from it a blessing: the name of Israel, meaning 'A Prince of God,' and founded the tribe of Israel."

"And his daughter Dinah got raped," the demon said, smiling as if with enjoyment.

This creature reminded Brother Paul strongly of Therion. He glanced back, but Therion was still standing there. On second thought, Therion would not approve of rape, not from consideration for the woman, but because he seemed to feel that the sexual act was a male sacrifice bestowed on the unworthy female. Why force this gift on a mere woman? "Rape is too strong a term," Brother Paul continued. "The young man was honorable, and begged to be allowed to marry Dinah formally, and even accepted the requirement of circumcision although he was a Gentile prince."

"Yeah, they covered up the record," the demon said. "Tried to make it out a good fuck in the end, so they wouldn't have to stone him for rape or her for acquiescence. A lot of juicy dirt got censored out of the Good Book."

Brother Paul started to make an angry retort, then realized that this was merely another aspect of the battle. Temptation fought with concepts as well as words, and truth was irrelevant. If distortion and vernacular caused Brother Paul to lose his temper, the victory would go to the dragon.

Indeed, these slights on Biblical accuracy were ones that Brother Paul himself had pondered privately. He liked to comprehend the full meaning of what he read, and much of the Bible remained tantalizingly opaque. Jacob's encounter with the Angel of God—there was an enigma! Why would an angel *want* to wrestle with a mortal man, and why would anything as pure of motive as an angel ever yield to the temptation? Yet Brother Paul knew he had to challenge the Bible with extreme caution, for it was a document that generations of scholars had not been able to question with certainty. Indeed, archaeological evidence continued to support the legitimacy of Biblical statements. Who was he, a minor novice in a minor Order, to set his puny judgment against the accumulated wisdom and revelation of the ages?

So he must vanquish Temptation here, too. It was not his place to debate any aspect of Scripture in public. It had been a mistake to invoke it here. What he did was his own responsibility; it should not be justified by reference to the Bible. That was a perversion, to adapt the Holy Book to individual purposes— though so many scoffers and special interests did.

203

"Enough of this," Brother Paul said. "If you will not let me pass, I must apply leverage."

The demon laughed. It was taller than Brother Paul, and heavier, and possessed a better physique. But how powerful was it, actually? Temptation could not be measured by external appearances.

Brother Paul stepped toward the castle, and of course the demon moved instantly to block him. This time Brother Paul stepped into it, shoved against the demon's right shoulder, and used his own right foot to sweep the demon's left foot out and forward. It was the *o uchi gari*, or "big inner reap" of judo.

The demon fell on the sand, as though its foot had slipped on a banana peel. Brother Paul stepped over it and resumed his march toward the castle. That had been amazingly easy!

And the demon stood before him again. "Very clever, mortal. But Temptation is not so readily put behind you. You could throw me a thousand times, and I would still be before you, for no single act of will defeats me."

Brother Paul stepped into it again. The demon braced against the maneuver that had brought it down before, but this time Brother Paul caught its right arm with both of his own and turned into *ippon seoi nage*, the one-armed shoulder throw. The demon's momentum carried it forward, and Brother Paul heaved it over his own shoulder to land on its back in the sand, hard.

This time Brother Paul followed it down and applied a neck lock. A simple choke would have cut off the demon's air, causing it to suffocate in a few minutes; this was a blood strangle that would deprive the creature's brain of oxygen, knocking it out in seconds.

The demon struggled, but it was useless. Brother Paul knew how to apply a stranglehold. He would not kill the creature, but would merely squeeze it unconscious. It would revive in a few minutes, unharmed—but too late to stop him from entering the castle. Temptation postponed might well be Temptation vanquished!

The seconds passed—and still the thing fought. The hold was tight, yet it seemed to have no effect. What was the matter?

The demon's arm came around, groping for Brother Paul's face. Sharp nails scraped across his cheek toward his right eye. He knew he would lose an eye if he did not get it out of reach in a hurry, but to do that he would have to release the strangle. This creature was not bound by polite rules of sport-combat!

Obviously the stranglehold had failed. The vascular system of demons seemed to be proof against the attack of mortals. Temptation could not be so simply nullified. Brother Paul let go and jumped up and away.

"I am a dragon," the demon said, standing. "I have no circulation, no blood. I operate magically. I need breath only to talk. You cannot throttle Temptation, fool!"

Evidently not! Brother Paul stepped toward the castle again, and the demon blocked his passage as before, grinning.

Brother Paul's left hand caught it by the right arm, jerking it forward. His right arm came up as if to circle the thing's impervious neck. The demon laughed contemptuously and pulled back, resisting both the throw and the strangle.

But Brother Paul's right arm went right on over the

demon's head, missing it entirely. He twisted around as though hopelessly tangled, falling to the sand. But the weight of his falling body jerked the demon forward over his back. It was *soto makikomi,* the outside wraparound throw, a strange and powerful sacrifice technique. The demon landed heavily, with Brother Paul on top; such was the power of the throw that an ordinary man could have been knocked unconscious. Immediately Brother Paul spun around, flipped the demon onto its face, and applied an excruciating armlock, one of the *kansetsu waza.* The demon might not have blood, but it had to have joints, and they were levered like those of a man. Such a joint could be broken, but he intended to apply only enough leverage to make the creature submit. In this position, there was no way the demon could strike back; no biting, no kicking, no gouging.

He levered the arm, bending the elbow back expertly. The demon screamed "Do you yield?" Brother Paul inquired, easing up slightly.

For answer, the demon changed back into the dragon, its original and perhaps natural form. Brother Paul had hold of one of its legs, but the ratios were different, and the lock could not be maintained. The monster's jaws opened, its orange tongue flicking out to lash at Brother Paul's face, whiplike. He had to let go quickly.

"So you couldn't take it," he said to the dragon. "You lost!"

"Temptation never loses; it is merely blunted, to return with renewed strength. I balk you yet." And the dragon moved to stand once again between Brother Paul and the castle.

Brother Paul turned to Therion, who had stood by

innocently while all of this occurred. "What do you say now, guide?"

"Have a drink," Therion said, presenting a tall, cool cup of liquid.

"I don't need any—" he started to reply, but he *was* thirsty, and in this situation the refreshment cup was appropriate and tempting. Maybe he was too hot and bothered to perceive the obvious—whatever that was. With a cooler, cleared head he might quickly figure out the solution to this maddening problem of the Dragon. He accepted the drink.

It was delicious, heady stuff, but after the first sip, he paused. "This is alcoholic!" he said accusingly.

"Naturally. The best stuff there is, for courage."

"Courage!" Brother Paul's wrath was near the explosion-point. "I don't need that kind! My Order disapproves of alcohol and other mind-affecting drugs. Get me some water."

"No water is available; this is a desert," Therion said imperturbably. "Does your Order actually ban alcohol?"

"No. The Holy Order of Vision bans nothing, for that would interfere with free will. It merely frowns on those things that are most commonly subject to abuse. Each person is expected to set his own standards in matters of the flesh. But only those persons of suitable standards progress within the Order."

"Uh-huh," Therion said disparagingly. "So you are a slave to your Order's inhibitions, and dare not even admit it."

"No!" Brother Paul gulped down the rest of the beverage, yielding to his consuming thirst.

The effect was instantaneous. His limbs tingled; his head felt pleasantly light. That was good stuff, after all!

Brother Paul faced the dragon, who was still between him and the castle, smirking. "I've had enough of you, Temptation. *Get out of my way!*"

"Make me, mushmind!"

Brother Paul drew his gleaming sword. He strode forward menacingly, bluffing the beast back. When the thing did not retreat, he smote the red dragon with all his strength—and cut its gruesome head in half. Sure enough, there was no blood, just a spongy material like foam plastic within the skull. The creature expired with a hiss like that of escaping steam and fell on its back in the sand, its little legs quivering convulsively.

"Well, I made it move," he said, wiping the green goo off his blade by rubbing it in the sand.

"You certainly did," Therion agreed.

"So let's get the hell on to that castle before the dragon revives."

"Well spoken!"

But now a new obstacle stood between them and the objective. It was another cup—the one containing the Victory Wreath. The braided twigs and leaves stood tall and green above the chalice, the two ends not quite meeting.

"Take it," Therion urged. "You have won it. You have slain Temptation!"

Brother Paul considered. "Yes, I suppose I have." Somehow he was not wholly satisfied, but the pleasure of the drink still buoyed him. "Why not?"

He reached out and lifted the wreath from the meter-tall cup. Strange that this, too, should appear in his vision of the castle; had his choice of one cup granted him *all* cups? Somehow his quest was not proceeding precisely as he had anticipated.

He set the wreath on his head. It settled nicely, feeling wonderful.

"Very handsome," Therion said approvingly. "You make a fitting Conqueror."

Yes, this *was* Key Seven, the Chariot, the Conqueror, wasn't it? With the Seven of Cups superimposed. Brother Paul bent down to view his image in the reflective surface of the polished golden cup. And froze, startled.

His image was a death's head. A grinning skull, with protruding yellow teeth and great square eye sockets.

Brother Paul rocked back, horrified. There was something he remembered, something so appalling—

No! He shut it off. This was only a reflection, nothing supernatural. He forced himself to look again. The death's head remained.

Experimentally, he moved his face. The skull moved too. He opened his mouth, and the bony jaw dropped. He blinked, but of course the skull could not blink, and if it could, how could he see it while his own eyes were closed?

His left hand came up to feel his face. A skeletal hand touched the skull in the cup. His nose and cheeks were there; the flesh was solid. The skull was merely an image, not reality. But what did it mean?

"Let's not dawdle," Therion said. "The dragon is not going to play dead all day."

Regretfully, Brother Paul stood up and circled around the cup. He was sure the skull meant something important. If it were part of the natural symbolism of this card, why hadn't he noticed it before? If not, why had it appeared now? He had encountered this card many times before coming to Planet Tarot; had the skull been on the cup then? He couldn't remember. There was something—something hidden and awful—but he *did* have a mission. Maybe the explanation would come to him.

He moved on. Then he realized he could have checked the blinking of the skull by winking one eye and watching with the other. He was thinking fuzzily, though his mind seemed perfectly clear. Well, it was of insufficient moment to make him return for another look at the cup. If it remained.

He glanced back. The huge cup was still there, and beyond it, the body of the dragon. He regretted the slaying; he really shouldn't have done it. He was not ordinarily a violent man. What had come over him?

His mouth had a bad taste, and a headache was starting. His stomach roiled as though wishing to disgorge its contents. "I don't feel well," he said.

"A little hangover," Therion said quickly. "Ignore it; it will pass."

Hangover? Oh—a reaction from the drink. Instant high, rapid low. It figured!

Now they were at the castle environs, mounting the winding pathway that led up the steep mountain upon which it perched. Progress was swift, for it was a very narrow mountain, but Brother Paul was tiring even more rapidly. Then he saw an inlet in the almost vertical cliff face, a kind of cave. And in this cave stood another cup. It was filled to overflowing with jewels: pearls, diamonds, and assorted other gems. Beautiful!

Brother Paul started for it, but found himself abruptly too tired to get all the way there. He also saw, now, that the cup was within a kind of cage, with a combination lock. In the lock was a picture of three lemons in a row.

"Oh—an ancient one-armed bandit," he muttered. "Well, I don't like to gamble."

"But look at the potential reward!" Therion exclaimed. "You could be rich—a multimillionaire in any currency you name!"

"Wealth means nothing to me. Brothers and Sisters of the Order dedicate their lives to nonmaterial things, to simplicity, to doing good."

"But think of all the good you could do with that fortune!"

"I just want to get into the castle and find the answer to my quest," Brother Paul said. "If I can only get up the strength to complete the climb . . ."

"Here, have a sniff of this," Therion said, opening a tiny but ornate silver box.

Brother Paul looked at it. The box was filled with a whitish powder. "What is it?"

"A stimulant. Used for centuries to enable people to work harder without fatigue. Completely safe, non-addictive. Try it." He shoved it under Brother Paul's nose, and Brother Paul sniffed almost involuntarily.

The effect was amazing. Suddenly he felt terrific strong, healthy, clear-minded. "Wow! What is it?"

"Cocaine."

"Cocaine! You lied to me! That's one of the worst of addictive drugs!"

Therion shook his head solemnly. "Not so. There is no physiological dependence. It is nature's purest stimulant, without harmful aftereffects. Much better than alcohol. But if you disbelieve, simply return the sample."

"Return the sniff? How can I do that?"

"It's your Animation. You can do anything."

Brother Paul wondered. If he could do anything, why couldn't he find his way *out* of this morass? Well, maybe he could, if he just willed it strongly enough. But he felt so good now, why change it? He did want to achieve the castle, after all, and he had already invested a lot of effort in that quest that would be wasted if he quit now. "Oh, let it stand."

His eyes returned to the cup of jewels. "But first, this detail." He strode across to the cage and reached for the handle of the one-armed bandit. "What do I have to put into this machine, to play the game?"

"A piddling price. Just one-seventh of your soul."

"Done!" Brother Paul said, laughing. And felt a strange wrenching that disconcerted him momentarily. If the price per cup were one-seventh, and there were seven cups in all, and he had already been through several . . . but he felt so good that he soon forgot it. He drew down powerfully on the handle.

The symbols spun blurringly past in the window of the lock. Swords, wands, disks, and something indistinct—perhaps lemniscates? What had happened to the lemons? Then they came to rest: one cup—two cups—three cups!

The cage door swung open. The cup tilted forward. Its riches spilled out over the floor of the cave. Jackpot!

"I gambled and won!" Brother Paul exclaimed.

Therion nodded. "It's your Animation," he repeated. "I merely show the way to your fulfillment."

There was something about that statement—oh, never mind! "Donate these jewels to the charities of the world," Brother Paul said. "I must proceed." He stepped carefully over the glittering gems in his path and left the cave.

The ascent was easy again. In moments he reached the front portal. It was open, and he marched into the castle.

"Like the palace of Sleeping Beauty," Therion remarked.

"Like a fairy tale, yes," Brother Paul agreed.

For some reason Therion found that gaspingly funny. "Show me what you laugh at, and I will show you what you are," he said between gasps. But it was he, not Brother Paul, who was laughing. Odd man!

"Strange," Brother Paul said, "how I start an Animation sequence to find out what is causing Animations, and find myself diverted into this fantasy world, where I must slay a dragon and see my reflection as a skull and gamble one-seventh of my soul on a worldly treasure I don't need. Why can't I just penetrate to the root immediately?"

"You could, if you knew how," Therion said.

"I acquired you as a guide! Why can't you show me the way?"

"I *am* showing you the way. In my fashion. But the impetus must be yours."

"*I* never sought to slay a dragon! Or gamble for riches! You and your damned drugs—"

"Apt description, that."

And why was he swearing, since he was not a swearing man? There was a lot of wrongness here, intertwined with the intrigue. "What do I do now?" Brother Paul demanded irritably.

"Do what thou wilt shall be the whole of the law."

"You said that before. But it doesn't help. It's from Rabelais, which I gather is prime source material for you. Here I am, restrained from doing what I wilt. What I wish, I mean. And you just tag along, spouting irrelevancies."

Therion turned to face him seriously. "However right you may be in your purpose, and in thinking that purpose important, you are wrong in forgetting the equal or greater importance of other things. The really important things are huge, silent, and inexorable."

"*What* things?"

"Your will."

"My will is to unriddle this Animation effect! Yet here I wander in this forsaken castle, as far from it as ever! What *is* this place, anyway?"

"Thelema."

"What?"

"This is the Abbey of Thelema, the place for the discovery of your True Will."

"I already *know* my will! I told you—"

"If you knew it, you would satisfy it."

Brother Paul paused. On one level, this was nonsense, but on another it seemed to make uncanny sense. "You're saying I only *think* I know my will, and I am getting nowhere because I am pursuing a false will? An illusion?"

Therion nodded. "Now you begin to perceive the problem. First you must truly understand your objective; only then can you achieve it."

"Well, I *thought* I understood it. But somehow I keep getting turned aside, as though I were a victim of Coriolis force." He paused, charmed by the revelation. Coriolis force—a prime determinant of weather on any planet. A mass of air might try to move from a high pressure zone near the equator to a low pressure zone to the north or south, but the shape and rotation of the planet diverted it to the side, because the surface velocity of rotation was greater at the equator than at the polar latitudes. Well, it was a difficult concept for the layman to grasp, but essential for the meteorologist. It was as though nature herself were fouled up by the system, causing the endless repercussions, instabilities, and changes that constituted the weather. Was there such a thing as a *mental* Coriolis force, so that a given urge could not be consummated directly unless the full nature of the human condition were understood? Yet this was hardly a perfect analogy, for the human mind was not a planetary surface, and human thoughts were not mere breezes. The situation was more dynamic, with force being diverted at right angles to—

"Precession!" he cried aloud.

Therion glanced up benignly. "Yes?"

"Precession. The factor that seems to change the direction of force applied to a gyroscope or a turning wheel. When properly exploited, as with a bicycle, it is a stabilizing influence, but when misunderstood, it stymies every effort to—"

Therion shook his head. "Can you explain it to me more precisely?"

"It is a technical term. It affects the Earth and all rotating things, and thus man's technology and mythology. The precession of the equinox . . ." He took a breath. "Simply, there is a great deal of rotational inertia in a spinning object, and when you apply an external force to change its orientation, you must deal with that inertia. If you understand this, and know the precise vectors—"

Therion smiled. "Thus your ignorance stops you here, because the inertial velocity of the mind is more complex than any casual survey can reveal. Know thyself—or as I prefer to put it, do what thou wilt."

"Yes," Brother Paul agreed, at last appreciating the man's meaning. A person could not do what he really wanted to do, unless he understood himself well enough to *know* what he wanted. What he *really* wanted, not what in his ignorance he thought he wanted. Many people were stuck on the ignorant

215

route, questing tirelessly for wealth or power that brought them only unhappiness. Others quested for happiness, but defined it purely in material terms. Still others, trying to correct for that, insisted on defining it in purely *non*material terms, seeking chimeras. As perhaps Brother Paul had been doing, himself. "My ultimate will is more subtle and devious than I myself can appreciate consciously. Since these Animations are at least in part drawn from my unconscious, I suffer precession when I attempt to direct them by purely conscious thought. Thus I wind up veering away at right angles, battling the Dragon of Temptation, and God only knows what else!"

Therion nodded again, looking like a somewhat seedy street philosopher. "I also know what else: it was your own conscience you battled."

"You know, you're not a bad guide, at that," Brother Paul said. "You have had a better notion of my true will than I. But as with leading a horse to water—"

"The whole of the law," Therion agreed.

They had been meandering through the gaunt, empty castle. Now they entered an upper chamber— and spied a woman. She reclined in a huge cup, so he knew this had to be another vision of the Seven of Cups, that he had to deal with one way or another. He suspected that the original cup he had chosen, that of the castle, had been merely an entry point; he was required to taste the contents of all seven before he was through. Had he chosen the lady first, he would have found the skull, Temptation, and the castle interposing, though perhaps in a different order. With precession, there was no direct or easy route to an objective. But now this woman; she was a marvel of organic symmetry and cultural aesthetics, with hair like summer wheat. . . .

"Amaranth!" Brother Paul breathed.

"Beg pardon?" Therion inquired.

Of course this man would not know about the private name Brother Paul had for the Breaker-lady. But now he was sure; Amaranth had gotten into this Animation, and here she was, the actress in a very special role. The major characters in these scenes *were* played by living people, reciting their lines, as it were, or perhaps extemporizing according to general guidelines. "A private thought, irrelevant," Brother Paul said, and knew he was lying. Since to him a lie was an abomination, he had to correct it immediately. "I believe I recognize this woman. She—"

"The female exists but to serve the male," Therion remarked.

So the man wasn't really interested in the identity of this woman. To him, women were interchangeable, covered by a general blanket of animosity. Well, Brother Paul was amenable to that game, in this case; from what he knew of Amaranth, she would quickly disabuse all comers of such notions.

Brother Paul approached the lady. "In what way do you reflect my hidden will?" he asked her.

She unfolded from the cup and stood before him, as lovely a creature as he could imagine. "I am Love."

Love. That was rather more than he had bargained on. "Sacred or profane?" he inquired somewhat warily. "I am here on a religious mission."

"He claims he loves God, not woman," Therion put in.

"I love God *and* woman!" Brother Paul snapped. "But my mission requires—"

Amaranth stretched, accentuating her miraculous

217

breasts, and Brother Paul recognized Temptation in another guise. He knew that Animation was not enhancing her appearance; it was every bit as enticing in life. A woman who was beautiful only in Animation—but of course physical appearance should not be the prime appeal.

"You fought valiantly to achieve this castle," Therion pointed out. "Do you now reject what it holds for you?"

"Precession brings this woman; what I seek is elsewhere."

"How do you know?"

Brother Paul considered that, uncertain. He had supposed he was overcoming Temptation—and a formidable Temptation it was!—but could it be that the physical side of Love was the essence of his search? It hardly seemed likely, but he could not be *sure*. There was a deep affinity between types of love, expressed on the highest plane as religion, and on the lowest as sex. It was often said that "God is Love." Could he achieve one form without the other?

He remembered the sour comments of the Hierophant. What was the nature of his belief? That the expression of physical love was inherently evil? The Hierophant's views had resembled a parody of—

"The Hierophant!" Brother Paul exclaimed, wheeling on Therion. "You!"

"So you caught on," Therion said smugly.

"You purposely distorted the religious attitude of—"

"Distorted? I would not say so," Therion said. "I had a role to play, so I played it with complete candor. I gave the essence instead of mere casuistry. Modern religion hates sex and pleasure and tries to suppress them, because a man with a stiff cock will

218

not seek a priest. The ancient religions were much more savvy; they knew that the 'alternate facet of divine love is physical love. It is a completely natural and necessary function."

"But not outside of marriage," Brother Paul said, shaken by the way he had been guided even before he had chosen the guide.

"Why not? What is marriage but a ceremony of society, establishing the proprietary rights of a particular male over a particular female? Does God *care* about the conventions of human culture? Who governs here, anyway—God or man?"

"Surely God does!" Brother Paul said.

"Then why didn't God make man impotent prior to the nuptial ceremony, or responsive only to some other key stimulus, like smell? Animals have no such trouble."

"Man is not precisely an animal!" Brother Paul retorted. "Man has a conscience. He controls his urges."

"The tail wags the dog, then. Man controls the natural urges God gave him, instead of allowing their expression in the way God intended."

"No! Man's conscience stems from God!"

"And God is created in the image of man."

Telling thrust! Of course, *man* was in the image of *God*, but if he argued that case, Therion would simply point out that God was therefore a sexual creature, and unmarried. Now Brother Paul was uncertain where the sacrament of marriage fitted into this scheme, for it was true that animals did not marry. Animals were completely natural, yet innocent.

Still, he had to believe that one of the things that distinguished man from animal was his morality, his higher consciousness. "I do not choose to argue with you about marriage," Brother Paul said, "or to abuse this young woman. I only wish to ascertain the reality behind the image."

"Still, you suffer precession," Therion said sadly. "You insist on carrying into this framework the private standards dictated by your Earthly existence, refusing to admit that they may be no longer applicable. You think you can penetrate the morass by plowing straight ahead. When will you realize that you cannot win unless you play the game by its rules? You have sampled only three cups."

Temptation, Victory, and Wealth. Apparently he did have to go through them all before gaining enlightenment. No shortcut! Yet did the presence of this woman, who had been accidentally trapped in the Animation, mean he had to use her sexually? Therion seemed to be arguing that case, which was odd, because Therion professed to hate women. Obviously he could not afford to be guided too closely by Therion's words, which did not necessarily reflect Therion's own will. This woman might be seductive, but he did not have to be seduced.

"I would like to talk with you," Brother Paul said to the lady. "What is your preference?"

"I adore thee, I A O," she replied.

"My name is Brother Paul, of the Holy Order of Vision," he said. That made a formal introduction within this Animation, in case that should help. "You—I believe we met before, in, er, real life. And you introduced the Brotherhood of Light Tarot deck, didn't you? What shall I call you now?"

She opened her robe. She was naked underneath, slim and pink-white and full-breasted. She was his physical ideal of woman, which was obviously what had first attracted him to her. He tried to seek the sublime understanding of God, but his flesh had other notions.

"I adore thee, I A O," she repeated.

Brother Paul refused to go along. "I understood you to say, in real life, that you worshipped a snake-footed God, called Abra—" He was unable to recall the full name.

"She refers to I A O, or Abraxas—literally, 'the God to be adored.' Therefore she adores him," Therion clarified. "He has human form, with the head of a cock and legs of serpents, and he is the god of healing. It would seem she believes you are that god."

"I!" Brother Paul exclaimed, appalled. "A pagan deity?"

"Abraxas was a most fashionable god, in the Roman Empire. She might see you as a modern incarnation. Perhaps if you showed her your feet—"

Brother Paul uttered an extremely un-Orderlike syllable. But Therion was studying Amaranth's torso. "She certainly is a healthy, well-fed specimen," he remarked, as though appraising a thoroughbred horse. "Most peoples of most times have been malnourished; only in the past century has good nutrition spread. One seldom sees as fine a form as that, however, even today."

To whom was he trying to sell that form? "You really do worship a pagan god?" Brother Paul demanded of the lady. He had somehow not appreciated the significance of this, or really believed it when, as a colonist, she had mentioned the matter.

"This is, after all, a free society," Therion remarked. "No person, according to the Covenant, may persecute any member of any other religion, whatever its nature. It is the only thing that prevents absolute internecine warfare throughout this colony. I'm sure I

221

A O has as much right to be here as any Christian god."

The girl shrugged out of her costume and stood before them, completely nude. The splendor of her body was dazzling, and not because she was well-fed; there was no fat on her where it didn't belong. She stepped toward Brother Paul.

He stepped back in alarm.

"The early priestesses led devotees to union with their god by the most direct means," Therion continued. "She wants to help you discover your true will; will you not oblige?"

"This is not the kind of union I seek!" Brother Paul protested. "Not with I A O, not—"

"Suppose I A O is the God of Tarot, and you refuse to meet Him?"

"Impossible!" But Brother Paul realized that it was *not* impossible. Improbable, perhaps, but theoretically possible. The whole problem on Planet Tarot, the reason he had come here, was to determine objectively (if circumstances permitted) which god was the guiding power behind the Animations, or whether *no* god was. He could not let his own religious prejudice interfere. For—he forced his mind to consider it—I A O Abraxas, the Adorable God, just might be the one. Even if I A O were not, he still had to ascertain that fact honestly. The assembled religions of Planet Tarot were awaiting his verdict. No one of their own representatives could make this survey, because every person among them was too firmly committed to his own particular concept of God to be objective. Those who had tried most sincerely had suffered the ravages of loss of faith, in some cases with fatal results.

Brother Paul had no intention of dying in this quest. But neither did he intend to participate in any whitewash or rehash of personal prejudice. The ethics of his Order, and his own pride, required that he seek only the truth. The mission transcended his petty personal scruples. He had to give I A O a fair hearing.

"But is it actually necessary to—?" he asked plaintively, viewing the nude priestess. "If she is a modern-day worshiper of Abraxas, it would be in her interest to convince me her God was the one, when in fact he might *not* be."

"True, true," Therion agreed. "I hardly envy you your task."

"And making love to her would not prove anything."

"Unless, as in the battle with Temptation, it were a route to the innermost truth," Therion said. "In that case it would be too bad not to call her bluff and leave this cup unsavored."

"That doesn't make sense!" But Brother Paul looked again at the priestess of Abraxas. If this *were* the God of Tarot, and if there were only one way to relate to that God, according to His ancient ritual of union . . .

"Have a sniff of this," Therion said, opening another little box.

"No! Not more cocaine! That doesn't solve anything!"

"This is not cocaine."

"Oh." Brother Paul relented and took a sniff.

"It is heroin," Therion concluded.

But already the drug was taking effect. Brother Paul turned to the priestess. "So you want interaction," he said boldly. "Well, I shall plumb you for the truth!" His own clothing fell away magically as he strode toward her.

He took her in his arms and kissed her deeply. Her

cool, firm breasts flattened excitingly against his chest. His hands traveled down her arching back and across her sleek haunches, finally cupping her firm yet soft buttocks. What a specimen she was!

The kiss was magical; he had never experienced anything like it! He knew it was enhanced by the heroin, but didn't care. He felt such mastery of himself that nothing mattered at all; he could enjoy this experience without any reservation.

Experience. There was man's most deeply seated instinct: the craving for new sensations, the satisfaction of curiosity, variety and excitement and fulfillment! Experience. Every minute, every second was precious; he had to indulge himself to the utmost, because this was the ultimate meaning of life. Why should he sow, and not reap?

He released the priestess just enough to look at her face. She smiled.

"Stab your demoniac smile to my brain," Therion said. "Soak me in cognac, kisses, cocaine." He pronounced "cognac" so that it rhymed directly with "demoniac."

This had the effect of stultifying Brother Paul's ardor, despite the heroin. "Don't you have somewhere to go?" he demanded.

"I am your guide. I must see you safely through this challenge."

" You are afraid I will make love to the priestess?"

"I fear you will *not*, unless I guide you."

"This is between me and my religion!"

"And your religion, like virtually all modern faiths, is fundamentally anti-sex. Your understanding of the subject is limited, though your instinct, were you ever to let it reign, is sound. Sex is good; love is the law; ignorance is evil."

"But casual, thoughtless sex—"

"No man can get along on a continual diet of abstinence. A man must be permitted normal sexual expression, as God intended. He *must* express his natural urges, of whatever type, or wither away."

"Still," Brother Paul said uncertainly. He had his beliefs, but they were being sorely besieged by this logic and the woman in his arms.

The priestess knelt before him, as though in supplication, her breasts sliding excruciatingly down the length of his torso. "I adore thee, I A O!" she repeated.

"Hey, that's not I A O!" Brother Paul protested. But then he realized that perhaps it *was*; she worshiped a serpent-legged God, so she sought the serpent in man.

Under her massage, that serpent rose and swelled like the forepart of a cobra. The skin of the head peeled back, releasing the faint scent generated in that special pocket—the scent that the knife denied to most Christians and all Moslems and Jews, in the guise of "health."

But Brother Paul had never been subjected to that unkindest cut. His member was whole, and it functioned as God had designed it to. The scent of arousal wafted out. She inhaled that aroma. A beatific smile spread across her face. "I A O!" she breathed ecstatically, her breath caressing the organ.

"Love is the law," Therion intoned. "Love under will."

"Enough of this!" Brother Paul cried, drawing her hands and face away from his anatomy. He lifted her up, but she spun away and sprawled half across the couch. (Couch? Where was the cup? Oh—they were the same.) He pursued her, caught her with both his

225

hands about her waist as she pushed herself up on the support, and brought his groin to her swelling posterior. Her hands, dislodged as her bottom was raised up, slid off the rim; the upper section of her body fell down inside the cup. Now she was bent forward at a right angle, her breasts flattening against the inner surface of the cup, her elbows braced at its depth, her face invisible within its shadow. But he didn't need her breasts or arms or face. He guided his member by hand, found the place, and thrust.

He had imagined easy penetration of her exposed vagina, but it was not easy. There was some pain for him as he forced entry past constricted muscles, without sufficient lubrication. But the drug spurred him on; he was, after all, the Conqueror!

The climax was explosive: a nuclear detonation in a subterranean vault. The recoil flung him backward, breaking the connection. Simultaneously his heroin high collapsed; he felt tired and sick, pumped out, without ambition, irritable, and disgusted. The priestess had fallen out of the cup to the floor, outstretched, supine. Therion was squatting beside her, almost over her head. Maybe she was hurt; it had been quite a blast. Brother Paul didn't care. He just wanted another sniff of H.

He staggered toward Therion. "Give it to me," he rasped.

"I'm busy!" Therion snapped, still squatting. "I have to give her—"

Brother Paul's nose was running and his stomach was cramping. Withdrawal symptoms, he knew. "Give me the stuff."

Therion ignored him, concentrating on the girl.

"I want more smack, more junk," Brother Paul insisted. "What do you call it these days? Horse? Snow? *Where is it?*"

Still Therion did not respond; he was still squatting.

Sudden rage engulfed Brother Paul. "You're paying more attention to *her* than to *me*! You're supposed to guide *me*!"

"Shit," Therion said.

Brother Paul remembered; that was another name for heroin. "Then give me shit!" he cried.

A cup appeared before him, but it contained no white powder. Angrily he swung his fist at it, knocking it over. A green snake fell out, hissing. A foot of the god Abraxas? No, this was merely the symbol of Jealousy.

He was getting nowhere. His hot flash was converting into a chill. What had he gotten into? "Why should *you* be so self-assured," Brother Paul demanded, "when *I* am so confused and sick! It isn't fair!"

Therion looked up. "I am content because I comprehend my own essential nature," he said. "I know what I am, and who I serve. I am at peace with myself. No victory, wealth, or woman can match that. 'Do what thou wilt shall be the whole of the law.'"

"Then show me how to comprehend *my* essential nature!" Brother Paul cried. "There is the key to ultimate power!"

"You must seek it within yourself, extricating yourself from the prison of the senses," Therion said. "Meditation, such as is sponsored by yoga—"

"No! I can't wait for that. I want it now!"

"Then take the shortcut." Therion held up a small capsule. "LSD."

Brother Paul snatched it and gulped it down.

It was like a headlong rush into a maelstrom. Sensations were coming at him from all directions, and seeming to go out from him similarly. Sights, sounds, smells, tastes, and touches. He saw the room. The girl was still lying on the floor, her mouth open. Therion was still squatting over her. He saw all the furniture. The patch of sunlight from the window. He heard the wheezing of wind around the parapet, the baying of some distant animal, the ticking of an unseen clock. He smelled the leather couch, and the brass of the inside of the big cup, and dust from the floor, and the faint, sweet scent of a flower outside, somewhere. He tasted the remains of the capsule. He felt the cool stone floor under his feet, the caress of a trifling breeze on his bare body. All distractions, to be dispensed with!

He focused his awareness, shutting all external stimuli out. Now he saw light behind his eyelids, for they were not thick enough to make total darkness. He heard the sound of his own breathing, and of his heartbeat. He smelled his own breath, a touch of whiskey still on it. Whiskey? Oh—from that first drink, back at Temptation. His tongue tasted slightly bitter. He felt the tension of his muscles as they tightened to keep him balanced.

Actually there were many more than five senses, but most of the unnamed ones could be lumped under touch: feeling of discomfort, muscle tension, orientation. Distractions.

He sat down on the floor, assuming the crosslegged yoga position favored for meditation, and consciously relaxed. Gradually his bodily tensions melted away, releasing his mind.

It was like flying low over a landscape toward the sunrise. His half-random thoughts zoomed past like technicolor clouds, some formless, some beautiful, some menacing. Below was the castle, with the priestess lying like Sleeping Beauty within it, awaiting the kiss to restore her to consciousness, except that that was an expurgation. It was really the sexual act that would rouse her, making the life within her quicken, only they couldn't tell children that (and why the hell *not*?) and in this case that act had put her to sleep instead. Priestess of Abraxas? What was such temple worship except ritualized prostitution? Prostitution, the oldest profession of woman. It would exist as long as men had the money and the urge and women had neither. How ironic that it should be combined with religion! Yet religion had about as great an affinity for the vices of man as any other institution.

The drug enhanced everything, providing a phenomenal visual, aural, and tactile experience. The Dragon of Temptation charged him, but was inflated like a hydrogen balloon until it exploded into harmless flame. Therion would say it had farted itself to death. The priestess of I A O again, opening her lovely body to him, crying, "I adore thee, I A O!" but he was no longer aroused. The suits of the Tarot, symbols flying up around him like the cards in *Alice in Wonderland*, male wands and swords thrusting through female cups and disks. Swiftly, in mere seconds, he abolished all these interfering thoughts. Gradually he oriented on his target: his own ultimate essence.

Now, in the distance, he saw the first glow of it— the effulgence of the Grail. Like the breaking of the dawn, that miraculous light expanded as he arrowed toward it. The disruptive presence of his superficial thoughts diminished, shining in pastel hues in the face of that solar brilliance; he coursed past them, unveiling the way to Nirvana.

At last the gleaming rim of it emerged, more splendid than any vision he had heretofore imagined. Onward he flew, bringing more into view: the magnificent curvature of the Holy Grail, hanging perfectly in the sky.

Now he saw that though the Cup itself glowed, as it had when it had floated past the astonished knights of King Arthur's Round Table, this was a faint glimmering compared to its principal illumination. This brilliance was by virtue of its content—that deeply veiled shape whose light spilled out between canopy and rim. The shape of his Essence!

Eagerly he moved toward it, certain now that he would perceive the glory that was his soul. What form would it take, that divine revelation? A giant, precious, bright crystal with myriad facets, a myriad-squared reflections? A godlike brilliance, gently blinding the mortal eye? An intangible aura of sheer wonder?

He came up to the monstrous chalice, that goblet of Jesus, the quintessence of ambition, and peeked under the glorious cover. There was an odor, awful and out of place, but he ignored it. Here at last was Truth, was Soul!

It was a huge, half-coiled, half-broken, steaming human turd.

8

Emotion

And Saul, yet breathing out threatenings and
slaughter against the disciples of the Lord, went
unto the high priest,

And desired of him letters to Damascus to the
synagogues, that if he found any of this way,
whether they were men or women, he might
bring them bound unto Jerusalem.

And as he journeyed, he came near Damascus: and suddenly there shined round about him
a light from heaven:

And he fell to the earth, and heard a voice
saying unto him, Saul, Saul, why persecutest
thou me?

And he said, Who art thou, Lord? And the
Lord said, I am Jesus whom thou persecutest: it
is hard for thee to kick against the pricks.*

* "to kick against the pricks"—i.e., to oppose
the pricks of conscience.

And he trembling and astonished said, Lord, what wilt thou have me to do? And the Lord said unto him, arise, and go into the city, and it shall be told thee what thou must do.

And the men which journeyed with him stood speechless, hearing a voice, but seeing no man.

And Saul arose from the earth; and when his eyes were opened, he saw no man: but they led him by the hand, and brought him into Damascus.

And he was three days without sight, and neither did eat nor drink.

THE BIBLE: King James Version ACTS IX: 1-9

Paul sniffed, trying to clear his nostrils of the stink of shit. He was driving a car, an old-fashioned internal combustion machine, wasteful of fuel. Therefore this was pre-MT Earth, oddly strange and just as oddly familiar. He knew this was another Animation, quite different from the last, but still a construct of some aspect of his imagination or his memory. Another direction governed by precession, whose laws he did not yet comprehend well enough to utilize consciously.

He seemed to recall having taken a drive like this, perhaps ten years ago, perhaps nine, but where had he come from then, and where had he been going? It would not come clear.

There were many other cars on the highway, traveling at the maximum velocity their governors permitted: 100 KPH, nice and even. All good things were governed by hundreds; it was the decimal, metric, percentage system. Easy to compute with, easy to verify, divisible by many numbers.

The cars were like his own: small hydrogen burners, streamlined, comfortable. The hydrogen was separated from water at various power plants; some of it was used for fusion into helium for major power, and some for combination with oxygen to make water again (clean water was precious), some treated for nonignition and put into transport blimps, and some burned explosively in motors. Hydrogen: the most versatile element. Paul was uncertain of the original source of power used to separate out the gas, but obviously it sufficed to run the system.

In just a few years all this would change, as the MT program burst upon them and co-opted all the convenient major energy sources. The creature from Sphere Antares, whose very presence was kept secret from the people of the world he so changed; what mischief was he to wreak on Sphere Sol? But right now people were indulging in their last fling; private transportation was still within the rights and means of the average citizen. Barely.

Paul himself could not afford this car. He had the use of it illicitly: he was drug-running. Hidden so well that even he had no notion of where it was, was a cache of mnem, pronounced "NEEM": the memory drug. Students used it when cramming for exams; when high on mnem their retention became almost total, enabling them to make very high marks on rotework without actually cheating. It did not enhance intelligence or give them lasting skills, but temporary memorization was so important in taking machine-graded examinations that this often made the difference in the competitive grade listings that determined eligibility for employment or promotion. Paul himself had never used mnem during his college days, not because of unavailability, expense, or ethics, but because he hadn't needed it. His college used no tests or grades. The drug had few side effects and could be detected in the human system only through extraordinary clinical procedures that cost more than the public clinics could afford. Therefore it was fairly safe to use, and much in demand.

There were only three drawbacks to mnem. First, it was illegal. That bothered very few people; when morality conflicted with convenience, morality suffered. Second, it was expensive, after the manner of addictive illegal drugs; the cost was not in the manufacture but in the illicit distribution system. That bothered more people, but not enough to seriously inhibit its use. The criminal element had a sharp eye for what the market would bear, just as did the business element. In fact, the abilities and scruples of the two elements were similar, and there was considerable overlapping. The mnem cartel proffered incentive options for those in critical need, such as Paul himself. For he, after college, had found a use for mnem. Third, mnem withdrawal caused not only the loss of the drug-enhanced memories, but a more general mnemonic deterioration, leading to disorientation and irregular amnesia. Thus the addiction was neither psychological nor physiological, but practical: once "hooked," a user could not function without mnem. That bothered most people, but they tended not to think about that aspect. It was a paradox of mnem, the subject of much folk humor, that it made people forget its chief drawback while it sharpened their memories enormously.

Which was why Paul was risking his freedom by running this shipment across state lines. He had used the drug to become expert in his sideline; now he could maintain his habit only by cooperating with the suppliers. Fortunately they did not require a particular person to do it often; this was not done from concern for the welfare of the individual, but as a precaution against discovery by the authorities. It might be a year before Paul would have to drive again, and in the interim his own supply of mnem was free. It was really a good deal.

There was someone standing at the margin of the highway; the figure seemed to be female. Other cars were rushing by, of course; it was dangerous to pick up a hitchhiker, male or female. But Paul sometimes got restless; though he did not drive often, this long trip bored him. Company would make a difference, particularly feminine company.

He stopped. The girl saw him and ran up. She was young, probably not out of her teens, but surprisingly well developed. Her clothing was scant and in disarray; in fact she was in a rather flimsy nightgown that outlined her heaving breasts with much stronger erotic appeal than she could have managed by any deliberate exposure. A natural girl in an unnatural situation.

"Oh, thank you!" she gasped, climbing into the seat next to him. "I was so afraid no one would stop before the police came."

"The police?" he asked with sudden nervousness. If she was a criminal—

"Oh, please, sir—drive!" she cried. "I'll explain, it's all right, no trouble for you, only lose us in the traffic. *Please!*"

But he hesitated, the car still parked. "I have no money worth taking, only a keyed credit you can't use. This car requires my thumbprint every half hour, or the motor locks and the automatic takes over, so you can't—"

She faced him, and he was surprised to see tears on

235

her cheeks. Her fair hair was bedraggled, yet she was lovely in her wild way. "You are in no danger from *me*, sir! I have no weapon. I have nothing. No food, no identification. I don't know how I can repay you, but please, *please* drive, or all is lost. I would rather die than go back there!"

Still ill-at-ease, he moved the car forward, gaining speed until he was able to merge into the traffic flow. "Where are you going?" he inquired.

"To the Barlowville Station," she said.

He started punching the coding into his computer terminal, seeking a clarification of the address. "Oh, no!" she protested. "Please, sir, don't ask the machine! They'll key it in to me, and in minutes the police—"

The demon in the machine. Paul's fingers froze. "You're on the criminal index?" he asked, alarmed. He had just about decided she was harmless, but he didn't like this. The last thing he needed was a police check on this car!

"I'm being deprogrammed," she explained hastily. "I belong to the Holy Order of Vision, and my folks sued—"

"They still deprogram religious nuts?" he asked thoughtlessly. "I thought that went out a decade ago, along with other forms of exorcism."

"It still happens," she said. "The established sects are all right—they finished their initiations years ago—but the new ones are still being persecuted."

The rite of passage, he thought. Any new religion had to pass through sufficient hazing to justify its existence, and when it became strong enough to fight back, as early Christianity had, it became legitimate and started hazing the religion that came next.

He shrugged. "I don't know much about it." Not in *his* business, he didn't—and he didn't care to. Religion held little interest for him, apart from morbid curiosity about the credulity of people. Still, this was a very pretty girl, who seemed somehow familiar. That flowing hair, those full breasts, the way she spoke— He was intrigued. "But if you really want to go back to this cult—"

"Oh, I do!" she exclaimed. "Somehow I'll return."

Paul made a decision. "I'll take you there, if it's not too far out of the way. But if you won't let me get the highway address from the travel computer—"

"I can tell you the way," she said eagerly. Then she faced him and smiled, the expression making her glow. "My name is Sister Beth."

"I'm Paul Cenji." What the hell had he expected her name to be? This seemed to be a memory, but it unfolded at its own pace; he could not remember what had happened that day in his past, so had to live it through again.

He drove on for a while, then asked, "How did you get caught away from your church?"

"My Station. We don't have churches as such, just centers of operation. My mother called me and told me my grandmother was dying, so I came at once. I never renounced my family ties; the Holy Order of Vision isn't like that. I wish my family belonged, too! But when I got there—"

"They grabbed you and hauled you off to the de-programming clinic," Paul finished for her.

"Yes. I suppose I should have suspected something, but I never thought my own mother would . . ." She shrugged sadly. "But I'm sure she thought she was doing the right thing. I forgive her. They tried to talk me out of going back, and when that didn't work, they said they were going to use mnem—"

"Mnem!" he exclaimed.

"It's a drug," she said, not appreciating the actual nature of his reaction. "They use it for rehabilitating incorrigible criminals. It's not supposed to be used for—" She broke off.

Paul's suspicions had been aroused again. Could it be coincidence, this reference to the drug he was hauling? Or was this a police trap? "I heard it was illegal," he said.

"Yes, for anything but the rehabilitation of criminals and some forms of mental illness. But there is a black market in mnem. It costs a lot that way, but my folks raised the credit."

Paul didn't like this at all. A seductively innocent girl in scant attire, planted on the highway to attract footloose rakes like him who might be supporting their lifestyles by dealing in contraband. A lot of fools were caught that way, he was sure. Now she was naming the subject, maybe probing for guilty reactions. It was all too easy to give away secrets while dazzled by offerings of this caliber. Already it seemed as if he had known her longer, in another place, by some other name—the perpetual mystery of the female. Maybe he only *wanted* to have known her. Her charm was already corrupting him; he had to get rid of this easy rider without arousing suspicion—if it was not already too late. "Which way is your—Station?"

"It's in the next state. You can go another hundred kilometers on this highway before turning off." Right. She had to be able to testify that he had actually crossed a state line. One of the niceties of the law. The police would be executing people on suspicion if they had the law all their own way. But America was not yet a total police state.

So he had until they reached the state line to act. He had to keep up the front until he knew what to do.

"Glad to have company for that hundred K," he said. The irony was that that would have been true, had she not brought up the subject of mnem. What a face, what a body, what a beguiling simplicity she showed! He was accustomed to a rather different sort of woman, and was now discovering that he had misjudged his own tastes.

"I really appreciate this, Mr. Cenji. When I learned of the mnem, I waited till night, then climbed out of my window in my nightdress, and here I am. They never thought I'd do that. If you hadn't stopped— there's probably an alarm out for me now."

Paul turned on the highway audio scan. If there was an announcement—but that would be part of the police bait; it would mean nothing. His best course would be to keep her talking while he figured out what to do with her. "I thought deprogramming itself was illegal now."

"It is, but they don't call it that. There are black-market professionals in that field too. I've been accused of stealing valuable jewelry. I would never steal! By the time it turns out that the charge is untrue, they will have me wiped out by the drug, and I won't even remember that I was ever a Sister—oh, I would die first!" She put her face in her hands.

What a touching display! She was good at her act, uncomfortably good; he wanted to put the car on automatic, take her in his arms, console her. Danger! She was surely planning to betray him, to add his scalp to the collection in her police locker.

Yet how could she do this, when he himself had no idea where the cache of mnem was hidden in the car? He was not even certain that there was a cache, this time; every so often the cartel made a blank run, to further confuse the enemy. If that happened to be the case this time, he had only to keep his nerve and he would win. He had no intention of telling her about his cargo, and if the police had known about it for sure, they would simply have arrested him outright. So this elaborate lure made no sense. Unless she was a trained observer, alert to the signs of mnem addiction. Such signs were trifling, but they did exist, and he was an addict. If he didn't get his fix tonight, he would begin to forget his way home tomorrow. So he had to be rid of her before then, bluffing it out. Stopping before the state line would not get him off this hook.

"Actually, I've heard the drug is not so bad—for criminals," he said. "It doesn't hurt. At least, I've heard it doesn't."

"Oh, it is very good for criminals," she said. "We of the Holy Order of Vision are concerned about the problem of criminality. We don't believe in taking life; it is as wrong for the state to kill as it is for the individual to kill. And we know our society cannot afford to maintain people in prison, yet some are incorrigible. Mnem is the answer to that. It resolves the conflict between the alternatives of killing the criminal and letting him go unpunished. We believe in forgiveness, but in certain cases correction is better. It makes the criminal a citizen again. Some of our Order members are mnem-erased rehabilitates—"

"It *erases* personality? I thought it improved memory!" How much did she know?

"In overdose it does. In trace dosages it actually enhances memory to an extraordinary degree, but then a person has to keep using it, never too much at a time. I could never stand to have all my memory taken away, or to be tied for life to such a drug. The Order could help me if I were an addict, but this single overdose would take me away from the Order, because I wouldn't *know*. I couldn't face that, so I fled."

"Yes. Understandable." She did know too much, for any ordinary young female citizen. She had to be a police-trained agent, with a near-perfect cover. Soon she would have him spotted.

Actually, part of what she said related to him very directly. He had never seriously thought about his future. He was bound for life to the drug, and to the criminal distribution system, and he could escape that prison only at the expense of his memory. Was that what he really wanted in life? It didn't matter; it was what he had. She, according to her story, had fled in time; for him it was too late. All he could do now was protect what he had—from her.

Yet he delayed in taking action, nagged by doubt. She was such a damned attractive girl, seeming so nice, representing the kind of life he would have chosen, had he been smart early. Like a fine racing car, styled right, with an engine to conjure with, capable of pushing a quarter mach 1 in heat, yet docile and comfortable when on idle. How could he kick her out without being *sure*? (And was she thinking: how could she arrest him as a mnem addict, without being *sure*?)

"Your cult—I mean, your religious order—what does it do? Is it like a commune or something?" (Where the women were shared among the men, and no person denied anything to any other? But surely he was dreaming!)

"The Holy Order of Vision is not really a religion," she said, and it was evident that now she was on familiar ground. But of course she would have her story straight. "Anyone can join, from any religion, and the Order does not interfere. We try to promote

241

the welfare of man and nature wherever we can. Many people come to us troubled in spirit, and for some the Tarot helps."

"The Tarot?" he asked. "I've used that deck."

"Oh?" Her interest seemed genuine. "For what purpose?"

"For business, of course. I deal cards for a licensed gambling franchise. Those twenty-two trumps add luster to the game; people like the pictures, and of course there are special prizes."

"For gambling," she murmured sadly. "That is all you see in the Tarot?"

"Oh, no. After I'd worked with the cards for a while, I found they were fun for general entertainment, too. There are many games. Sometimes when I'm driving from one stand to another, like now, I put the car on auto and play solitaire." That established his own cover, for what it was worth. Not much, if they ran an employment check.

"We use them for meditation," she said. "The contemplation of a single Arcanum, or a group of Arcana, can bring special insights, well worth the effort. I never really understood my purpose in life until I meditated with the guidance of the Tarot. We also study the deck as a whole, analyzing the distinctions between individual cards, and between the concepts of different experts. Whole separate philosophies are revealed, leading to insights on the nature of human thought."

Paul smiled. "Interesting how one deck can have four different uses," he observed. "Meditation and study for you, business and entertainment for me. A purpose for every person."

"True," she agreed with a small, fetching smile of

242

resignation. "I wish I had my Tarot with me. But the deprogrammers took it away, calling it a crutch."

Paul did have his deck with him, but decided not to mention that. There was yet another use of the Tarot, he remembered: character reading or divination, and that could be unnervingly accurate. He did not believe in the supernatural (except as it might relate to the limited area of inexplicable runs of luck, good or bad), but he was not about to risk any analysis of his character through the Tarot. Besides that, his prints and sweat were all over that deck; a policewoman could take a sample or sliver from one card and give the laboratory enough to indentify him readily. It had been a mistake to give her his name, but he could change that. It was a mistake to keep talking to her; she might be recording his voice through some hidden device. (A bracelet? No, she wore no jewelry. But women had so many secret places . . .) Regardless, he was getting to like her too well. She might be a religious nut, but there was an odd appeal to her philosophy. That could mean either that this Order of Vision really was a sensible organization, or that this policewoman had done her homework extremely well.

Enough. He had to act—now.

Paul put the car on auto and removed his hands from the wheel. He turned to her, smiling somewhat crookedly. "I guess you know why I picked you up," he said, forcing a leer. A woman with a body like hers had to have encountered this expression many times before, and had to recognize it instantly.

Sister Beth's eyes widened. She did not pretend to misunderstand. "Oh, Mr. Cenji, I—I hoped it wouldn't be that way. You seemed so nice."

Paul felt like a complete heel. But he had to do it, or she would finish him. He had to play the part of the callous male who had nothing on his mind but sex. This was not really far from the mark; any man near to this girl would react similarly, differing only in the manner he expressed it. He was being purposely crude, and hating it, for if by some freak she was what she claimed to be, a gentle, circuitous approach just might land her. "I *am* nice. Give me a try."

She shrank back as far as the crashproof seat permitted. Her bosom heaved within the seat's embrace. "I don't have the strength to resist you, but at the Order we prefer chastity before marriage."

Marriage? Hell! He took hold of her arm, drawing her in for a kiss as the seats leveled out in response to his pressure, forming into a bed. Her lips trembled as his own lips touched them. "Please," she whispered. "Will you let me go? Nothing you could gain for yourself could match what you would take from me. Put me back on the highway; maybe I can get another ride before the police net closes."

That was exactly what he had wanted: her voluntary departure. It would mean he had fooled her, that she was satisfied he had no serious commitments—such as to mnem. Thus her time would be better spent baiting some other sucker, while that police net hung loose, waiting for her signal.

But now the touch of her aroused him. Disheveled and frightened as she seemed, she remained a compelling figure of a young woman. He could force her; he was sure of that. She might be a policewoman, but he was trained in physical combat himself. A wrist-twist would keep her hand from her weapon, wherever it was, and make her submit without physical struggle. Yes, he could do it. . . .

And she would know him for a mnemdict. It always showed, somehow, in the passion of lovemaking. All addicts and dealers were agreed on that, and he had been spotted himself once that way. The woman in that case had had no intention of turning him in, but she had adamantly refused to enlighten him on what had given him away. "Women have secrets," she had murmured smugly. Men had them too, but he had never been able to spot another mnemdict. Probably with further experience—but he was drifting from the subject, as he did chronically. If "Sister Beth" were a police fishhook, sex would mean nothing to her; she would be right up on her a-preg, a-veedee, a-allergy shots. She probably intended to seduce him, by her most artful protests, and read the telltale traces then.

"I can drop you off right now," he said. He put his left hand on her smooth leg where the nightie was hiked up. This was very like the leg he had seen—where? When? But the translucent material made it more exciting than full exposure would have been. The leg was classic, like the rest of her. Suddenly the sexual compulsion was almost overpowering. Maybe it would be *worth* betrayal. . . .

"Please do," she whispered. He could see the cloth over her bosom shaking with the force of her elevated heartbeat. Of course she protested; that was part of the role. Her excitement could even be genuine because she was on the verge of nailing him. What normal man could resist as delectable a morsel as this, so provocatively packaged and with such an ingenious story? A girl fleeing deprogramming, ready to do anything for a private ride, unable to protest even rape, lest she be erased by the drug. A decent law-abiding citizen would turn her in; a soft-hearted one would give her a ride to her Station. A callous or criminal one would take advantage of her.

Paul was none of these. Not precisely. Now he was

about to prove that. He twisted around to touch the STOP key, and the car slowed, picked its way out of the traffic flow, and came to a stop at the roadside. The seats elevated to normal sitting posture and released their clasps. "Goodbye," Paul said.

Sister Beth looked at him with surprise and something else. "I'm sorry I wasn't what you expected," she said, then quickly got out. "God bless you, Mr. Cenji."

God bless you. Those unfamiliar words struck him with peculiar impact. Even to him, the brutalizer, she gave her prayer. Was she, after all, genuine?

The door closed. Automatically he punched DRIVE, and the car glided forward, still guiding itself. Paul turned in the seat to peer back at her.

Forlorn and lovely, Sister Beth was standing on the gravel shoulder, the wind tugging at her hair and gown. Paul felt a wrenching urge to go back to pick her up again, and to hell with the consequences; there was always the chance she was legitimate.

Then he saw a traffic hoverer descending toward her. The police had spotted her, and might spot *him* if he didn't lose himself in a hurry. He merged with the flow and sweated it out. Probably she had a homing signal, so her employers could always locate her. He had had a narrow escape.

Yet, unbidden, he repeated her words. "God bless you." He believed neither in God nor in Sister Beth, but the power of that unexpected benediction had shaken him.

Paul completed the trip uneventfully and delivered the car. He waited in the plush office for his payment—in the form of a boosted credit rating that would gain him unofficial but valuable privileges in a number of legitimate businesses, and of course his renewal supply of mnem, concealed in the hollow tines of his pocket comb. It took the warehouse a little while to unload the car and verify the potency and purity of the stock and make sure no police were tracing the vehicle. As soon as they had satisfied themselves in a businesslike manner about these things, they would settle with him. It was a most professional operation.

In fact, the whole black-market mnem industry was professional—more so than many legitimate enterprises. Paul had gotten into it gradually, his philosophy of life bending in small increments to accommodate the needs of an expanding lifestyle. He had left college with a liberal arts degree, but had found no suitable employment. Clever with his hands, he had used them to do tricks with cards. That had led him into contact with legitimate gambling interests. One of the popular games, not really gambling but more of a warmup for those not ready to take the full plunge, was said to be a medieval revival, *Tarocchi*, using the seventy-eight-card Tarot deck instead of the fifty-three-card standard deck. The Joker of the regular deck had been expanded into twenty-two trumps for the Tarot, basically. He had adapted that deck to other games, partly luck and partly skill. A really sharp memory decreased the former factor and increased the latter, which had led him to mnem. A casino, irritated by his penchant for winning, had attempted to have him summarily bounced. That had been their mistake, for Paul was more nearly professional in his unarmed combat than in his gambling. The casino manager, no dummy, had quickly changed tactics and bought Paul off with a job. Now Paul was well set, so long as he rocked no jetboats.

God bless you. . . .

The news was on the video outlet. Suddenly an item caught his attention: "A young woman committed suicide last night by flinging herself from a police craft," the announcer said. "She has been identified as Sister Beth, for the past year a resident at a station of a religious cult, the Holy Order of Vision. Apparently she was depressed over the prospect of drug-assisted deprogramming necessitated by her theft of jewelry. . . ."

"She didn't steal those jewels!" Paul exclaimed, then caught himself, feeling foolish. A picture flashed on the screen. It was the girl he had picked up, almost exactly as he had seen her last, her translucent nightgown resisting the wind. Even robocameras had a sharp eye for detail, especially when it was associated with something genuinely morbid, such as death.

"She seemed so quiet," a uniformed police officer was saying apologetically. "I never thought she'd pull a stunt like that, or I'da cuffed her." He tapped the handcuffs hanging like genitalia at his crotch.

Paul felt disbelief. It *couldn't* be her; he had seen her only yesterday. She had been a police hooker with a sharp cover. Then he felt anger. How could this have happened? Why hadn't the police taken proper care of her? But even if they had, she would be just as dead, with her complete memory erased.

Could it be part of the set-up? No, that made no sense; no policewoman would blow her cover by such a newsflash, even a faked death. Her picture would alert her potential victims to the threat. She was too memorable, with that lush body, that innocent face. Man's dream of heaven! She *had* to be legitimate— and therefore dead.

Why hadn't he believed her, believed *in* her, when it had counted? He knew why; he was cynical about

248

the legitimacy of any religious association. He had listened to the incredibly selfish appeals of religious messages: Support Us, Give Us Credit, so that You will go to Heaven and Live Forever in Bliss, Free from Sin. That sort of thing. How anyone could have simultaneous bliss and freedom from sin was a mystery to him.

Yet Sister Beth had seemed different, as though she really believed in the particular salvation she sought. She had not invoked Heaven once. If only he had paid attention to her words as well as to her body!

But if she had really been a Sister, why hadn't her God protected her? Surely He would have struck some bargain with the authorities. He would have arranged it somehow, fixing it so she would recover. It was only necessary to have faith. . . .

Paul had no faith. He was the cause of her demise. He had attacked her sexually and dumped her back on the roadside. They had been watching for her, and zeroed in rapidly.

If he had only trusted her as she had trusted him. He could so easily have delivered her safely to her Station. There had been too little decency in his recent life. He had been given the opportunity to help a better human being than himself, and instead he had—

"Sir, your account has been verified," the secretary informed him dulcetly.

Paul looked at her, and for a moment saw the image of Sister Beth. Something horrible boiled up inside him, a depression verging on violence. But what could he do? This was only an ordinary secretary, a conformist shell covering a formless soul, not worth even his passing attention. *Sister Beth was already dead*.

Paul stood with abrupt and terrible decision. "I am

closing my account," he said. "All prior dealings shall be canceled without prejudice and forgotten."

She never flinched. Why should she? She was flesh and blood, with the mind of a robot. "This will have to be approved by the front office," she said.

"Fuck the front office." He whirled and walked out.

Outside, the reality of what he had done struck him. In the language of this business, he had informed the drug magnates that he was quitting, that he expected no severance pay, and would not talk to the police. He was through with mnem.

Unfortunately, he was now in trouble. He would no longer have the perquisites of his secondary employment—and that meant his lifestyle would suffer. His primary employment at the casino would rapidly suffer too, for he was out of mnem and would soon feel the effects of withdrawal.

It was a good evening at the casino. The clients were present in force, and free with their credit. Paul took his stint at the blackjack table, dealing the cards with the dispatch of long experience. His responses to the clients' calls were automatic, while his thoughts were elsewhere. "Hit me." He dealt that man an extra card. *Why did Sister Beth do it?* "Hit me." He gave the lady one too. She had a peek-a-boo decolletage, but today he wasn't interested. *If only I had known!* He hit her again, noting the jellylike quiver of one breast as she reached for the card. With increasing age, such jelly either liquified or solidified, and this was beginning to age. Sister Beth's breast would have quivered true. *Sister Beth could have been the one.* Not sensational and cheap and fading, like this gambling addict.

The routine became interminable. He had suddenly lost all zest for it. Yet this was the way he earned his living, bringing in the house percentage. Where would he go from here?

"I cry foul!" a gravelly voice said, cutting into Paul's reverie. "He's dealing seconds!"

Dealing seconds: giving other players the second card in the pack, saving the top one for himself. One of the oldest and slickest devices in the arsenal of the mechanic, or slick dealer.

Paul's hands froze in place. All eyes were on the deck he held. The charge of cheating was serious. "The casino computer stores a record of every shuffled deck put into play," Paul said without rancor. There were established procedures to handle such charges, just as there were for the play. "Do you want the printout?"

"I don't care about the shuffle," the man snapped. He was tall, slender, and of indeterminate age. He did not look like the gambling type, but Paul had long since learned that there were no sure indicators. A person was the gambling type if he gambled; that was all. "It's the *dealing* that counts. You gave me an eight to put me over, saving the low card for yourself. I saw you! No wonder my luck's been bad."

"Select someone to handle the verification deck," Paul told him coldly. "I think we can satisfy you that the game is honest."

"No! You've got shills all over the place! *I'll* handle it!"

Paul nodded equably. If the man was honest, he would soon realize he had been mistaken. If he tried to frame Paul by misdealing himself, the computer record of the cards would catch him and discredit him. "Take the deck from the hopper and deal it out slowly, face up. The cards will match those I have dealt."

251

"Of *course* they will!" the man exclaimed angrily. "You dealt them, all right, but in what order? You got an advance printout, so you knew what cards were coming, and you—"

"We want you to be satisfied, sir," Paul said. But he saw that a rational demonstration would not satisfy this man. Was he a troublemaker from a rival casino? Paul touched the alarm button with his foot.

The casino's closed-circuit screen came on. "What's the problem?" the floor manager inquired, his gaze piercing even in the televised image.

"Accusation of dealing seconds," Paul said, nodding at the accuser.

The manager looked at the man. "We do not need to cheat, sir. The house percentage takes care of us. The verification deck will—"

"No!" the man said.

The manager grasped the situation. He was quick on the uptake; that was what *he* was paid for. His range of options was greater than Paul's, and he drew on them with cool nerve. "Play it again, Paul. Your way. Show him."

Paul smiled. His reins had just been loosened. "Here is the way it would have gone, had I been cheating," he said, taking the verification deck. "None of these replay hands is eligible for betting; this is a demonstration only." And the NEGATION sign lit.

He dealt the cards as he had before, to the same people in the same order. Miss Peek-a-boo was fascinated; this was the closest she had come to excitement all evening. This time Paul's hands worked their hidden magic; his own display always came up high, making the house a one hundred-percent winner. Yet it looked exactly as though it were an honest deal.

"We hire the best mechanics, so that they will not

be used against us," the manager said from the screen. Perhaps he was remembering the circumstances surrounding Paul's own hiring. "But our games are honest. We take twenty percent, and our records are open to public inspection. We have no need to cheat anyone, and no desire to, but we cannot afford to let anyone cheat *us,* either. Are you satisfied, sir? Or do you wish to force us to lodge a charge of slander against you?"

The manager was hitting hard! No charge of slander could stick, but with luck the client would not know that. The manager was showing how the professionals gambled, with nerve and flair.

Grudgingly the challenger turned away. The manager's eyes flicked toward Paul. "Take a break; the flow has been interrupted here." Client flow was important; people had to feel at ease as they moved from game to game and entertainment to entertainment, spending their credit. Client flow meant cash flow.

Paul closed down the table. Miss Peek-a-boo lingered, evidently toying with the notion of making a pass, but he ignored her rather pointedly. She shrugged and took her wares elsewhere.

But the irate gambler was not finished. He was a poor loser, through and through. He followed Paul— not too obviously, because he didn't want to be booted out of the casino, but not too subtly either.

Paul ambled past the ballroom area, where the decade of the seventies was in vogue at this hour; mildly dissonant groups of singers and instrumentalists performed on a raised stage, their emphasis on volume rather than finesse, while people danced singly and in pairs. A young woman in a tight-fitting costume sang into a microphone whose head and stem were compellingly phallic; she held it with both hands, close to her shaped bosom, and virtually mouthed it. Mikes, of course, had been superfluous in the seventies and since; the need being served was symbolic, not practical.

Paul glanced at his pursuer as he circled the stage. The man seemed indifferent to the presentation. Paul found a table at the side and sat down, forcing the man to sit at another table within range of the show, where the decibels were deafening. Loud noise had erotic appeal, of course; that was the secret. Those old-time singing groups had been notorious for their seductions, and perhaps the "groupies" who had so eagerly sought those seductions had not understood the basis of that appeal. Those who disliked sex were similarly turned off by the volume, without understanding why; their protestations that it was only "poor music" to which they objected were pitiful from the point of view of succeeding generations.

Naturally a waitress came immediately—a physical, human, female one, another period piece, rather than the efficient modern keyboard table terminal. "Vodka—straight," Paul told her, making a tiny motion with one hand to signal negation. She recognized him as an employee and nodded; in a moment she brought him pure water in a vodka glass. He proffered his credit card, and she touched it to her credit terminal, recording NO SALE. But none of this was evident to the client at the other table. The man had to buy a legitimate drink—and Paul suspected that he was a teetotaler. That kind tended to be. This was becoming fun.

The banjo player stepped forward on the stage for his solo stint, squatting low so that the swollen bulk of the instrument hung between his spread legs, with the neck angling forward and up at a forty-five-degree angle. His fingers jerked on the taut strings at his crotch while the instrument thrust up and down orgasmically, blasting out the sound. Paul smiled; they might not have been much for quality music in those days, but they had really animated their symbols!

At the other table, the client was averting his gaze, but the sound was striking at him mercilessly. Sure enough, he was a prude. The question was, why had he come to an establishment like this? Was he the agent of a rival casino? That seemed unlikely; he was too clumsy, and would not have bungled the blackjack challenge like that. Could he be an inspector from the feds, checking on possible cheating or other scalping of clients? Again, too clumsy. The days of readily identifiable government agents were long gone; the feds hired real professionals, like anyone else. Could he be someone from the mnem front, making sure Paul was not about to betray them?

No, the only thing that made sense was that he was a poor loser, looking for a way to get even. The man had not even dropped a large sum of credit; his loss was one of status, because he had been outbluffed by Paul and the management, as he should have anticipated. No amateur had a chance against the professionals. The games *were* honest, and any that were not would be too subtly rigged for a person like him to expose that way. Paul himself could win at blackjack without manipulating the cards at all, simply by keeping track of the cards played and hedging his bets according to the prospects for the remaining cards. Sometimes he shilled for the management by doing just that, demonstrating tangibly that the house could be beaten, drawing in many more clients. Of course it was his mnem-boosted memory that made this possible; the regular clients, as a class, could not beat the odds. Lucky individuals sometimes did, of course, but they were more than balanced by the unlucky ones.

That thought saddened him. He would not be able to do that anymore, beat the odds. He had given up a lot when he had quit mnem. Had it really been worth it?

He visualized a young woman falling from a cop-copter. Maybe the mnem backlash would wipe out *that* memory!

Paul finished his water and got up. The client followed. They walked past the wheel of fortune—and that reminded Paul of the Tarot. Key Ten was the Wheel of Fortune. Certainly these wheels uplifted the clients' fortunes—and dashed them down again! But the Tarot, in turn, reminded him again of Sister Beth of the Holy Order of Vision, the girl he had killed. Full circle, as the wheel of fortune turned. He could not escape himself. And that destroyed something in him.

Paul turned around. The man was right behind him. "What do you want?"

"I want my money back," the man said.

Paul brought out his credit card. "What are your losses?"

"Not that way. I want to *win* it back. I want to beat you."

What an idiot! "You can't beat me. I deal for the house; the percentage is with me, in the long run."

"I *can* beat you—playing man-to-man."

"All right," Paul agreed, desiring only to be rid of this nuisance. "Man-to-man. Name your game."

"Do you know Accordion?"

"I know it. I never lose, if it is played my way."

"Your way," the man agreed. His foolish, pointless pride was really driving him.

"The Tarot deck. Trumps half-wild."

"*Half*-wild?"

"Each of the twenty-two Trumps takes any suit card—but no Trump has a number, so it can't jump *to* any suit card. Trumps are passively wild; all they do is disappear."

"What if the last card's a Trump?"

Not entirely naive! "That one card's full-wild until designated. Then it freezes."

The man shook his head in wonder. "Half-wild Tarot Accordion!"

"Is the challenge still on?" Paul prodded him.

The man scowled. "Still on. Identical deals, separate cubes, cheat-meters on."

"Naturally," Paul agreed. "For the amount of your previous losses." This might be fun after all—and the mark had asked for it. "One game only," Paul said, to prevent rechallenges.

They went to the Accordion table. They sat in facing cubicles. The mechanical dealer dealt them identical layouts, but they could not see each other's plays.

Paul could almost always win an "open" Accordion game, because success depended largely on a player's memory of the cards he dealt. If he were allowed to see the order of the cards before play, on the printout screen, even for a single second, his mnem-enhanced memory made it seem as though the entire deck were laid out in a line. He could thus plan his strategy on a seventy-eight-card basis. But even in a "closed" game like this, where the fall of the cards was unknown, he could still do well, because as each card was played, his memory checked it off, and he had a better notion of what remained to be played. Thus, as with blackjack, his play got sharper in the later stages, while that of the average person did not.

But now Paul found himself in trouble. The mnem was fading from his system, so that he no longer had reliable eidetic recall. He was still a good player, long familiar with the strategies for aligning suits and numbers in potential chains so as to extend his options without giving away his position to his opponent, but he had not realized how much he now depended on his perfect memory. He felt naked without it, uncertain, weak. *He could lose*—and that bothered him far more than it should have. He had almost forgotten what it felt like to be a loser, and the prospect of returning to that status was not at all attractive. To lose on occasion during one's strength, as a result of the breaks, was one thing; to lose as the result of one's weakness was another. That was what had driven the other man.

Should he return to mnem? He could still do that, he knew. He would hardly be the first—or the tenth or the hundredth—person to try to drop mnem, and fail. The addiction was more subtle than that of physiological-dependence drugs. Some experts still refused to classify mnem as addictive at all. But those people were ivory-tower fools; addiction was more than a physical dependency, as cocaine users knew. A person's fundamental perception of self was involved; if he lost his memory, he lost his identity. That was Sister Beth's nemesis. So Paul could admit his error and go back and—

No! This was his penance for killing the innocent girl; it might not be rational, but it was final. He would live or die a free man—as she had sought to be free.

Meanwhile, he played. Seven of Cups on Five of Cups; Five of Wands on Tower Trump—oops, he had misplayed. He should have aligned the two fives—no, it didn't make a difference in this case. But he should at least have considered the fives before choosing the other option. On such decisions wins and losses were determined.

Paul moved on, concentrating his play more efficiently, matching suits and numbers to second or fourth piles down, condensing his spread in the fashion that gave this game its name. The frequent half-wild Trumps gave him valuable spacing, enabling him to keep the accordion contracted, but of course his opponent had the same advantage. And the man was pushing him, for in match-Accordion both players had to agree to the lay-down of each new card. Paul's opponent had evidently seen a play Paul had missed, and had his layout contracted one card smaller than Paul's, so that he could draw two or three cards while Paul's layout was hung up. He knew how to play competitive Accordion, all right! He had Paul on the ropes and knew it, and never let up. Try as he might, Paul could not regain the initiative.

The final card was a Trump: the High Priestess, ironically associated with memory. Memory—now his liability. Sure enough, she was reversed. The Tarot had uncanny ability to turn up significant associations! So now the Priestess was full-wild, ready to help him compress his spread impressively. But he had not anticipated this, simple as it would have been to count Trumps, and was able to knock off only two piles. He was left with eight piles: not a good score, for him.

Sure enough: his opponent had seven piles. Paul had lost. He scowled and brought out his credit card.

"No," the man said, becoming slightly magnanimous in victory. "Settle in private."

What did that mean? An exchange of credit was inherently *un*private; it became a matter of instant

259

record in the broadest computer network in the world. So the man did not want money. But the bet had been for money; Paul was not obliged to make any other type of payment.

He shrugged. They left the casino. In the street the man began talking, softly and rapidly. "You are a mnem addict on crash-cure. I am a federal drug agent. Your credit will be cut off soon, if it has not been already. That's why I kept you from making any credit transactions; we don't want anyone to know yet. You're in trouble. Turn state's evidence and we will guarantee that no one ever *will* know."

A federal narc! So deliberately clumsy that Paul had entirely misread him!

"I don't know what you're talking about," Paul said, knowing protest was useless.

"You carried a load that you delivered this morning for the cartel," the man insisted. "We've been watching you for six months, along with a hundred other addicts. We didn't nail you because we don't want *you*, we want the wheels. Your psych profile indicated you were one of our best prospects, because you're honest and intelligent; mnem is a dead end for you. Sooner or later you'd have to break with it, and you had the courage to carry through when you did. Something happened, triggering that break, and now you're out of it. Was it that female you turned in, that cult nut?"

"She was no cult nut!" Paul snapped. "She was a nice girl!"

"Very well, she was a nice girl, too unstable to sit still in a police copter. *Very* nice for us, because she must have done what we couldn't do, and set you up for your break with mnem. Her fanaticism infected you, maybe. She was a pretty girl, I hear. Now we're moving in on you because you're ready to turn against the wheels. With your help we can break this thing open, and close mnem down permanently."

"No," Paul said.

"I know you're off it; I saw the signs at blackjack. Your mind was drifting. I broke that game up and took you out of circulation before your casino employer caught on. It was worse in the Accordion game. You've lost your enhancement, and soon you'll suffer withdrawal lapses. Talk to me now; finger the wheels. Give me the data while you can still remember it, and we'll take care of you. There are counter-drugs we can use to ease the transition and protect much of your memory. My recorder is on. It's your only chance."

For a moment Paul was tempted. But he realized that this man was just as likely to be a mnem cartel agent as a fed narc. The cartel might be testing him, making sure he was keeping the faith. And he *had* to keep the faith, or he might be rapidly dead. "I don't know anything about it," he said. "Leave me alone."

"You can't make a living anymore," the narc (mnem agent?) insisted. "You're finished. We can help you if you'll help us. Right now—while you can."

Paul ducked into the crowd, leaving the man. He wove around and through knots of people until he had lost the narc. Soon he was on a different street. A huge nova-neon sign illuminated as his approach activated its mechanism: CHRIST=GUILT.

Paul smiled. Was this unintentional irony? One never could tell with religious cults. He passed under it and glanced back. From this side it said: SEX=SIN. No mistake, evidently; to many religionists, any form of pleasure was immoral, and no person could be holy

261

unless he felt guilty. Even in the joy of true faith, he had to feel guilt for that very emotion of joy.

Yet in some people it assumed an attractively demure quality, and there could be a certain allurement, the security of belonging. What was that one Sister Beth was in? The Holy Order of Vision. His memory had not failed! Maybe that was just another repressive cult, reacting to repressive society—but she had been one sweet girl. Why had she had to die?

Paul paused, feeling a kind of explosion in his chest. Heat erupted and spread out under his ribcage, a burning tide, slowly fading. Suddenly he understood what was popularly called heartbreak. There was no physical pain; the sensation was oddly pleasant. But something that had been subtly vital to him was gone, even as he realized its existence. In its place was—guilt.

There was a moment of confusion, then it was late afternoon and he was alone, entering a rundown building. It was unmarked, but everyone who had business here knew its name. It was the Dozens—the hangout of the disowned. More specifically, it was the expressly nonwhite enclave of an age when there was, by law, no societal discrimination based on race or creed. So this institution had no legal foundation. But neither did the mnem cartel. Legality deviated from fact, and no white person was foolish enough to set foot inside the Dozens.

Paul's presence caused an immediate stir. In moments, three husky men blocked his progress. One was the reddish hue of an almost full-blooded Amerind; another was Oriental; the third was black. "Maybe you just lost your way, snowball?" Black inquired softly.

A snowball was a hundred-percent white person,

and would not survive long in this colored hell. Paul dropped into a balanced crouch whose meaning could not be misinterpreted. "No." He refrained from using the counter-insult, "Pitchball."

"Mine," Yellow said. The two others gave way. The Oriental stood opposite Paul, standing naturally. "Karate?"

"Judo."

"Kodokan?"

"Ikyu," Paul replied.

"Nidan," Yellow said.

They bowed to each other, a stiff little motion from the waist. They had just identified their schools of martial arts and respective ranks. Yellow outranked Paul by two grades, and these grades were not casually acquired things; he was quite likely to tromp Paul in a normal match. Paul could fight Yellow if he wished, but he would not remain long on the Dozens premises. It would be better to desist from this approach. He had, at any rate, obtained his hearing, which was his purpose.

"I belong," Paul said. "I am one-eighth black. I'm a casino dealer, a skilled mechanic, and the feds are after me. Mnemdict." This was the one place where he would have nothing to fear from either fed or cartel; the Dozens took care of its own with fiendish efficiency, and its resources extended as far as nonwhite blood did. But first Paul had to gain admittance.

Yellow stepped back and Black came forward. "We can use a mechanic. But you're seven-eighths *white*." The tone made it an insult.

"Yes. My name is Paul Cenji. I was raised white. But you can verify my ancestry with the bureau of records."

Black produced a button transceiver. "Paul Cenji," he said into it.

In a moment it responded. "Twelve-point-five percent black. Three percent yellow. Trace admixture of other nonwhite. On the lam from fed and cartel this date."

Black studied him critically. "You are in trouble. Your body makes it, by the skin of your prick. But your soul is white."

"Try me," Paul said. He knew they would—and before they were through, the truth would be known.

Black spoke into his unit again. This was evidently no standard computer terminal; the Dozens had information more current and extensive than he had believed possible. They knew about his mnem complication and the federal man's offer already! And that three-percent Oriental ancestry; this was the first Paul had heard of that. It must derive from somewhere in his white component; he had not checked that out as thoroughly as the black. "Karrie."

In another moment a brown-skinned girl about six years of age joined them. Black gave way to her with a certain formal courtesy reminiscent of the martial arts practice. What was developing?

The child gazed at Paul with open contempt. She had a slightly crooked lip that lent itself admirably to a sneer. "Know the dozens?" she asked.

She was not referring to this building. Not directly. Disconcerted, Paul raised his hands in partial negation. "I know it some—but not with women or children."

"Then haul your white ass home," the girl said.

Paul stared at her. He *did* know the "dirty dozens," or contests in insult, a typically black form of ordeal. Black humor, in a very special sense. The name of this club derived from it. This was a most appropriate challenge; if he could beat the house champion, he would prove the blackness of his soul, for Whites seldom competed and were not good at this. He had come prepared. But he had thought of it strictly as man-to-man. This man-vs.-female-child situation was extremely awkward.

Yet this was the way they had set it up. If he wanted to join the club, he would have to perform.

He focused on the child, Karrie. She had demonstrated her readiness to fight with shocking directness. This was as real an encounter as the prospective judo match with Yellow, and rather more to the point. Little Karrie had invited him to depart with an unkind reference to the color of his ass. He had to refute this, turning the insult on his opponent, and rhyme it if he could.

"I'll haul ass home/when you learn to use a comb," he said—and was immediately disgusted with himself. He had gotten the refutation and rhyme, but it was a pretty weak attack. A girl her age would use a comb—if she chose to. Often it was a point of pride to need no comb, or to borrow one from a male companion. So he hadn't really scored. He had merely entered the lists.

She snapped right back: "I'll take that comb/and jam it through your chrome." She paused, then struck hard: "With foam."

This was no innocent, despite her age! Chrome generally reflected white, not black. Foaming agents were still used by minority groups for prophylactic purposes. Score a couple of points for her; she had adapted his concept to his disadvantage.

"If your mama had put foam *in*, you'd never have come *out*," he told her. No rhyme—but the insult was

265

stronger: the suggestion that she had been an accidental, unwanted baby. It was hard to put it all together, relevance, rhyme, and insult, without time for thought. But that was what made it such a challenge. Even many blacks could not perform well at the dozens, lacking the ready wit. If he could handle it, it would more than compensate for the marginal quality of his genetic score. Now, too late, he thought of the rhyme: "you'd never have *been*."

A crowd was gathering. This was their kind of entertainment. Not all of them were against him; he was beginning to prove himself by fighting dozens-style, and a number of them were light-skinned blacks like himself. A dozen or so. A pun, perhaps; the dozens had nothing to do with the figure twelve. It derived from a white expression applying to stunning or stupefying. If he won this contest, he would have instant friends, and his future would be feasible, if not absolutely secure. "Good shot," one murmured.

Stung, Karrie came back viciously: "Your ma's foam squirted out/when she fucked that white lout."

"Reversed," one spectator commented with professional acumen. He meant she had taken Paul's insult and applied it to *him*, reinforced by rhyme and another racial reference. Those "white" shots were hurting him, here!

He had to take off the gloves. He could not afford to think of Karrie as either female or child; she was the enemy, out to destroy him. "That was no lout, that was her man. *Your* ma got two bucks for baring her can."

There was a smattering of applause. Paul had topped her verse with his own, implying that her mother was a prostitute. The mother was always the target of choice in such contests, the vulnerability of every living person. "Two bucks!" someone muttered appreciatively. That figure had been traditional half a century ago; now it denoted impossible cheapness, barely the price of the required shot of foam—which improved the quality of the gibe. He was hitting his stride now, after a shaky start.

The girl felt the thrust and knew she had been wounded. Maybe she *was* the accidental child of a prostitute. The insults were not intended to be accurate reflections on one's opponent, but if one struck close enough to home to make a person lose his composure, he was also losing the contest. "Get out of here, seven-eighths ball!" she screamed. "Go back to your ma's lily-white cunt!"

"Hoo!" someone exclaimed admiringly. Losing ground, Karrie had struck hard indeed, producing a marvelous eight-ball pun on his white ancestry, and calling him a motherfucker. That was close to the ultimate insult, almost impossible to top in the normal course of the game, and in this case he was unable to reply in kind. *She* could not convincingly be called a motherfucker. He realized now that the match had been weighted against him; some prime insults did not apply to females or children. Karrie presented a disconcertingly small target.

Still, he was warmed up now, and not out of it by any means. "My ma's in Africa; I never saw her cunt./And it's none of your business, you little black runt."

No comment from the gallery. Paul had defended himself aptly enough, but had not taken the attack to her. He had lost the initiative.

Karrie sensed victory. She went for the kill. "Her ass is in Africa so she can see/how to get the cure for your pa's veedee."

Making him the child of venereal disease. How was he to top that?

Suddenly it came to him: the irrefutable implication, utterly dastardly. The fecal connection! "When your pa fucked your ma, he missed the slit;/he peed up her ass and didn't quit;/and you came out as brown as shit." A triple rhyme, yet!

Karrie stared at him, defeated, unable to respond. He had really nailed her, making her the spawn of urine and defecation. But there was no applause from the audience; all stood in stony silence.

Then he realized: he had won the dozens, but lost his objective. For he had by implication likened *all* brown people to feces, and yellow people to urine, including his own nonwhite components. In his heat to win, he had let the means justify the end, and so destroyed the value of that end. Only a white soul would have conceived and executed that insult.

Once again, he had grasped salvation—and discovered a turd.

It seemed only a moment before it happened. He found himself standing in the street, wondering where he was going. He knew that hours had passed, for now the city's shadows were long, and he was hungry. The mnem was draining from his system, and he had no replacement; his memory was going. He must have suffered a blackout; the drug was like that. Sometimes the fading was perceptible; at other times it was in chunks.

He smelled shit. And he knew. This was the Animation that revealed his inner worth, the sources of his feculence. The woman Amaranth had played the part of Sister Beth—but the memory was genuine. He had murdered an innocent girl, ten years ago. Or nine, or eight. Mnem had shrouded his memory, and now Animation had brought it back, his dirtiest secret. He was worthless.

A window lighted. He stood before a residential building, and the shade was not drawn on this ground-level aperture, or else he was up on a fire escape, snooping. It wasn't clear, and it didn't matter. He peered in, and saw Therion standing naked while the girl squatted, clothed, in the corner. Call her Amaranth, call her Light, call her Sister Beth or a cartel secretary or an anonymous casino waitress; she was Everygirl, the focus of man's eye and penis. This was the castle of discovery of human interrelations.

Something nagged him about the positioning of the two in the room. It was the same room he had shared with them, and he understood why he himself was absent, because now he was out here looking in, seeing it all from another perspective. But he had made love to her in the center, not the corner. And she had been nude, not clothed. Here it was Therion who was in the center, naked.

Now Paul heard Therion's voice: "Stab your demoniac smile to my brain; soak me in cony-ack, cunt, and cocaine." And the paunchy man pushed out his flabby rear.

The smell of shit became overpowering. Paul's gorge rose; he tried to suppress it, but could not. He turned away from the window, teetering vertiginously over the abyss of the alley. Vomit spewed out of his mouth and nose, heave after heave, brown in this light, trailing yellow strings of mucus that would not let go. Yet even so, he smelled the shit.

The dart, imperfectly thrown in the dark, struck his belt and was turned aside. The needle had not penetrated his flesh, by sheer chance and the motion of his heaving body. But Paul clapped his hand to his flank and cried out as if in pain.

A man emerged from the shadows. "Nothing personal about this," he said. "I guess you thought you could just quit the cartel, and in a few days you wouldn't remember nothing about it anyway."

Paul realized he had suffered another memory lapse. Now it was full night, and the vomit stains on his shirt were dry; the smell of shit was faint. What had he done in the intervening hours? He had no notion; mnem had taken that away, as cleanly as the knife took away the infant's foreskin. The dart had jogged him into full awareness, though; he knew its significance. The survival instinct was more basic than these routine events; all his faculties were being marshalled to meet this threat. The dart bore an anesthetic, to make his body lethargic and uncoordinated so that he could be conveniently dispatched. It had happened to others he knew.

"Now you just come along with me," the man said, unaware that the dart had missed and that he faced an alert, dangerous man. "A nice little ride. See, if you turned up with a mnem-wash, the police'd pick you up in no time and check you out, and then they'd know you was an addict. And that'd be bad nuts for us all. So we can't afford for them to find you. Ever." He reached for Paul's shoulder.

Paul put up his right arm to ward him off, forearm to forearm. He spun to the right, stretching the man out, overbalancing him, then closed his right hand around the man's right, his fingers grasping the knife-edge of the man's hand. Paul turned under his own arm as if doing a figure in a minuet. As he completed his turn, his two hands were gripping the man's arm, bending the wrist cruelly. He applied leverage.

With an exclamation of surprise and pain, the man went down. As well he might; had he resisted, his arm would have been wrenched out of joint. A child could bring down a 180-kilogram sumo wrestler with this hold.

Paul twisted the man's arm, forcing him to lie facedown on the pavement. He picked up the fallen dart and jabbed it into the flesh of the man's exposed neck. He waited a few seconds until the man relaxed, then let go and stepped back. The man did not get up. "Nothing personal, friend," Paul said, adding, "God bless you." He walked away.

So now he knew what should have been obvious before: the cartel would not let him quit. His life was in peril, regardless of the fate of his mind. He would have to hide, before the next goon squad caught up with him. Or the feds.

She was a fortune-teller of the age-old school: a woman of indeterminate years and large, dark eyes, wearing a long gown decorated with enigmatic symbols, seated in a curtained, gloom-shrouded compartment, at a table with a genuinely faked crystal ball. Modern technology had insinuated itself into the act. The crystal contained an illuminated holograph of a twilight landscape, with a full moon rising over gnarled oaks.

"Your card," she murmured.

"No, I—have no card," Paul said. He knew his credit had been cut off, and even attempted use of his card would alert his pursuers to his whereabouts. It had been a great hour for the technocracy when credit had become universal, for every person had to spend to live, and when he spent he was identified. Convenience had increased, but freedom had suffered.

The fear that Sister Beth had expressed, of being caught through the computer system, was now his own fear.

Sister who? Pursuit? Was he in some sort of trouble? He couldn't remember.

"Money, then," she said with resignation. Physical cash was an uncertain tool; it was too easy to counterfeit, and it offered no inherent proof of identity. But a fortune-teller couldn't be choosy.

Paul delved into a pocket and came up with what small change he had: two fifty-dollar bills and a twenty-five. He laid them on the table beside the crystal ball.

She sighed. It wasn't enough—but again, she was constrained to accept what she could get. This was evidently a slow day. "Sit down."

Paul sat. "I don't know why I'm here," he said.

"We shall find out." She looked into the crystal, and the holograph changed, becoming a swirl of colors. That was the thing about multiple-facet holography: the slightest motion of the globe changed the viewing angle, bringing out a new image. But this could be tricky, because the three-dimensional effect suffered if the shift occurred on the vertical plane between the two eyes, making different pictures. There had to be some leeway. Generally the facet-lines were horizontal, so that both eyes showed the same view, and the ball was rotated on a horizontal axis. The colors spiraled hypnotically, and Paul knew it, but didn't care.

"You are confused, tired, hungry, alone," the fortune-teller said. "You need help, but do not know how or where to seek it."

Paul nodded. "Programming," he said, in a small

flash of memory. "Deprogramming—must escape—drug—"

Her eyes narrowed slightly. "Let me have your hand."

Paul put out his hand. She turned it palm upward and studied the lines. "Mixed type, unclassifiable, but with indications of psychic gifts," she said, reading as if from a text. "Long Line of Life, broken . . ." She paused, looking very closely. "But there is a faint Line of Mars. And a fork at the lower end." She looked up, her eyes meeting his. "You have a long life ahead, but soon—even now—an accident or a very serious illness. You will survive, but in changed form. Your life will never be the same as before, and you will live and die in a country or manner alien to your birth."

"Quite likely," Paul agreed.

"Clear Line of the Head, rising from the Mount of Jupiter, tangent to the Line of Life, branching to the Mount of the Moon. You have an exceptionally powerful intellect and strong ambition, and will succeed through imagination and psychic awareness."

"At the moment I seem to have failed," Paul said.

"Your hand knows better than your mind," she assured him. "You may be in flux at the moment, but you have formidable powers." She returned to the hand. "The Line of the Heart rises between the Mounts of Jupiter and Saturn. You have the capacity for both idealistic and passionate love—and that love is exceptionally strong." She looked into his eyes again. "In fact, you are a most attractive man. I could make you an offer . . ." She shrugged, letting her shawl slide down to expose her bosom. Amaranth, in a new role, turning on her sex appeal again.

"I just want to know my future," he said.

She sighed. "Line of Fate—very short, not rising at

273

all until the middle of the palm, then well-marked and forked. You have had an extremely difficult early life, but will win success through your own efforts, especially through your imagination. The Line of Fortune, clear and sharp across the Mount of Apollo. You will have good fortune and contentment in the later years of your life."

"Aren't you just telling me what I want to hear?" Paul demanded. "I don't *want* to hear what I want to hear! I mean—what *do* I mean?"

"I am telling you what your own hand tells me," she insisted. "Would you prefer another mode? The Tarot—"

"No, not the Tarot!"

"I Ching?"

Paul didn't know what that was, at this stage of his life, so he was suspicious. "No."

"Then the ouija board."

Paul had bad associations with that; he regarded it as a child's game, not to be taken seriously. "No."

"Then it will have to be astrology."

Paul rose, confused and disturbed. "No. I don't want to know any more! I just want . . ." But he could not continue, because he did not know what he wanted, other than relief from—what? Some terrible feeling . . .

"Or divination by dreams," she suggested. "Or the tea leaves. Or by the forehead—you have a very expressive forehead, with good lines of Saturn and Jupiter."

But Paul was moving out, fleeing her. He knew there were a hundred or a thousand modes of divination, and they might all be valid, but just now he was afraid of his future and wanted to avoid it.

274

Dawn. His legs were weary, one arm was bruised, and dust and dried vomit filmed his clothing. He was hungry and sleepy, but he couldn't sleep. He must have been running all night, wearing himself out, and now he had no memory of it and no knowledge of where he was. He must have had to fight again, and he knew he was not safe yet. But where could he go?

Where had he *been* going, during his lapse? He must have been conscious and thinking, and he was not stupid. Maybe he had figured out a good hiding place, and was almost there—if only he could remember. But maybe he could figure it out again; maybe he had already figured it out half a dozen times in the course of the night, and made further progress toward it each time before lapsing out.

Oooff! He stumbled forward. Then the slow pain started. He saw the brick bounce on the pavement. It had hit him on the back of the head, but it hadn't knocked him out. He staggered, feeling his consciousness waning; the mnem withdrawal was complicating it, making his brain react inadequately. He put out a hand to brace himself against a brick wall.

Children emerged from alcoves, carrying scrounged weapons. A sub-teen gang, out for thrills, money, and maybe a fat commission from a bootleg organ bank. Artificial blood and organs made natural ones unnecessary, but some patients insisted on the genuine article. Lungs, kidneys, and livers fetched excellent prices if they were fresh and healthy, and his own were.

Paul tried to organize himself to flee, but he had trouble remembering *why* he was fleeing or what the immediate threat was. Deprogramming—was that it? No, that was the girl, Sister Who, and she was dead, and he had killed her, and a strange man had defecated on her face, and what could he do now to bring her back? He was guilty of persecuting an innocent person, and he had to pay—the penalty had to fit the crime. Christ equaled guilt. *He* had to be sacrificed to the inanities of this society—a tooth for a tooth, a life for a life, shit for shit—yet that was capital punishment, and she didn't like that—

"Now, that isn't nice," a gentle voice said.

Abashed, the children faded into the crannies from which they had issued. A strange young man took Paul's arm, supporting him. "Come, sir, I fear you are injured. We can help you."

"No, no," Paul protested weakly. "I have somewhere to go—"

"You are bleeding from the head, you are dead tired, filth-encrusted, and—" the man paused, examining him sharply. "You have the aspect of a mnemdict in the throes of sudden withdrawal. You are in trouble, sir."

"Can't remember," Paul said. "Who—"

"I am Brother John of the Holy Order of Vision," the man said. "We understand mnem addiction; we can help you. Trust us."

The Holy Order of Vision! *That* was where he had been headed! And he had almost made it, before lapsing out. But what would they do when they learned of his part in the death of Sister Beth? For he would have to tell them. Before he forgot his guilt.

Guilt! That was the thing pursuing him! How could he ever escape it?

"You can't help me," he said. "My life is shit. My innermost self—my soul—is a steaming turd. Worthless. Don't soil your hands on me."

Brother John neither flinched nor scowled. "Fecal matter is the raw material for compost," he said. "A vital stage in the cycle of renewal. Soil, the fundament; without it, most life on this and any other planet would soon stifle and become extinct. There must be death and rebirth, and between them is the soil. Your soul serves God's purpose there, and there need be no shame in that."

No shame! If only he could believe that! Still, the other matter, the death of— "I can't."

Brother John held out a deck of cards. "Will the Tarot help?"

Bemused, Paul took a card at random. He turned it up. It was the Eight of Wands: eight sprouting poles flying through the air, coming to rest on the ground. Their force was spent. "My force is spent," Paul repeated.

"Because you are swiftly approaching your goal, your true desire?" Brother John inquired.

His goal. Suddenly it was as though a great light shone about him, blindingly. Paul knew what he had to do.

"Do not stare into the morning sun, sir," Brother John cautioned him. "That will injure your eyes."

But that didn't matter. What was physical sight, compared to the phenomenal revelation he was experiencing? He had persecuted and taken the life of a member of the Holy Order of Vision; he must return a life to that Order. His own life. There had been death; there would be renewal. Between them was the soil. His soul.

He had found—home. "God bless you, Brother," Paul said.

Appendix
ANIMATION TAROT

The Animation Tarot deck of concepts as recreated by Brother Paul of the Holy Order of Vision consists of thirty Triumphs roughly equivalent to the twenty-two Trumps of contemporary conventional Tarot decks, together with five variously tilted suits roughly equivalent to the four conventional suits plus Aura. Each suit is numbered from one through ten, with the addition of four "Court" cards. The thirty Triumphs are represented by the table of contents of this novel, and keys to their complex meanings and derivations are to be found within the applicable chapters. For convenience the Triumphs are presented below, followed by a tabular representation of the suits, with their meanings or sets of meanings (for upright and reversed fall of the cards); the symbols are described by the italicized words. Since the suits are more than mere collections of concepts, five essays relating to their fundamental nature follow the chart.

No Animation Tarot deck exists in published form at present. Brother Paul used a pack of three-by-five-inch file cards to represent the one hundred concepts, simply writing the meanings on each card and sketching the symbols himself, together with any other notes he found pertinent. These were not as pretty or convenient as published cards, but were satisfactory for divination, study, entertainment, business and meditation as required. A full discussion of each card and the special conventions relating to the Animation deck would be too complicated to cover here, but those who wish to make up their own decks and use them should discover revelations of their own. According to Brother Paul's vision of the future, this deck will eventually be published, perhaps in both archaic (Waldens) and future (Cluster) forms, utilizing in the first case medieval images and in the second case images drawn from the myriad cultures of the Galactic Cluster, circa 4500 A.D. It hardly seems worthwhile for interested persons to wait for that.

	NATURE	SCIENCE	FAITH	TRADE	ART
1	Do *Scepter*	Think *Sword*	Feel *Cup*	Have *Coin*	Be *Lemniscate*
2	Ambition Drive *Torch*	Health Sickness *Scalpel*	Quest Dream *Grail*	Inclusion Exclusion *Ring*	Soul Self *Aura*
3	Grow Shrink *Tree*	Intelligence Curiosity *Maze*	Bounty Windfall *Cornucopia*	Gain Loss *Wheel*	Perspective Experience *Holograph*
4	Leverage Travel *Lever*	Decision Commitment *Pen*	Joy Sorrow *Pandora's Box*	Investment Inheritance *Gears*	Information Literacy *Book*
5	Innovation Suspicion *Hand of Glory*	Equilibrium Stasis *Kite*	Security Confinement *Lock*	Permanence Evanescence *Pentacle*	Balance Judgment *Scales*
6	Advance Retreat *Bridge*	Freedom Restraint *Balloon*	Temptation Guilt *Bottle*	Gift Theft *Package*	Change Stagnation *Möbius Strip*
7	Effort Error *Ladder*	Peace War *Plow*	Promise Threat *Ship*	Defense Vulnerability *Shield*	Beauty Ugliness *Face*
8	Power Impotence *Rocket*	Victory Defeat *Flag*	Satisfaction Disappointment *Mirror*	Success Failure *Crown*	Conscience Ruthlessness *Yin-Yang*
9	Accomplishment Conservation *Trophy*	Truth Error *Key*	Love Hate *Klein Bottle*	Wealth Poverty *Money*	Light Dark *Lamp*

SUIT CARDS (Continued)

NATURE	SCIENCE	FAITH	TRADE	ART
Hunger *Phallus*	Survival *Seed*	Reproduction *Womb*	Dignity *Egg*	Image *Compost*
ENERGY	GAS	LIQUID	SOLID	PLASMA

COURT CARDS

	NATURE	SCIENCE	FAITH	TRADE	ART
PAGE	Child of Fire	Child of Air	Child of Water	Child of Earth	Child of Aura
KNIGHT	Youth of Work	Youth of Trouble	Youth of Love	Youth of Money	Youth of Spirit
QUEEN	Lady of Activity	Lady of Conflict	Lady of Emotion	Lady of Status	Lady of Expression
KING	Man of Nature	Man of Science	Man of Faith	Man of Trade	Man of Art
	ENERGY	GAS	LIQUID	SOLID	PLASMA

TRIUMPHS

0 Folly (Fool)
1 Skill (Magician)
2 Memory (High Priestess)
∞ Unknown (Ghost)
3 Action (Empress)
4 Power (Emperor)
5 Intuition (Hierophant)
6 Choice (Lovers)
7 Precession (Chariot)
8 Emotion (Desire)
9 Discipline (Strength)
10 Nature (Family)
11 Chance (Wheel of Fortune)
12 Time (Sphinx)
13 Reflection (Past)
14 Will (Future)

15 Honor (Justice)
16 Sacrifice (Hanged Man)
17 Change (Death)
18 Vision (Imagination)
19 Transfer (Temperence)
20 Violence (Devil)
21 Revelation (Lightning-Struck Tower)
22 Hope/Fear (Star)
23 Deception (Moon)
24 Triumph (Sun)
25 Reason (Thought)
26 Decision (Judgment)
27 Wisdom (Savant)
28 Completion (Universe)

NATURE

The Goddess of Fertility was popular in spring. Primitive peoples believed in sympathetic magic: that the examples of men affect the processes of nature—that human sexuality makes the plants more fruitful. To make sure nature got the message, they set up the Tree of Life, which was a giant phallus, twice the height of a man, pointing stiffly into the sky. Nubile young women capered about it, singing and wrapping it with bright ribbons. This celebration settled on the first day of May, and so was called May Day, and the phallus was called the Maypole. The modern promotion of May Day by Communist countries has led to its decline in the Western world, but its underlying principle remains strong. The Maypole is the same Tree of Life found in the Garden of Eden, and is represented in the Tarot deck of cards as the symbol for the Suit of Nature: an upright rod formed of living, often sprouting wood. This suit is variously titled Wands, Staffs, Scepters, Batons, or, in conventional cards, Clubs. Life permeates it; it is the male principle, always ready to grow and plant its seed. It also relates to the classic "element" of Fire, and associates with all manner of firearms, rockets, and explosives. In religion, this rod becomes the scepter or crozier, and it can also be considered the measuring rod of faith, the "canon."

FAITH

The true source of the multiple legends of the Grail is unknown. Perhaps this famous chalice was originally a female symbol used in pagan fertility rites, a counterpart to the phallic Maypole. But it is best known in Christian mythology as the goblet formed from a single large emerald, from which Jesus Christ drank at the Last Supper. It was stolen by a servant of Pontius Pilate, who washed his hands from it when the case of the presumptuous King of the Jews came before him. When Christ was crucified, a rich Jew, who had been afraid before to confess his belief, used this cup to catch some of the blood that flowed from Jesus's wounds. This man Joseph deposited Jesus's body in his own tomb, from which Jesus was resurrected a few days later. But Joseph himself was punished; he was imprisoned for years without proper care. He received food, drink and spiritual sustenance from the Grail, which he retained, so that he survived. When he was released, he took the Grail to England, where he settled in 63 A.D. He began the conversion of that region to Christianity. The Grail was handed to his successors from generation to generation until it came at last to Sir Galahad of King Arthur's Round Table. Only the chaste were able even to perceive it. The Grail may also relate to the Cornucopia, or Horn of Plenty, the ancient symbol of the bounty of growing things. It is the cup of love and faith and fruitfulness, the container of the classic "element" of water, and the symbol of the essential female nature (i.e., the womb) represented in the Suit of Cups of the Tarot.

Trade

It is intriguing to conjecture which of the human instincts is strongest. Many people assume it is sex, the reproductve urge—but an interesting experiment seems to refute that. A group of volunteers including several married couples was systematically starved. As hunger intensified, the pin-up pictures of girls were replaced by pictures of food. The sex impulse decreased, and some couples broke up. Food dominated the conversation. This suggests that hunger is stronger than sex. Similarly, survival—the instinct of self preservation—seems stronger than hunger, for a starving person will not eat food he knows is poisoned, or drink salt water when dehydrating on a raft in the ocean. This hierarchy of instincts seems reasonable, for any species must secure its survival before it can successfully reproduce its kind. Yet there may be an even more fundamental instinct than these. When the Jews were confined brutally in Nazi concentration death-camps, they cooperated with each other as well as they could, sharing their belongings and scraps of food in a civilized manner. There, the last thing to go was personal dignity. The Nazis did their utmost to destroy the dignity of the captives, for people who retained their pride had not been truly conquered. Thus dignity, or status, or the perception of self-worth, may be the strongest human instinct. It is represented in the Tarot as the Suit of Disks, or Pentacles, or Coins, and associates with the "element" Earth, and with money (the ignorant person's status), and business or trade. Probably the original symbol was the blank disk of the Sun (gold) or Moon (silver).

Magic

In the Garden of Eden, Adam and Eve were tempted by the Serpent to eat of the fruit of the Tree of Knowledge of Good and Evil. The fruit is unidentified; popularly it is said to be the apple (i.e., breast), but was more probably the banana (i.e., phallus). Obviously the forbidden knowledge was sexual. There was a second special Tree in the Garden: the Tree of Life, which seems to have been related. Since the human couple's acquisition of sexual knowledge and shame caused them to be expelled from Eden and subject to the mortality of Earthly existence, they had to be provided an alternate means to preserve their kind. This was procreation—linked punitively to their sexual transgression. Thus the fruit of "knowledge" led to the fruit of "life," forever tainted by the Original Sin.

Naturally the couple would have escaped this fate if they could, by sneaking back into Eden. To prevent re-entry to the Garden, God set a flaming sword in the way. This was perhaps the origin of the symbol of the Suit of Swords of the Tarot, representing the "element" of air. The Sword associates with violence (war), and with science (scalpel) and intellect (intangible): God's manifest masculinity. Yet this vengeful if versatile weapon was transformed in Christian tradition into the symbol of Salvation: the Crucifix, in turn transformed by the bending of its extremities into the Nazi Swastica. And so as man proceeds from the ancient faith of Magic to the modern speculation of Science, the Sword proceeds inevitably from the Garden of Eden . . . to Hell.

Art

Man is frightened and fascinated by the unknown. He seeks in diverse ways to fathom what he does not comprehend, and when it is beyond his power to do this, he invents some rationale to serve in lieu of the truth. Perhaps the religious urge can be accounted for in this way, and also man's progress into civilization: man's insatiable curiosity driving him to the ultimate reaches of experience. Yet there remain secrets: the origin of the universe, the smallest unit of matter, the nature of God, and a number of odd phenomena. Do psychics really commune with the dead? How does water dowsing work? Is telepathy possible? What about faith healing? Casting out demons? Love at first contact? Divination? Ghosts?

Many of these inexplicable phenomena become explicable through the concept of aura. If the spirit or soul of man is a patterned force permiating the body and extending out from it with diminishing intensity, the proximity of two or more people would cause their surrounding auras to interpenetrate. They could thus become aware of each other on more than a physical basis. They might pick up each other's thoughts or feelings, much as an electronic receiver picks up broadcasts or the coil of a magnetic transformer picks up power. A dowser might feel his aura interacting with water deep in the ground, and so know the water's location. A person with a strong aura might touch one who was ill, and the strong aura could recharge the weak one and help the ill person recover the will to live. A man and a woman might find they had highly compatible auras, and be strongly attracted to each other. An evil aura might impinge on a person, and have to be exorcised. And after the physical death of the body, or host, an aura might float free, a spirit or ghost, able to communicate only with specially receptive individuals, or mediums.

In short, the concept of aura or spirit can make much of the supernatural become natural. It is represented in the Animation Tarot deck as the Suit of Aura, symbolized in medieval times by a lamp and in modern times by a lemniscate (infinity symbol: ∞), and embracing a fifth major human instinct or drive: art, or expression. Only man, of all the living creatures on Earth, cares about the esthetic nature of things. Only man appreciates painting, and sculpture, and music, and dancing, and literature, and mathematical harmonies, and ethical proprieties, and all the other forms and variants of artistic expression. Where man exists, these things exist—and when man passes on, these thing remain as evidence of his unique nature. Man's soul, symbolized as art, distinguishes him from the animals.